A proper lady, a rake in disguise — and dangerous desire.

Rafe Atherton, the Duke of Devonshire, has managed to muck up his life, and rather grandly. A dalliance with the wrong woman has put him at the center of a scandal that could bring down the next Prime Minister of England. Desperate to remove the threat to his peer — and to himself by way of being skewered by said peer, he agrees to disappear from London life. Begrudgingly, he accepts his friend's suggestion to act the part of a butler at the fellow's cousin's country estate.

Lady Isabella FitzHugh is nothing if not a practical, logical, orderly young woman. Having her lifelong butler just retire and being informed by her cousin, surely in an attempt to help, that she was to host a butler-in-training, is beyond annoying. A small, self-contained estate needs no ripples to mar the necessary smooth waters. But, when the new butler, one Mr. Easton, arrives, her home and her emotions become one stormy mess. And Isabella finds herself breaking all the rules and happily opens her heart to the chaos of love.

The Country Butler

True to the Heart, Vol. 2

LORI LYN

THE COUNTRY BUTLER
True to the Heart, Vol. 2

Copyright ©2014 by Lori Lyn
Trifecta Publishing House edition, 2015

All rights reserved. Except as permitted under the U.S. Copyright Act of 1976, no part of this publication may be reproduced, distributed, or transmitted in any form or by any means now known or hereafter invented, or stored in a database or retrieval system, without the prior written permission of the publisher, Trifecta Publishing House.

This book is a work of fiction Names, characters, places, and incidents are the product of the author's imagination or are used fictitiously. Any resemblance to actual persons, living or dead, business establishments, events, or locales is coincidental.

Published in the United States of America
First Printing: 2015
Print Book
ISBN: 978-1-943407-01-9

Trifecta Publishing House
871 Coronado Center Drive
Suite 200
Henderson, Nevada 89052-3977

TRIFECTA PUBLISHING HOUSE

Edited By: Elizabeth Jewell
Cover Art By: April Rickard
Formatted By: Cyber Witch Press

Dedicated to my readers who asked for more!
Enjoy, peeps.

Dear Reader ~

This is the prequel to *The Archery Contest* and tells you of Rafe, the first of our young gentlemen to succumb to true love. Now Rafe, being a young Duke, is quite sure he knows the truth about love — that it doesn't exist and is only a ruse created by women to assuage their guilt at feeling passion. Luckily for him, our old friend Alex Fitzhugh is also his friend and devises a plot to save Rafe from scandal and probably death by duel — and from his own foolish notions of love.

    Isabella, the young Baroness and ruler of her family estate, is quite sure she knows what is best for her people and of course for herself. Order rules her life as well as her heart. But when her meddling cousin Alex sends a handsome young man to her country estate to act as temporary butler, Isabella finds herself breaking all the rules and happily opens her heart to the chaos of love.

    I hope you will once again forgive me for playing fast and loose with some of the social customs of the Regency times. To me, the stories are all about the characters. They tend to take over and dictate how things will unfold and allow me only the privilege of telling it to you.

    And please know that my Duke of Devonshire has nothing to do with the actual existing Duke — whom I only just found out is really real! My apologies, Your Grace.

    I hope you enjoy reading this story as much as I did telling you about Bella and Rafe. I, too, hope you enjoy hearing more about Alex and Whit as they help Rafe and Bella on their course to true love. Please do let me know what you think. I love to hear from fellow readers. And after you've read *The Country Butler*, I would be most grateful if you took just a few moments and write up an honest review.

Cheers ~ Lori

P.S. ~ Look for the next in the *True To The Heart* series in early 2016 called *The Betrothal Contract*.

The Country Butler

Chapter 1

"Good God, Rafe! You've really done it this time." Lord Whitmore Langley stripped off his gloves as he strode into the cavernous library, his golden brown eyes sparkling with amusement. "Melanie Evanston, of all the women — *Baroness* du Champs, the wife of the next prime minister, no less." He tossed the fine gray gloves onto Rafe's mahogany desk.

"Her husband will bloody well kill you." Despite the early hour of the day, he moved to the liquor cart and poured himself a healthy serving of brandy.

His Grace, Lord Raefiel Woodrow Atherton, seventh Duke of Devonshire, fifth Earl of Easton, made no response to his long-time friend's observation, save to groan — loudly. His dark head fell to his desktop, no doubt smudging his housekeeper's careful polishing.

Yes, he really had done it this time. What a bloody mess.

Whit, his close friend, the 26-year-old Viscount Langley, shook his head.

"Well, chum, I'm quite anxious to find out how you're going to get yourself out of this muck." He sipped the brandy and leaned against the side of the desk. "It is quite difficult to fathom why Melanie plans to tell every member of the *Ton* just what went on between you two. She must know that her husband will kill you, then her."

Rafe gave another groan from his still prostrate position.

"You must have done her some horrible grievance."

"Sweet Mother," was Rafe's only response. He really should have known better than to verbally lambaste Melanie when she had finally confessed who she really was. Behind his closed eyes, he could again picture her in the peach negligee he had only just purchased for her, her face red with rage, breasts heaving and her usually enticing mouth curled in a snarl, screaming she'd ruin him if it were the last thing she did. She had gone so far as to say she would convince her husband that Rafe had abducted her and forced himself on her! He had snarled in reply that a common street whore had more integrity than she. He really should have handled her with more tact.

"I was so angry to find out I'd been cuckolding a good friend, I couldn't think straight." Rafe slowly raised his head, finally looking at his visitor. "Damn it all, Whit, I really let my wounded pride make an ass of me." He ran his fingers through already disheveled hair. "Melanie had told me she needed a new protector when we met at Drury Lane last month. I thought she was an actress, you know." He saw he had Whit's full attention. "She told me the truth last night. She was finding married life boring, what with du Champs away so much and her being used to the vagabond's life she had before. I do believe I called her a bitch." Yes, that, and worse — much worse.

"Why did she do it? Why did she let you believe she was a mistress, rather than a *mistress*. I would have thought she would be content with her lot, since du Champs overlooked her slightly sordid past and married her."

"She said it was just to have a *bit of fun*, while her husband was away." Rafe leaned forward in his chair, steepling his fingers under his chin. His vivid blue eyes narrowed. "Just a bit of fun, she said. She hadn't meant to be unfaithful, but she said she couldn't 'pass me up'." He snorted with contempt. Women could profess undying love to their husbands through honeyed lips one moment, and the next would be entreating him to their bed.

"She said that?" Whit replied, not appearing surprised. He often said how most women would give their dowry to have even a chance of capturing Rafe's wandering gaze, being that he was the choicest of available men, titled to the gills and filthy rich. Why, the duke, Whit would chuckle, could charm the stays off any female.

"Can you believe her nerve?" Rafe nodded, as if he knew Whit could.

Why couldn't he have recognized her before things went too far? Damn that veil she had worn so demurely during her wedding ceremony just five months ago!

Would he never meet a female who was beyond such trickery simply to get into his bed, most with the ultimate hopes of snaring him in marriage?

"So why did she confess, when she could have simply ended the affair and no one would have been the wiser?"

"Pour me one of those." Rafe said, indicating the drink in his friend's hand. "She said she'd *fallen in love* with me." He slammed his fist down on the desktop. "Bah! Stupid female rot." Why women insisted on this drivel of love, he'd never understand. How could any sensible female be so self-deprecating?

"Why can't they just own up to having the same carnal lusts as men? I see no reason to wrap it up in the archaic notion of *love*." He took a fortifying swallow of the brandy Whit handed him.

Whit rolled his eyes.

"They are faithless creatures, the lot of them. Now, I adore women. You know how much I *adore* them, Whit. But the darlings are completely addled over this business. It is beyond logical reasoning that they continue to believe such drivel. Lust is lust — pure and simple."

Rafe was just getting warmed up when there was a rap on his library door. It opened and Tilbot, his butler, stuck in his shiny bald head.

"Your Grace, Lord Langley," he nodded to both men, "Lord Stapleton is asking to join you in lamenting and brandy, Your Grace."

"Send him in, Tilbot," Rafe's grin at his elderly servant's phrasing quickly turned into a grimace. "Well, it didn't take long for word to spread."

"Oh, no, I sent Alex a message before coming myself." Whit explained to Rafe how he had been told very early this morning by his valet, who was just coming in, that the lovely Baroness was now confiding all at Madam Rosette's. Whit had then dashed off a note to the earl before coming to see Rafe himself. How Whit's valet knew was simple — he was seeing the Madam's maid.

The door to the room was flung open, startling the two

occupants.

"Damn me, Rafe! You are an idiot!"

"Thank you, I'm sure, Alex. Do come join us in our lamenting, as Tilbot calls it." Rafe replied dryly and held up his snifter. "Whit was just toasting me on my choice of female companions."

Alexander Fitzhugh, the Earl of Stapleton, smacked himself on the forehead with the palm of his hand. "You've really buggered things this time, Rafe, me boy. Baron du Champs' wife, indeed! Not only is he a Whig but the bloke's to be the next prime minister of bloody England! Whatever were you thinking? And, yes, I'll join you in that illegal French swill." The tall, burly lord sat down in one of the two chairs facing the desk.

Whit poured another round for himself and Rafe, including a double measure for their new guest, while Alex continued.

"Really, I don't know why I've even bothered with you. I take the time to teach you all I know about seduction, and you waste it on a woman like her! It's beyond belief."

Whit laughed as he handed the slightly older earl the drink. "She duped him, old boy. Quite pulled the cap over his eyes."

At Rafe's scowl, Whit laughed again. "Come now, we need to be honest here. Otherwise, how can Alex use his considerable brain power to get you out of this?"

"*I* am to rescue this puling boy?" Alex looked at them, mockingly incredulous as he hooked his thumb in the fob pocket of his bright yellow vest.

"Come now, it won't be the first time you've extricated one of us from a mess." Whit grinned. "Remember Eton and that caning we never got?"

Rafe recalled the time Alex had dreamed up a clever plot to get them out of a caning by the headmaster at Eton. What was amazing was that it had actually worked.

Of course, it had also been one of Alex's schemes that had gotten them in the soup to begin with.

"Well, true, I *am* a genius," Alex said.

While the other two bantered, recalling the boyhood escapade, the duke pondered women. Women had no integrity, that was their problem. It took integrity to enter into an obligation like marriage.

Now, Rafe could certainly appreciate a woman who wanted to flit from man to man. But, if ladies swear before God and kin that they will cleave only to that particular man, then they had bloody well better do it. Just because men had the right to seek pleasure outside the marriage, didn't mean a woman could. Why have to doubt if your heir is truly your heir? Rafe's head throbbed as the thoughts scurried around. Of course, he hoped he would marry a woman he could trust. But the more he encountered the gender, the more he seriously doubted it.

"Will you both be still? I've a headache." Rafe scowled into his drink. "She thought that, upon her confession, I would be willing to run away with her." He looked up at his two confidantes. "Can you believe such nonsense? She thought I'd just toss away everything, because she had supposedly fallen in love with me. Didn't she even *think* about what would happen? That we'd both be completely ostracized by society should have come into her *tiny* little mind. And just what the blazes did she think her poor husband would have to say? 'Oh, well. Better luck next time. So my political career is over and

I'm the laughing stock of Europe'?" He set down the untouched refill. "Faithless, I tell you, gentlemen. And, now, because of some silly notion she has, I am in quite a rough spot!"

Whit shrugged and Alex studied his fingernails.

"Well? Don't either of you have any ideas on what I'm supposed to do about it?"

"I thought you wanted us to shut up." Whit replied, an amused smile hovering about his mouth.

"Yes, you appear to want to do all the lamenting by yourself." Alex didn't look up from his well-manicured hands but couldn't suppress his grin.

Rafe sighed. He fervently wished he'd never laid eyes on the lovely Melanie. But, of course, that did absolutely no good. "*Useless thoughts are wasted thoughts*", his dear father had often said. It was a shame he'd died eighteen months ago and wasn't here to get a good chuckle from his son's misdeeds. Father certainly had *his* share of affairs, goodness knows. His father had probably gotten himself into a similar situation in his youth.

"All right, then," Alex slowly sat up in his chair and laid his palms on his velvet-clothed knees.

Rafe saw the gleam in his friend's eyes, and knew the earl was formulating a plan. He leaned forward and noticed Whit, who had settled himself in the other chair, also watching Alex. All three were silent for several minutes.

"You've got to go to ground for a while." Alex spoke finally, then paused, obviously still working out his plot to free Rafe from Melanie and scandal. "Yes, you've got to hide out until this can be defused. But it has to be where no-one knows you and no-one will know to look for you."

"Good luck, there." Whit leaned back in the chair. "Where is Rafe supposed to go? Du Champs will look everywhere when he learns of this. He'll even look to our properties, Alex. He knows how close we are."

Whit was right. Rafe would be hard pressed to find a place where no-one knew him, not only due to his birthright, but also because his father had been a hero and admired by all Englishmen for his part in saving the king from an assassination attempt some years ago. And Rafe was the spitting image of his sire — from his thick black hair and cobalt blue eyes, to his impressive height.

"True, boy-o. He would be known within a hundred miles of any of *our* properties. But, if we sent him to, say, me plain country cousin's estate in North Bindlefork, and if he don't go as himself ... " Alex was still turning over details in his quick-witted head. "Yes, he shall have to impersonate someone else."

"And, pray tell, just whom am I supposed to impersonate?"

Just then, there was another knock at the library door and Tilbot once again stuck in his hairless head.

"Your Grace, there is a gentleman from the drapier here to see your valet but he is out attending other business. Shall I send him away to lament on his own or shall I see to it, You Grace?"

Rafe waved at his servant. "See to it, Tilbot."

The door had just clicked shut when Alex shot out of his chair. It always surprised Rafe that such a huge man could move with such speed and grace.

"That's it, old man!"

"Good God, what's 'it'?" Whit asked in alarm. "He's not to pose as a *drapier?*"

Alex leaned down and peered into Rafe's face, his fisted hands planted on his hips. "You'll be me cousin's new butler." At the shocked expression of his younger friend, the earl laughed heartily, his head thrown back.

"A butler?" Whit, mouth gaping, looked from Rafe to the giant in hysterics. "*Rafe*, a *butler?*" He shook his head, a disbelieving frown settling on his face. "A pity to go mad so young in life."

"Really, it's perfect." Alex choked back his laughter. "Shut your mouth, dear boy. It will only be for a few weeks, at best a month. Who will be looking for a butler in North Bindlefork?" He crossed his arms over his massive chest, grinning like a lunatic at Rafe.

"Good Lord, you're serious, aren't you?" Rafe was dumbfounded.

"Of course I am." Alex sat back down, quite pleased with himself, by the smug expression on his face.

"How the in blazes am *I* supposed to play a butler? I don't know the slightest thing about being a servant!" Rafe thought this the most absurd idea Alex had ever come up with. "Couldn't I simply go *stay* with your cousin, and perhaps pretend to be some distant relative from Ireland?"

"No."

"But why a bloody butler? I could be a horse trainer. Now there's something I know a bit about." A butler? Bloody hell!

"She don't *need* one of those." Alex replied before picking up his glass from the desk and draining the contents. "Besides" he said, "she is an heiress in her own right. Her family was granted their land and title from William the Conqueror himself. The plain little lady is quite orphaned and has no mamma or papa to interfere."

Rafe looked at Whit, who was obviously as perplexed as he at this idea.

"Look, Alex, how is Rafe here, privileged to his very toes, supposed to pass himself off as a *servant?*"

"Really, Alex, it's absurd. Why don't I just go to France for a few months?"

"Du Champs would find you in a heartbeat, in France or Ireland or Scotland, and you know it, you sod. You'd have to fight a duel and you'd die."

Alex spoke calmly now, but Rafe could see the concern in his brown eyes. They all knew du Champs well, and anything the baron considered his, he would guard with his life — and that definitely included his new, beautiful wife. Rafe was again furious with himself for not realizing why the lady had looked so familiar. Of course, he had only met her that one time and hadn't seen her since. Still, he felt quite the fool.

"Why is it you assume *I* would be the one to die?" Rafe asked defensively, annoyed at what he saw as his friend's lack of loyalty.

"Come now, Rafe," Whit replied for Alex. "You may be tough to beat in the ring, but you're only a passable marksman and you can't fence for beans."

Rafe scowled.

Whit's response was to shrug before continuing. "Now is not the time to forget that du Champs is a superior swordsman and shooter." He turned to their big friend. "But, what is Rafe supposed to do — hide forever?"

"I object to hiding at all, truth be known," Rafe grumbled, not used to avoiding confrontations. He liked to meet a task head on. His life was banal enough with the restrictions society tried to impose on a man of such standing that he hated the thought of turning tail and running from a challenge in any guise.

"While you are, shall we say, being inconspicuous, Whit and I will endeavor to change lovely Melanie's devious little mind about the whole affair and tamp down any nasty gossip she may have started."

"We will? And how will we?"

"Leave that to me, puppy. I have a *strategy*." Alex waggled a finger in the air, emphasizing his point.

"I'm doomed," Rafe groaned and allowed his head to again drop to the desktop, further smudging it, no doubt.

"Nonsense, dear boy. Your fate is in these paws, and they're much too large to let even the smallest detail slip through."

Chapter 2

The letter lay in her lap, already creased from repeated readings — and not only by her but, undoubtedly, also by every staff member of the manor. The message was easy enough to understand, yet there seemed to be some other implication to the words. It quite puzzled her.

> Dearest Cousin Isabella,
>
> I have found a perfect solution to the dilemma at hand. Within two days of receiving this note, there shall arrive at Kirkwood a young man whom I propose to you as a temporary candidate for your butler. Although not yet fully trained, I believe him quite capable of pulling this off.
>
> Do show him any errors in his ways, but do not fault him his haughty airs, as he is headstrong and young.
>
> Me thanks to you in advance, as I remember your sweetness and kindness from our younger days. Hopefully, circumstances will improve here and he will not be required

to remain overly long in your employ.

Your Grateful Cousin,
Alexander Fitzhugh

Isabella Fitzhugh, Baroness Kirkwood, shook her head as she read the note again. Whatever did her cousin mean by his odd words? Alex had always been strange, touting his great intellect and making outlandish jokes. Isabella supposed she should just attribute it to his nature.

She frowned at his crisp writing. Being a city man, he knew nothing of country life and what a hardship a haughty servant could cause a relatively self-contained estate. Why on earth would the fellow be coming way out here for only a temporary situation? Isabella needed a permanent replacement, and it would be a bother to have to go through the training of several men. She sighed and rose from the dainty desk situated beneath the windows in her small day room, overlooking the rose garden. She was briskly shaking the wrinkles from her pale lavender day dress when there was a knock at the door.

"Enter, Mrs. Combs."

The small, plump, gray-haired woman entered and curtseyed.

"My Lady," Mrs. Combs smiled. "It is time for your ride, my lady. Alice is busy in the laundry. I shall assist you in dressing."

They walked to Isabella's room just down the wide, mahogany-paneled hallway. Mrs. Combs, who had been housekeeper for the Fitzhugh family for more than thirty years, quickly moved to the armoire and took out a dark green riding outfit with matching boots and hat. "Would you wear this, my lady?"

"Oh, yes, that's fine." Isabella absently changed, all the while speculating on the young man who was to be her new butler. Cousin Alex had not even mentioned the fellow's name!

As Isabella strode to the stables, now dressed in the forest green riding habit, she thought about old Bent. It was indeed a shame he had been forced to retire to Bath to seek relief from his gout some months ago. He had been with her family for more years than any could remember and had served them very well indeed. He had always anticipated the master's needs and had been the epitome of diplomacy. How could some pompous young boy be expected to fill such shoes?

Isabella greeted the head stable lad as he led out her mount and cooed to the horse in some secret language.

"Good day, Harry. How is Dilly today?" She smiled as her horse whinnied to her.

"Full o' fire today, m'lady!" The young boy patted the horse's neck. "Ain't you, m'sweet pet?" The mare tossed her head in response.

Isabella mounted easily by herself. She was as comfortable in the saddle as she was behind her desk. "I shall be back within the hour, as we are expecting the new butler today."

"Aye, m'lady." Harry removed the woolen cap from his pale brown hair and scratched his head. "We is all mighty curious 'bout 'im, m'lady."

"So am I, Harry." She shrugged with practiced nonchalance. "We shall see what we shall see, I suppose."

It was a perfect day for a ride, and Isabella decided to visit the small lake on the north side of her vast estate. She loved the land surrounding quaint Kirkwood Manor. It was lush and fertile, and extremely prosperous for her and her tenants. She was a lucky girl, no doubt, even if she was an orphan. *Thank you, William The Conquorer, once again for bequeathing the title to our family!*

When Isabella returned home from her ride, Harry was practically hopping about, he appeared so excited.

"Harry, whatever is the matter?" Isabella slid from Dilly's back and handed the groom the reins. "Don't tell me Cook threatened to roast Petunia again!"

Petunia, the estate's pet goose had a fondness for radish greens and was forever stealing into Cook's garden to uproot the vegetables. Cook could oft be heard shouting how he would roast the offensive fowl.

"It's 'im, m' lady! The new butler just arrived an' on a fine lookin' steed!"

"Ah, finally." Isabella calmly removed her riding gloves. "What do you think, Harry? Will he do for North Bindlefork and Kirkwood Manor?"

Harry snorted. "He acts like a bloomin' gent, beggin' yer forgiveness at me crude tongue, m'lady."

"Hmm, a 'blooming gent.' Interesting." She smiled at the boy and walked quickly across the yard, up the wide stone steps and through the massive doors held open by a footman. As soon as she was inside the spacious entry, Mrs. Combs was at her elbow.

"He's in the study, my lady."

The usually unflustered Mrs. Combs was quite flushed.

"Is he?" Isabella removed her hat and handed it and her gloves to her housekeeper. "Well, am I presentable, as such?" She absently ran a hand over her thick hair, tucking in a few loose tendrils.

"Quite, my lady. You look lovely as the day itself."

Isabella chuckled as she made her way to the study. Lovely

indeed! She paused but a moment at the door, realizing she hadn't asked Mrs. Combs what name the fellow had given. She shrugged, assumed her haughty mistress-of-the-manor demeanor and marched into the room. Even as she moved behind the desk, she began speaking in her most brisk tone.

"I am Lady Kirkwood. You undoubtedly are familiar with —" She could only look at the man who had just risen from the chair before her desk. Good heavens, he was breathtaking! His hair was black as sin and his face strong and arrogant. And his eyes! They shone with intelligence and she thought more than a hint of wicked amusement. Those incredibly blue eyes locked with her own green and she could not look away.

Get a hold of yourself, Bella! She shook her head, then promptly sat. She thought she heard him chuckle. She struggled to regain her composure. It wasn't easy, but she managed. Still, her heart seemed to be beating awfully fast.

"As I was saying, you are familiar with my cousin, the Earl of Stapleton, I take it?"

"Yes, my lady."

His voice was deep and smooth, reminding her of the taste of fine brandy. Gooseflesh rippled over her arms.

"He has written to me recommending I employ you as butler here." She looked up at him, annoyed to find he was smiling. My, but he was sinfully handsome, with broad shoulders and a lean body. He had a firm chin and generous lips. Oh, dear. "I regret that he did not think to supply your name."

"I am Woodrow Easton, my lady."

"Easton, I understand that you are still something of an apprentice butler?"

"Yes, my lady."

"Well, you'll find things here are not overly taxing, even if your skills are still being developed. I assure you the other staff members will be quite willing and able to assist you, should you have any questions as to specific duties. Mrs. Combs is the housekeeper and she has been with my family for a number of years. You can direct any questions to her."

"Yes, my lady."

"We don't receive many callers here at Kirkwood Manor, as you can imagine being so far from any large city." She leaned back in her chair, which squeaked with age. "When callers do arrive, I prefer to greet them in the front parlor." For the first time, she noticed he was wearing the clothes of a proper gentleman, not a servant. The jacket was navy blue, the trousers a shade darker and his shirt whiter than the star on Dilly's nose. He really should have presented himself in uniform. Mind you, he looked quite *nice* in those gentleman's clothes.

"Do you have a uniform?"

"Yes, my lady."

Goodness, was that all he could say? He certainly wasn't a conversationalist — but then, it wouldn't have spoken well of him if he had attempted to engage in idle chatter.

"Easton, do you have any questions?"

"No, my lady."

"Well, then," she said, rising and signaling an end to the brief interview. She nearly gasped seeing how tall he was. Goodness! She was 5 foot, 4 inches, whereas he must be well over 6 feet tall.

"Thank you, my lady." He bowed to her. "I shall go and find Mrs. Combs now, my lady."

"Yes, that will be fine, Easton." Those cobalt eyes locked

with hers again as he straightened, and she saw merriment sparkling in them.

"If I may, my lady," he spoke softly, the barest hint of a smile on those magnificent lips, "I think I shall greatly enjoy my time here."

"Why, I hope you do, Easton."

And then he was gone, the door closing quietly behind him. Isabella sank down into the chair that has been her father's and was now hers. Goodness, butlers simply shouldn't be that handsome. It was quite unnerving.

RAFE lay stretched out on the small, narrow bed that would be his for at least the next few weeks. His hands laced together behind his head, he contemplated Lady Isabella.

Alex hadn't painted a very flattering picture of the young woman. He'd repeatedly called her plain yet Lady Isabella was anything *but* "plain," in Rafe's esteemed opinion. He'd been quite surprised when she'd entered the study. Such a lovely little thing, not quite coming to his shoulders. Her green eyes had an exotic slant, her full lips were red and very tempting, and her hair — ah, beautiful, thick auburn hair he would bet was long and soft as silk. And her figure was the capper — a tiny waist, full breasts, and, he just knew, shapely legs. Yes, the lady was quite a dish. Too bad he wasn't in the position to attempt a little seduction.

His arrival had been quite amusing, with servants peeking out of various rooms as he was ushered through the massive entry and down the wide hall into the den to await the mistress.

And then the lovely baroness had swept into the room, her chin in the air and back ramrod straight, like a bloody little general. Her initial reaction was one he was used to from women, but she had been quick to recover, he'd give her that.

While she spoke in a clipped manner, he studied her, looking beyond the surprising beauty. Rafe could see that she was used to giving orders and had every expectation they would be adhered to. She was a serious, proper little miss, to be sure. Even her dress was prim, although very tasteful. She kept their interview brief and to the point, dismissing him within moments. It had been quite amusing, really. He had never encountered such treatment before in his life, especially not from a member of the fairer sex.

Later, as a footman was leading him to his room, he caught the eye of a pretty maid on the back stairs. The look she had given him had been more than inviting. Well, if he had to spend time in isolation, he supposed this was as good a place as any. The natives seemed friendly enough.

His room, however, was abysmal. Back home, his armoire was more spacious than this. He lifted his head and frowned, seeing his feet dangling off the end of the bed. This really wouldn't do. But, as a lowly servant, he couldn't very well order a bigger bed, could he? No, Tilbot had told him quite explicitly that servants did not request things.

"Simply say 'yes, my lord,' or 'no, my lady,' and do the best you can to keep from being noticed. And, what ever you do, do not 'demand' *anything*. That, for you, Your Grace, should be challenge enough."

Not very encouraging, mind you, but it was advice Rafe would attempt to adhere to.

He rose, realizing it was getting close to the dinner hour, and began changing into one of the uniforms Alex and Whit had taken great pleasure in procuring for him. It was your standard butler attire, black trousers and coat with tails, with a white shirt and simple cravat. His black shoes were polished nicely, thanks to his valet, who had nearly fainted when told what his distinguished master planned to do.

"Your Grace, it cannot be borne!" Simpson, a slim little man, had wrung his hands and hopped about from one foot to the other. "You are an Atherton, a *duke*. Is there no other way, Your Grace? Must you actually *serve*, Your Grace?"

This was followed by more hand-wringing and hopping, until finally Rafe told him to take a vacation for the next two weeks, starting immediately.

It took Rafe some time to be satisfied his attire was correctly put together. He would not have considered himself so inept before today, never having given dressing a thought. He had always had a valet and must have simply taken cravat-tying for granted. When he emerged from his room, he almost collided with a young footman.

"Oh, blimey! There you are, Gov." The boy was sweating and tugged at the collar of his dark green jacket. "I was sent to fetch you and was told to be right smart 'bout it. Dinner's nearly served and you're needed."

"Of course, boy. Lead the way, if you would be so kind. I'm not yet familiar with my surroundings." Rafe brushed a stray piece of thread from his shiny black satin lapel. He looked up to see the little fellow eyeing him oddly. "Well, let's go then. Her ladyship mustn't be kept waiting."

Was he so obviously out of his element that even the footman realized it? This plan of Alex's was truly insane.

Rafe managed to keep up with the chap as he led the way down one corridor after another on fleet feet. Shortly they arrived in the main hallway, where Rafe was to wait for the appearance of Lady Isabella. He stood at the base of the stairs and adjusted the cuffs of his shirt. Satisfied, he looked toward the top of the steps, trying not to appear bored and amused. Within a moment, the baroness was gliding down the huge curved stairway, dressed most becomingly in a soft burgundy muslin gown, her cream underskirt just peeking through. Her lovely hair was piled atop her head in a mass of ringlets. She saw him and paused in mid-step but so briefly he wondered if he had imagined it. She was at his side an instant later. Rafe resisted the urge to compliment her and take her arm. Instead, he bowed to her, murmured a "my lady" and proceeded her to the doors he was fairly sure opened into the dining room. Luckily, he was correct. After closing the portal behind her, he held her chair at the head of the table and signaled the footman to begin serving. Good heavens, he was actually doing it! Wouldn't Tilbot be proud of his butlering?

ISABELLA could not believe how handsome Easton was in his uniform. The tailored jacket hugged his broad shoulders and she could tell he had no need of padding. His cravat was just a bit crooked but she overlooked that one tiny flaw in the otherwise perfect appearance of him. Her eyes were drawn to him repeatedly while he stood in the corner, observing with veiled amusement every dish and its placement on the long table. The stark black-and-white attire enhanced his ebony hair and those arresting blue eyes too well.

Suddenly, Isabella realized she had never before felt so alone sitting here as she did now. Here she was — an heiress surrounded by all the comforts one could wish for and the only thing she lacked was someone to share her company.

The thought that Easton might pity her popped into her

head, and she wished Lisbeth had dropped by. She often did of late, as her mother was currently residing in London with her eldest daughter. Her friend's elder sister was having her debut this Season. Bubbly Lisbeth would be a very welcome presence right now.

She jumped when suddenly Easton was right beside her, pouring more of the rich cabernet into her wineglass.

"I beg your pardon, my lady. I didn't mean to startle you."

His deep voice caressed her, his warm breath stirring the stray tendrils of hair at her nape. She shivered, despite the warmth of the room.

"Thank you, Easton."

"My lady."

Dinner was finally over, and Isabella decided to retire early. Her nerves felt near to breaking, they were stretched so taut. Easton escorted her to the foot of the stairs and bowed low over her hand.

"Good night, my lady."

"Good night, Easton." She was almost disappointed he hadn't kissed her hand.

Nonsense, that was silly. Why should she be disappointed the butler hadn't kissed her hand? Despite his devastating good looks, he was a *butler*, not a gentleman caller trying to woo her. It was nonsense indeed! She must be overly tired.

Chapter 3

Rafe soon discovered that the work of a butler was quite busy. He seemed forever to be dashing here or there in anticipation of someone coming or going, making some dire decision or other, or assisting Mrs. Combs with a task. The dear housekeeper had taken quite a shine to him and was pleasant company. He was able to take an hour each day to ride his horse, Julius. And in the evenings, he stood watch over Lady Isabella's table, taking any excuse to stand near her and to smell her subtle scent of roses, and to hopefully see to her full lips curve upward as she bestowed on him one of her dazzling, if rare smiles. He observed each graceful movement, and heard each small sigh of pleasure, he was so attuned to her innocent sensuality. Every night she held him transfixed and left him aching with desire. It was sweet torture he looked forward to and it was the perfect test for his resolve. He could not seduce a young woman of good family, and certainly not the cousin of a friend ... oh, but how he wanted to!

He found he rather liked this grand but cozy country estate and the inhabitants, now that they were beginning to warm up to him. He was pleased to find that Lady Isabella was highly regarded and seemed more than capable of keeping the place well run. He had met with several of the local farmers, when they came to deliver goods to the manor, and it was gratifying to hear their praises of the lady.

On his fifth day, he discovered the lake at the far north edge of the property. It was such a beautiful spot, so peaceful. It reminded him of his country estate. He had spent many happy days of his childhood there. He remarked on the area to Mrs. Combs one afternoon. She had smiled and nodded at his description.

"Oh my, yes. That's one of her ladyship's favorite places. She often rides there. When the afternoons grow hot, I suspect she dips her toes in the water." The elderly woman gave him a conspiratorial wink.

That evening, at the usual appointed dinner hour, Isabella again glided down the wide staircase, this time dressed in a demure gown of deep gold. Her lovely hair was entwined with matching ribbons and piled atop her head. As usual, she held herself as if she were a general who was about to survey her troops, sure she would find some lacking. As she passed him, she nodded and the scent of roses invaded his senses.

During dinner, Rafe's imagination took flight and he spent the time tormenting himself with visions of Isabella swimming in the clear cool pool, her naked form cutting through the sun-dappled water like a nymph.

He did not sleep well that night.

Late the next morning, Rafe opened the massive front door and discovered a very pretty blonde young lady standing there. She stared at him with amusingly blatant admiration. He quickly remembered his newfound place and bowed low to her.

"May I help you, miss?" It was difficult, but he managed to keep his face as somber as a vicar's even as she began blushing profusely.

"Goodness! Why, I'm Miss Lisbeth Tetherly, here to see the Baroness." She continued to stare at him, her soft blue eyes round.

"Do come in, Miss Lisbeth. I shall announce you at once." He closed the door after she had stepped into the green marbled entry, took her light summer spencer, and led her to the front parlor. He chuckled. So, that was Lady Isabella's best friend and closest neighbor, whom he had heard about through Mrs. Combs. Rafe gave the spencer to a passing footman and quickly sought out his "mistress."

AS usual at this time of day, Isabella was ensconced in her private day room, a room she preferred to the large study that had been her father's domain. She sat poring over account ledgers and correspondence, considering an offer from a neighboring estate to purchase fifty of her sheep. It was a tempting proposal, but there weren't nearly as many ewes this year as there had been in the past and she wasn't sure about parting with quite so many of the animals. Absently, she called out "enter" at the knock on her door.

She turned to look at the servant and her pulse quickened.

"Oh, Easton." Seeing him standing there, she quickly rose from behind her small desk. No man had the right to so completely steal a girl's breath away. She felt an urge to reach up to brush back an errant lock of hair falling across his brow and had to clutch her hands together to stop herself.

"My lady, Miss Tetherly is awaiting you in the front parlor. Shall I order refreshments?"

"Oh, yes, thank you." Isabella hadn't ever imagined him in this room. He seemed to dwarf her dainty furniture, making it look childlike. As usual, the sound of his deep rich voice made her pulse skip a beat.

Isabella drew herself together and quickly moved past him, mortified to realize she had been gawking at him. It happened every time she saw him, for heaven's sake. Why, only yesterday, she had been walking toward the kitchen to inventory with Cook the supplies needing to be replenished, when she had caught sight of the butler through the open doorway of the dining room. He had been talking with Mrs. Combs, only his profile visible to her, but Isabella found herself staring at the angles of his chin, his lips, at the curl to his thick dark lashes. Her fingers had itched to smooth his black brows, to stroke his firm jaw. Thoughts of him touching her, of kissing her, filled her mind and she blushed at her own silly musings before tearing herself away from the sight of him and continuing on to the kitchen. The images of him had stayed in her mind all during her discussion with Cook.

Now, a once-again composed Isabella entered the parlor and was greeted by her long-time friend with enthusiasm.

"Oh, my gracious, Bella," Lisbeth squealed. "He is too scrumptious! Wherever did you find him?"

There was no need to ask to whom Lisbeth referred. Isabella sat on the edge of a chair close to the gold and green couch, her back stiff. "My cousin Alexander sent him."

The blonde threw herself down onto the small settee. "I

visit my Aunt Estelle for only a few days and come back to find an Adonis has arrived in North Bindlefork! I would love to have such a gorgeous man in my employ. Just imagine, he would be at my every beck and call." She sighed, then sat up abruptly. "No, you don't have to imagine! You have the real thing." She bit her lip and wrapped her arms around herself. "Perhaps I shall poison our Jeffreys."

"Please, Lisbeth, no dramatics." Isabella waggled her finger at her friend. "I have enough problems with Easton."

"Easton? Easton," Lisbeth said softly, as if tasting his name. "How could someone so superb be a problem?"

Isabella plucked at the sleeve of her gown with practiced nonchalance. "The maids do nothing but swoon, Cook only makes dishes he prefers, the stable boy defers to his judgment — must I go on?" She stood suddenly, unable to face her childhood friend, lest the other girl see the truth in her eyes. "This place is becoming a shambles, truly." It was *she* who couldn't seem to get anything accomplished. The household had never run more smoothly, as the servants seemed to be vying for Easton's approval. She had read over the reports from the easterly lands some three times and didn't have a clue what they said. She still had made no decision about the sheep. Each time she attempted to concentrate, she found her thoughts soon drifting to the dark and dangerous man. And he was dangerous, at least to her and her sanity.

"Oh, honestly, Bella," Lisbeth giggled. "Now who is being dramatic?"

Just then there was a brisk rap on the door, and Easton entered directly, pushing a small trolley loaded with cakes and a pot of tea.

"My lady, Miss Lisbeth," the new butler nodded to the

grinning blonde seated on the pale green couch.

He quickly located her, standing across the room behind a large matching wing chair.

"My lady, do you wish me to serve?"

"No."

"Oh, yes!" Lisbeth clapped her hands and smiled most charmingly. "Do let the lovely Easton serve us our tea, Bella."

Isabella rolled her eyes, but knew Lisbeth would have her way. Her friend could charm the birds from the trees, if she felt so inclined.

"My lady?"

"If you don't mind, Easton?" Isabella was embarrassed to her toes by Beth's comment. One simply didn't refer to a butler as "lovely," especially within said servant's hearing.

"Of course, my lady."

She could barely contain her fidgeting until he was finished pouring.

"Thank you, Easton, that will be all." Isabella simply could not relax while the man was in the room. His eyes held such wicked amusement each time they met hers, she was sure if he didn't leave, she would end up with a lap full of the hot beverage.

The handsome butler finally bowed his way out of the room.

"Lisbeth, I should strangle you," she said after the door clicked shut.

"What?" Her slim friend feigned all that was innocent, then promptly ruined the act by giggling.

Isabella gave her a stern look before sighing. "Damnation, he's too handsome for a girl's frame of mind."

"How long do you get to keep him?"

"My, that sounds odd. I don't really know. Cousin Alex only said it was for a while, until Easton's situation improved in London."

Isabella chose a lemon tart from the plate of goodies and nibbled it daintily.

"What situation?" Lisbeth, who was partial to apricots, selected an apricot cake.

"Again, I don't know." She frowned down at the pastry with its thin yellow glaze. "Alex's words seemed to have a double meaning. I would assume Easton found himself in some trouble or other." What had her cousin been implying in his strange missive? And how was it that Easton seemed to know the rules of etiquette so well, but was so obviously at sea when it came to where to find the silver polish and linen cupboard? Why, he directed the footmen to begin serving even before she had signaled she was ready!

"He probably got caught in bed with someone's wife."

"Beth!"

"What now?" She licked the last of the filling from her slender fingers, ignoring Bella's frown.

"You know more than a young lady ought, that's what."

"Well, Sheila Dooley told me all *sorts* of things as soon as she got back from her wedding trip. She said 'lovemaking' was much sought after, even by *ladies*, and that it was *delightful*. She said that in London, every man has a least one mistress and no-one bats an eye about it."

"Bosh, Sheila Dooley is a ninny."

"She may be a ninny, but your previous chaperone is now a married one, so I put my groats on what she says." Lisbeth suddenly sat up. "I almost forgot! Father is bored and wants to have a party. Could you come this Saturday?"

"Whyever does your father want a party? He only grouses when your mother plans one."

Lisbeth giggled. "Actually, I want one and convinced him it was his idea. He *is* dying to show off his new mare. And I don't badger him with the details like Mother. I just do everything my way."

Isabella agreed to come. They visited for a while longer and she listened while Lisbeth rehashed the latest local gossip. Lisbeth adored gossip and Isabella had learned to put up with her dear friend's bad habit, as she saw it. At least the blonde wasn't given to repeating cruel misinformation.

Long ago, Bella had given up trying to discuss any of the trials of running the estate with the other girl, who would only shake her head and look bored and puzzled at the same time. The friends stuck to more ladylike topics.

After being summoned by the pull bell, Bella's new servant showed Lisbeth out. The blonde coyly fluttered her lashes at him, and he obligingly smiled.

After observing the flirtatious smile pass between her butler and friend, Isabella had a hard time remaining still until the door was closed behind the other girl. She suddenly found she was furious.

"I'm going for a ride, Easton. Please tell Harry to saddle Dilly." Isabella turned and briskly mounted the stairs. She had to get out of this house, had to get away from that man! How dare he smile at Lisbeth with such masculine appreciation? He never smiled at her that way. It had been so knowing, so *intimate*.

Half an hour later, Isabella, wearing a soft peach riding habit, was galloping toward her lake, her auburn hair unbound and streaming out behind her. The wind cooled her heated cheeks, and the solitude calmed her ire.

It really was absurd of her to be angry at Lisbeth for doing what came naturally to her — flirting with any handsome man, butler or not. It wasn't Easton's fault for smiling at the irresistible Beth. Was any man immune to her friend's charm? No, even her father, a very logical fellow, had been wrapped round Lisbeth's little finger.

As soon as the lake was in sight, Isabella felt her spirits lift. Today she would indulge in a refreshing swim. It was just what she needed to sooth her frazzled nerves. Within moments, she was off Dilly and stripping off her clothes, carefully hanging them over several branches.

Isabella dove into the water with a shout of pure joy, loving the feel of the coolness enveloping her naked body. As she broke the surface of the water, she pictured Easton in her mind's eye, his eyes regarding her with devilish amusement, his firm sensuous mouth smiling a wicked smile. She closed her eyes and embraced the image, scissoring her legs to tread the water. She tried to imagine what it would feel like to have those lips pressed to her own. How would his long fingers feel touching her, caressing her bare skin? The action of her legs made currents swirl about her body and she thought that this must be what it was like, to have fingers brushing against her skin and touching her intimately. She bit her lip as a tingling sensation began to flutter low in her belly.

"But it cannot be," she whispered to the reeds and the willows as she opened her eyes. Chagrined at herself and at her wicked thoughts, she dove back under the surface.

Some while later, she was back on the shore, dressed once again, save for her riding jacket and boots. She tried to keep thoughts of her handsome butler out of her mind, but it was impossible. Her swim had not soothed her this time, it only enflamed her yearning for the man. She sat upon the carpeting of soft moss beneath a huge, old willow and braided her damp hair loosely. The warm, filtrating sunlight and cool, soft breeze invited her to lean back against the gnarled trunk and shut her eyes.

She issued a frustrated sigh. Easton could never find her attractive, surely. And even if he did, there was nothing the broad-shouldered, virile dark man could do about it, was there? It was all too absurd.

Just who was Easton, really?

RAFE waited a moment longer before emerging from his hiding place only a few yards from Isabella's sleeping body. Thank God he was no longer nearly panting with lust; however, his body was still painfully aroused. Well, he'd asked for it, hadn't he, coming here on a warm afternoon, *knowing* she might take a swim? Yes, he deserved this excruciating state. But, good God, she was lovelier than he'd imagined! Her body was utter perfection. He'd been right to think her legs shapely, and that exquisite little derriere of hers begged for the touch of his hands. He knew each cheek would fit just right in his palms. Her breasts were full and firm with dark pink jutting nipples that made his mouth water, her hips flared enticingly and her stomach was smooth. She was bloody Venus incarnate.

He watched her a moment longer, trying to figure out what to do. He was sorely tempted to make love to her, but knew it would be a selfish act, and surely he was above that. He was an experienced man, not some randy young boy who might take advantage of such an opportunity. And she was an innocent, a proper little virgin.

Albeit, an incredibly alluring one, but still a virgin.

This was the perfect instance to test himself, to prove, if only to himself, that he was above acting on a simple case of lust. Surely he could keep his resolve, no matter the situation?

Perhaps he could satisfy at least one curiosity and steal a kiss? What was the harm in that? She was fast asleep, dreaming chaste little dreams, no doubt. He needed to prove to himself that she didn't taste or feel nearly as exquisite as he kept imaging.

Rafe quietly approached her figure on the spongy ground, then eased himself down beside her. He wished her hair wasn't braided so that he could run his fingers through her tresses. He studied her beautiful face, relaxed completely in slumber. She had a proud, stubborn chin, and a pert little nose. Her cheekbones were high, accentuating her slanted eyes. And those lips were simply made for tasting, full and red, like the ripest of strawberries. She was stunning. He eased closer, watching her carefully for signs of awakening. Slowly, he lowered his head until his mouth was but a whisper away from her own. He breathed in the smell of her and was engulfed with wanting. Gently, he touched his lips hers. God, her mouth was soft and seemed made to mold to his. He desperately wished she would open her mouth so that he could taste her sweetness, but knew he must be content with only this. Still this was heaven, the feel of her, so warm and yielding, so very supple. Unable to resist, he touched his tongue to her lips, running it feather-soft against her lower lip. He shuddered, and regretfully, withdrew from her heat. She sighed in her sleep and turned her face toward him, as if seeking his mouth again.

Damn, she tasted even more divine than he'd fantasized.

Lightly, but with intense yearning, he brushed his knuckles against her petal-soft cheek, something he'd wanted to do countless times since he'd met her. Smiling wryly at his own behavior, he rose and took his place back in the trees to keep watch over her while she continued her nap.

ISABELLA felt strange when she awoke, oddly restless and yearning, but for what exactly, she didn't know. Her lips tingled and she raised her fingertips to touch them. She had dreamt a kiss, yes, she remembered now. And how silly, it had been Easton kissing her. Even her subconscious couldn't resist the man! It was bad enough she daydreamed about him, but even a peaceful nap wasn't safe.

Goodness, it was as if she were becoming obsessed with the butler. She found herself anticipating of dinner, as he would be close at hand looking devilishly handsome in the soft candlelight, his ebony hair gleaming and such an intense look in his eyes that she trembled when their gaze would lock. She sighed. How pathetic she was, getting jealous over so mild a flirtation between him and Beth! At this rate, she was surely to become a bitter old maid, with only cats and probably a senile Mrs. Combs for company.

The angle of the sun told her she hadn't slept for too long. She stretched, rose and pulled on her spencer, then her boots. A sharp whistle brought Dilly to her, and she easily swung up into the saddle. She absently wondered which gown she should wear this evening to dinner, caught herself in her musings, and called herself a fool.

Chapter 4

"Please, my lady! You must hold still or I'll never get your hair right." Alice, Isabella's maid who worked wonders with coiffures, was nearly cross-eyed with irritation.

"I'm sorry, Alice," Isabella said sheepishly, knowing she was being difficult, but she was too excited that Saturday evening had finally arrived to feel much remorse. It had been months since she had been able to attend a party. She couldn't wait to try on her new gown, which had just that day been completed by Alice and Mrs. Combs' daughter. It was a dreamy silk confection in midnight blue with an opalescent, sheer overskirt and off-the-shoulder cap sleeves. The deep scoop neck was not like her other ballgowns. She hoped it reflected her emerging maturity. After all, she was no longer a young girl. She was her own mistress now, the baroness, and had been for more than two years. It was time she stopped dressing in the demure gowns of a young miss and began to present herself as the lady of the manor she was.

"There," Alice was finally satisfied with her handiwork. "There won't be no other lady lookin' so pretty, I'll wager, my lady." She stepped back, her hands splayed on her full hips, and allowed Isabella to see her reflection in the large oval mirror hung above the small dressing table.

Isabella could only stare at her image. She actually looked lovely! Her thick hair was pulled up away from her face, accentuating her almond-shaped eyes and high cheekbones, and then cascaded down her back in loose curling waves. Alice had added small sprigs of pure white baby's breath and blue silk ribbons at each temple, which added luster to her auburn tresses, and, once again, drew attention to her eyes.

"Oh, Alice," she breathed, "it's wonderful!"

Alice, who knew too well how gifted she was, smirked with pride, then hurriedly helped Isabella on with the new gown. When she was dressed, complete with matching slippers and gloves, Alice couldn't resist applauding.

"You're fit to sit at court, right beside the Regent, you are, my lady."

Isabella laughed in delight, then blushed, realizing she had never before revealed so much décolletage. "You don't think I'm just a bit *too* much on display?" she asked her maid, indicating the swell of her bosom.

"Bosh, I've seen Miss Lisbeth show more 'charms' than that in a day dress. You look a proper lady, you do indeed." Alice knelt to smooth a wrinkle from the back, muttering under her breath, "you'll take a little wind right out 'o *her* sails tonight."

"Alice, please go and tell Easton to have the coach brought around. I cannot wait another moment to be on my way." Isabella ignored her maid's mumbling, all thoughts focused on the party. She decided to wear only the diamond earrings her father had given her on her sixteenth birthday. They were the only truly nice pieces of jewelry she owned, anyway. What need was there for a lot a flash way out here in North Bindlefork? No, such money was better spent on plows and oxen and grain.

What was she to do about those dratted fifty sheep, anyway?

A few moments later, Isabella, with a silken cape of midnight blue lined in white over her arm, nearly skipped down the grand staircase. She had reached the last step when she saw her handsome butler near the front door. He was looking at her in a most peculiar way which immediately had her pulse racing.

"Easton, is the coach ready?" He said nothing as he stepped closer to her. "Easton?" She cocked her head in puzzlement at his intense stare.

"My lady, the carriage is waiting, as you requested." He stepped closer still and laid the cape over her shoulders. "You have no escort, my lady, nor a protector."

Isabella stood still, feeling a little uneasy, wondering at the harshness in his tone. "I'm sure I shall be quite alright, Easton. I am only going to my dear friend's home, where I have known every person who will be in attendance since my birth."

It wasn't as if she were going off alone to the city for goodness sake! Why was he acting so disapproving of her? It really wasn't his place to judge her. Did he think she would make a fool of herself? Did he, with his haughty London ways, think a simple country lady such as her could not comport herself properly?

"Shall I go with you, my lady?" He seemed to realize the absurdity of what he said the moment he had uttered it, snapping his jaw together and stepping back.

"Really, Easton, how preposterous." She frowned at him as she pulled the cloak closer around her. "Good night."

"Good night, my lady. Have a pleasant evening, I'm sure." He yanked the heavy door open and practically shoved her out.

Isabella was more than a little perplexed by her new butler's attitude. Why on earth did he seem so angry with her? He was odd, that was it. That must be why he had to leave London. He had become too familiar with his employer and had been sacked, surely. Yes, he was *definitely* odd, indeed.

She sighed. Odd or not, he was too attractive for any girl's sanity to endure. Even when he scowled at her, as she saw he was doing from the doorway, he was beyond compare.

Isabella tried to dismiss Easton's strange behavior from her mind and focus on the lovely evening as the coach traveled down the long country road. The moon had just risen and the countryside was set aglow in its soft light. Young Harry, her driver, whistled a jaunty tune as they traveled along. It really was a shame Easton *couldn't* have accompanied her.

It didn't seem long before they arrived at Lisbeth's large family home, which was brightly lit, the sounds of the orchestra spilling out into the night. Isabella was so excited, she could barely wait long enough for the footman to open her door.

The moment she stepped foot in the festooned entry, Lisbeth was on her. "Goodness, simply *everyone* is here! Charming Mr. Dalton is back from town and is currently sipping punch with Sheila Dooley." She paused in her mindless chatter to gape at Isabella, who had removed her cloak and handed it to a footman. "Oh my gracious! Isabella!"

Isabella adopted her cultivated nonchalance as she pulled her gloves off. "Yes, dear, what is it?" It really was hard not to laugh at her friend's astonished look.

"You're breathtaking!" Lisbeth looked near to tears. She glanced down at her own very pretty and alluring pink dress. "I look positively dowdy standing next to you."

Isabella laughed at the absurdity of her friend's remark. "Nonsense, Lisbeth, you couldn't look 'dowdy' in a burlap sack with ashes on your nose."

Lisbeth didn't look convinced.

"Really, you know that you outshine every other woman here. You're just not used to me wearing a grown-up female's gown."

"Grown up and out," Lisbeth murmured, then grinned. "You look smashing, and I can't hate you for it. I love you too much." She grasped Isabella's hand and led her over to where her father stood, expounding on his latest horse purchase. Soon, both young women were surrounded by gentlemen and remained so the rest of the evening.

IT was quite late when Isabella mounted the steps to her own home. Her feet ached, and she was bone weary from having danced so much. Lisbeth's "charming Mr. Dalton" had trod upon her feet several times, obviously distracted by her bosom, which he had practically drooled upon. It amazed her that men would overlook her plain face if enough décolletage was revealed. But obviously, some things were more appealing to men than a pair of dimples or a pretty bow mouth. It was nonsense, really.

Isabella was startled when the door opened for her. She

had assumed all the servants were asleep, as the house was dark and still. But, there was Easton. She mentally shrugged, realizing that Bent had always been on hand to do just the same, despite the hour of day or night.

As she stepped inside and past him, she thought she smelled liquor.

"Did you enjoy yourself tonight, my sweet lady fair?"

"I beg your pardon, Easton?" Isabella could barely credit her ears. *What* had he called her?

"Did an appropriate number of young gentlemen fawn over your ample charms, my lady? Did they all vie for the chance to dance with you and flatter you shamelessly? Did any manage to maneuver you behind a potted fern and steal a kiss, or *more?*"

Isabella could only stare at him. Goodness, he was looking at her arrogantly, one black brow arched. She suddenly noticed that he wore no coat or cravat, and the top buttons of his shirt were undone. Never had respectable Bent been seen in such a state. Of course, it only made Easton appear more handsome and perhaps a bit like a rake.

"I do believe you are foxed, Easton."

"Nonsense. Butlers don't get foxed." He frowned. "I shall, of course, have to ask Tilbot to be sure. But I feel quite confident that while butlers may occasionally become tipsy, they never get foxed." He shook his head emphatically.

"I think it best you find your bed now, Easton." Isabella began edging toward the stairs. Given the predatory gleam in his eyes, escaping her attractive butler seemed a very sensible thing to do right now. And heaven only knew, if she was anything, she was a sensible person.

"No, *my* bed is too bloody *small.*"

Easton, now grinning wickedly, was advancing on her. Oh, dear. She would swoon, surely, if he touched her. She'd never swooned before in her life, of course, but she had a feeling that this was truly a swoon-worthy situation if there ever was one.

"I'll bet my groats that *your* bed is big and soft, my lady fair. I'll bet it has room enough for *two*."

"Easton," Isabella squared her shoulders and attempted to look at him haughtily. "My bed is of no concern of yours. You are obviously in no frame of mind to converse in a reasonable fashion, and so I bid you goodnight." She turned and nearly ran to the foot of the stairs. She swung around to see if Easton had yet toppled over and found she was almost touching his shirtfront.

Without a word, he gently cupped her chin with his hand and lifted her face up to him. Isabella couldn't breath; the touch of his fingers caused her skin to tingle.

"Sweet lady fair," he murmured as his mouth settled over hers.

The feel of his warm lips was heaven. She knew she should push him away, knew allowing him such a liberty was wrong, but it felt so good, so *right*. And then his arms pulled her against him, and she gasped at the heat from his body.

He flicked his tongue against her parted lips. He kissed her again and again, his teeth nibbling at her full lower lip, his tongue caressing her; his hands stroked up and down her silk-clad back and then settled on her hips.

Isabella stiffened against him and tried to push him away. This was wrong, it was too much. He groaned again into her mouth. Desperate, she tore her lips away from his and threw back her head. "Easton, you mustn't," she rasped out in a weak voice.

"Bella, sweet Lady Bella," he licked the hollow of her throat where her pulse was beating madly. "You can't know how I've wanted to do this, to touch you, taste you." His hands roamed over her derriere. "You've been driving me mad."

Frightened and more than a little angry at his forwardness, Isabella shoved against him as hard as she could. He fell back onto the marble floor.

"How dare you! You touched my bottom!"

As she raced up the stairs and dashed to her room, Isabella could hear the sounds of his drunken laughter mocking her.

Chapter 5

"Good morning, Easton," Isabella loudly called out to her butler as she descended the staircase. She smiled as she saw him wince. It served him right to be incapacitated. She wondered if he remembered the outrageous things he had done to her last night. *She* certainly did. She had been awake the better part of the night thinking about how he had touched her and kissed her — and then had spent the rest of the night trying not to think about it as her traitorous body throbbed with the yearning he stirred in her. He was quite unlike any man she had ever met before.

"My lady."

"Is breakfast ready? I believe I shall enjoy some kippered herring and haggis this morning." Isabella remembered how her father had turned quite green just thinking about kippered herring or haggis after a night of imbibing too much liquor. Of course, Father had *always* become ill at the idea of haggis, a tasty Scottish dish involving most unappetizing animal body parts.

"Yes, and some fresh goat's milk." She could have sworn she heard a gagging sound from the man proceeding her to the dining room. Her mood drastically improved.

After spending close to an hour torturing Easton while she slowly ate her meal (which was actually kippers and eggs, but she didn't let *him* know that) and making sure to remark at nearly every bite how delicious it was, Isabella withdrew to her day room. It was almost time for luncheon when the footman rapped on her door, having just received a letter from her cousin Alex's courier. It was a thick packet, and she was somewhat apprehensive about opening it. Was he summoning Easton back so soon? It had only been a week, after all.

After picking up and putting down the envelope a good half dozen times with unusual indecisiveness, Isabella finally ripped it open. Inside was a letter to her and another envelope, this one addressed to Woodrow Easton. She took a deep breath then read her note.

Dearest Cousin Isabella,

Me gratitude knows no bounds that you have managed to put up with our young butler-in-training thus far. I pray he has not upset your fine sensibilities too much with his coarse ways.

Isabella snorted, thinking that if her cousin only knew how her "fine sensibilities" had been treated last night, he would surely shoot Easton. She read on.

Although it is not yet time for him to return to us here in London, things do look brighter for his future. I hope to have issues resolved within a week. I shall, of course, write you the moment I know for certain. Perhaps I shall come meself to fetch the puppy, as it has been overly long since I have looked in on you. I hope that you will forgive me imposition, but I shall come, with me friend Whit. All right, then, me dear, it's settled.

Until we meet in a week,
Your Cousin,
Alexander Fitzhugh

Goodness, he wrote strangely, and his speech certainly hadn't improved with the years. Ah, only a week left of Easton's company. She felt oddly depressed now. Life could be so very disappointing at times.

A footman delivered a letter to Rafe while he lay suffering in his room. Cook had given him a tonic earlier, which he had been assured would temper the worst of his headache but as yet it had not had much effect. Upon recognizing Alex's handwriting, he sat bolt upright, despite the agony it caused him. He eagerly tore open the envelope.

Dear Easton (ha!),
You will be most gratified to learn lovely Melanie is rapidly falling in love with first Whit and then me, of course. We are taking turns at wearing her down. The lengths we are willing to go for you, old boy! It boggles me mind.

Du Champs remains in the country, or wherever, which makes things much easier. We should have this matter resolved by the end of the week, when the poor sod is due home. I have written to plain little Isabella that Whit and I will come then to fetch you, thus relieving her of your tedious presence. We are so very kind.

Try to behave until then, and "limit your lamenting", as Tilbot suggests.

Your friend,
Alex

Rafe grinned at first, then frowned. He only had a week left with "plain little" Isabella.

He leaned back and closed his eyes, remembering vividly how beautiful she had looked last night in her dark blue gown with its revealing neckline. Bloody hell, he had actually squeezed her round little bottom.

He had brooded for a while after she left for the party, only too aware at how he would have treated her had he been himself and seen her in such a setting. He would have used his carefully crafted skills to flatter her, get her alone — the veranda always being a nice place — and seduce her as thoroughly as possible without *completely* compromising her, of course.

Cook had finally found him pacing among the thick tomes in the library, wanting to see if he was up for a game of cards and a pint of grog. The drink had sounded like just what Rafe needed. Perhaps the liquor would set him right again. Heaven knew he had never been one to sulk over a female, and he didn't much care to start now.

As he sat with the cook and a few other staff members, the cards were soon forgotten as the grog flowed and he learned quite a bit more about their lady.

"Och, she was a wee lit'le bairn when her lady mother birthed her." Cook had needed little prodding on the subject of their mistress. "She done come out wi' a head o' red fuzz, she did. A plain lit'le mite, sure eno'. Her da, the laird, feared she'd ne're catch a mon, sae he taught her all he ken o' managing the land." Cook chuckled and refilled his tankard. "Sure eno', she learned quick as a sprite, and then she *blossomed*." The others nodded, sighing with fondness for their lovely lady.

"So, she really was plain once?"

"Och, aye. Plain as day auld bread, she was. Boot such a smart and sweet lass, i' t'were easy tae o'erlook. Her da doted on her, boot ne'er did she spoil. She always has time fer yea, always remembers a birthday, and always has a kind word for work well done. Why, e'ery Christmas, besides a hearty helping o' coin, she gives her lasses each a bar o' fine rose soap, made by her own hands, nay less, and material fer a new frock." The heavyset cook nodded, then tapped a thick finger on the scarred wooden tabletop. "And, don't ye ken, each mon gets a fine new pair o' woolen mitts *wi'* matchin' scarves and a new pair o' boots."

"Really." Rafe was vastly enjoying the man's thick accent. He poured himself a refill of the tasty brew.

"Och, tae be sure. Mind ye, she expects a decent days labor, boot she treats ye fair fer it." The other men joined the chef in raising their mugs in salute. "'Course, there were some what didn't ken the pur lit'le lass could fill her da's shoes, once he passed o'er." His chest puffed up with pride. "But, she did now, didn't she lads, and right fine, tae."

Rafe had listened for a while longer to tales of the "sweet

lass" of her kindness, loyalty and bravery. Of how she nursed old farmer Danny when the fever was on him or how she pitched right in when the freeze came too early and nearly destroyed the crops. And any time there was a dispute between farmers or tradesmen, she was quick to offer the perfect solution. Silently, as he knew his dry remark would not be well met, Rafe had wondered if she shouldn't be put up for sainthood.

It was after the others had retired that he got to sulking and worrying again. He kept seeing her, attempting to fight off some lecherous old squire who had managed to corner her behind a pot of ivy. He remembered pacing and talking to the portraits high on the wall that he assumed were her long dead relatives, but about what, he couldn't quite remember.

Then, when he had been torturing himself with images of her *enjoying* some other man's attentions, she finally came home. And that's when he had completely lost control.

He groaned, then laughed. Her obvious attempts to make him uncomfortable this morning were quite adorable. Goat's milk and haggis? Good Lord. If he had thought he could have withstood the noise, he would have applauded her.

"WHATEVER is the matter with you, Bella?" Lisbeth frowned toward her.

Isabella turned to stare out the large windows of the parlor that overlooked the vast lawn and beyond. Her friend had only just arrived for tea and already Bella couldn't focus on her friend's gossip.

"Where is Easton today? I was very disappointed he wasn't here to show me in."

Isabella glanced at the blonde, whose pretty bow mouth

was set in a pout, and snorted. "He's probably still puking on his boots." She looked back out across the green lawn, toward the fields and woods stretching on. If only she wasn't responsible for the care of all this, she could—.

"Bella! What has happened — is Easton ill?"

Isabella turned from the window and took a seat on the light green settee beside Lisbeth. How much should she confide to her best friend? Dare she tell her of how thrilling it had felt to be in Easton's arms last night? How his tongue had flickered in her mouth and ... goodness.

"Nonsense, nothing happened."

"Now Bella," Lisbeth's tone was scolding, "you can't pull that on *me*, of all people. I know you too well." The other woman studied her heated cheeks. Suddenly, her visitor leaned back, her eyes wide with understanding. "Gracious!"

"What?" Isabella absently toyed with a tart on the tray before her. Their tea was still untouched. What was she to do about the man?

"He kissed you, didn't he?" Seeing Isabella's cheeks turn even redder, Lisbeth shouted with triumph.

Isabella placed her hands on her burning face, glanced at her friend, then nodded. "Yes," she whispered, before covering her eyes. She had never been so embarrassed. Gracious, she had actually let the man fondle her on the stairs! It had been a remarkable disregard of ladylike comportment. She couldn't help but wonder what he might have done next, if she hadn't run from him.

Lisbeth started giggling. "You lucky girl!"

"Beth! How can you think me lucky? Do you know what he *did* to me?" She groaned. Lucky, ha! He was leaving in only a week. How lucky was that? What was she to do?

Lisbeth sat forward, her pale blue eyes shining with excitement. "Tell me, Bella. What *did* he do to you?"

Isabella flung her head back against the couch, her arms wrapped around her. She sighed. "He kissed me."

Lisbeth let her irritation show. "I *know* he kissed you, but what *else*? There's more to it than that."

"His hands." Isabella faltered, thinking of his large warm hands caressing her back, his fingertips gently tracing her spine. She shivered as she recalled the feel of him grasping her hips.

"What about his hands?"

"They touched … my back." Isabella gave the blonde a meaningful look. "My *back*."

"Goodness."

She sighed. "And his, well, his tongue … "

"Oh, my." Lisbeth began fanning herself with her napkin. "His *tongue?*"

"On my neck … and … my mouth." She was feeling rather warm, herself. Her body was reliving each thrill as she talked about it.

"What actually happened?" The fair woman suddenly recalled Bella's earlier remark, which must seem at obvious discord with the kissing parts. "Why would he vomit on his shoes for heavens sake?"

"Oh," Isabella stiffened, and answered, "because he was foxed."

"No!"

"Yes," Isabella nodded. "He advanced on me, said outrageous things, and then kissed me."

"And," Lisbeth was leaning so far forward, she was in danger of toppling over.

"And then he embraced me." She looked down at her

white hands, fidgeting in her lap. "His big hands pressed me to him and I pushed at him, but he was too strong. I told him to stop, but then he began kissing my neck and I ... " She swallowed, hard. The feel of him pressed against her, the heat of his hands and mouth on her. She was wicked, surely, as she wanted to feel those sensations again.

"What?"

Isabella suddenly grinned, remembering just what had happened next. "I pushed him on his arse!"

"You did what?" Incredulous, Lisbeth's mouth hung open and her eyes were wide.

Isabella couldn't help it, she started laughing.

"Bella, really! That gorgeous piece of manhood kisses and caresses you and you knock him *down*? What is *wrong* with you?"

Isabella sobered. "Nonsense! What else was I supposed to do? He was drunk and making love to me on the stairs, for heaven's sake!"

"Well, I don't really know, but I think shoving him down was silly." Her friend gave her an indignant snort. "*I* would have let him continue a bit more, unless," the blonde looked suddenly concerned. "Was he being a clod? Did he bruise you or tear at your bodice?"

"No, no." Isabella waved her hand, dismissing the notion. "Nothing like that." White teeth worried her lower lip. "Truth be told, Beth, it was wonderful. I just got frightened when he, well, *grabbed* me *there*." She knew she was blushing again. "I just felt so out of control and I didn't know what would happen next if I didn't stop him. He was quite smashed."

"That's understandable, I suppose."

"I've never been kissed before, Beth." Isabella felt

woefully inadequate. Here she was at the ripe old age of nineteen, an age when most girls were married, for goodness sake, and she was having her first romantic encounter with her *butler*, of all people.

"Never?" The flirtatious girl appeared surprised. "Not even by Eddie Philpott? He was constantly after you before he went off to study."

Isabella shook head, her curls bouncing. "Goodness, no. Oh, he tried a time or two, but I only had to give him a stern look and he behaved himself again."

"I did wonder if you would marry him."

"Mr. Philpott?" Isabella laughed. "Nonsense! He's a weak little troll. He only wanted my money, after all."

"Oh, I doubt that was *all* he wanted, Bella." Lisbeth gave her a knowing look. "You'd quite begun to fill out by then." She laughed at the face Isabella made. "Really, you've become quite lovely. Father was going on just this morning about how you're even more beautiful than your mother was."

"Oh, please, Beth."

"Don't look so disbelieving. Haven't you got a mirror? Weren't you hounded last night, and not only at the party?" Lisbeth giggled.

"Bosh and rot."

"Goodness, Bella, I'm quite serious." The blonde looked at her in puzzlement. "You really don't see how lovely you've grown to be, do you? You have no idea."

"You are my dear friend and it's your duty to say sweet things to me." Isabella was embarrassed by this talk. She had known all her life how plain she was. Even her dear papa, who had loved her more than anything, had not harbored false thoughts.

"We'll not fool ourselves, dearest," Father had told her. "You're no head turner, like your sainted mother was, but you're smarter than most men. You've got that. Rely on your brains and eventually you'll settle a decent match."

She had been all of twelve at the time and the next year, the details of managing the estate were added, at her father behest, to her ladylike studies. She had quite enjoyed it, actually, earning praise from her tutor and her beloved father at her successes. She had decided then that perhaps it was a good thing God had traded her comeliness for brains.

Isabella altered the topic of conversation, bringing up that which was at the forefront in her mind. "He'll be leaving in a week."

"Who? Easton?"

"Yes, my cousin is coming to fetch him. I had a letter from him just this morning that he and his friend Lord Langley would be visiting."

"Why is Lord Stapleton taking such an interest in a butler?"

Isabella shrugged. She had wondered about it as well, but Alex was strange enough that anything was possible. Hadn't he named that fine hound of his 'Dog,' and refused to even consider changing it to something much more normal?

"Well, it's odd. They are of a similar age. Hmm," Lisbeth tapped a finger against her cheek while she thought. "Perhaps Easton is your uncle's bastard?"

"Well, it's possible but I don't think so. He doesn't act very much like the lower class, does he?" Finally, she poured herself and her guest a cup of tepid tea. "Alex's note was worded strangely. Something about situations righting themselves, and Easton's future looking brighter now."

"Perhaps he's a penniless count or something, and Alex is helping him out?"

"Nonsense, that sounds too fanciful, by far. Maybe he *is* a bastard. It would explain his haughty ways, if he had been gently raised."

"Well, this tea is cold, and it's growing late." Lisbeth stood and shook out the wrinkles from her sky blue day dress. As was her nature, her thoughts flew from one subject to another. "Father is expecting the vicar for dinner, and you know the evening will end in a row if I'm not there." Lisbeth's father and the vicar were rivals in the local horse races. Invariably, their discussion would turn into a shouting match of just who had the better mount. "I shall come by early tomorrow so that we can ride and further discuss delicious Easton."

Chapter 6

Although she had been thinking about him all day, Isabella didn't see Easton until the evening meal. He was at his usual post, awaiting her at the bottom of the staircase, when she emerged from her room and descended the stairs. He looked much better now. His color appeared normal and, upon closer inspection, she could see that his eyes were no longer nearly so bloodshot. In fact, they positively sparkled with amusement and devilment.

"My lady." He smiled and bowed to her, then surprised her by lifting her hand to his lips.

"Easton!" Isabella trembled at the feel of his warm breath on her skin. She snatched her hand away from his, shook her skirt with a snap and stomped past him. She had every right to be angry with him, and she wouldn't let him spoil it by behaving gallantly. She would not succumb to his seductive eyes and knowing smiles. She most definitely would not! She could ignore these silly tinglings emanating from the spot where his lips had caressed her hand and that now ran up her arm.

"You look lovely tonight, my lady." He reached out and opened the door for her, then bowed again. He grinned as he caught the glare she gave him as she marched past. "I do believe Cook has prepared one of your favorites tonight, my lady. Would you like to know what tempting morsels Cook has made for you?"

His breath stirred the loose tendrils of hair brushing her neck, causing her to shiver.

"I suppose I could wait and be surprised." Isabella strove for a dry tone. He was toying with her, she was sure. What was his game? To humiliate her yet again? She heard him chuckle, a low, wicked sound that made her want to kiss him, heaven help her.

"No, I won't keep you in suspense. He has prepared roast duck with raspberry sauce."

If only there was a terrine of soup handy she could conveniently dump upon his head.

Isabella sat very still, since he was still leaning over her shoulder. It was tempting to throw her head back and possibly give him a bloody nose, but then she might ruin her dress and the deep violet was one of her favorites. It was equally tempting to lean back and lift her face to his, to touch lips with him. She sighed.

"Easton, do please direct the footmen to serve." She felt a sudden sense of loss as he straightened and stepped away. She didn't want to spend yet another night eating alone, yearning for the companionship of the handsome man who stood silently regarding her through hooded eyes. There would be too many lonely nights after he was gone. She wondered what it would be like to have him seated across from her, sharing the meal. Unconsciously, she tilted her head to one side, while she considered it. It was insane, outlandish.

"Easton, I realize this is quite absurd, but would you care to join me this evening? I do believe I heard your mouth watering as you said 'roast duck with raspberry sauce'."

There, let's see if he dared to accept. She recalled her conversation with Lisbeth about the truth behind Easton and Alex's interest in him. She could use this opportunity to see if he revealed anything. Of course, he wouldn't dare accept, more's the pity.

Would he call her bluff? There wasn't a terrine of soup to be seen, after all.

"I would be delighted, my lady, to impose my poor self on you for this evening's meal. Do you have a preference as to where I should sit?"

"No," she almost gulped aloud. Goodness, what would the other servants think? She was too impulsive around this devilishly handsome man. What on earth had she been thinking to invite him to join her? And what the devil was he thinking to accept?

"You may sit where you will. It is of no matter to me." Surely he would exercise tact and sit a good distance down the table from her? Perhaps not too far, though.

"Thank you, my lady."

"Shall I pour your wine, my lady?" He waited for her nod, then filled her glass.

She realized he had no glass, nor even a plate. This situation was comical indeed.

"Oh, John," Isabella called out. A small footman poked his head in the side door. "Do fetch Easton a place setting."

There, that wasn't so hard. John had barely gaped at her, his eyes only just bugging out the tiniest bit. She glanced at Easton, and gave him a nervous smile. "It shouldn't be a moment." Goodness, what had she gotten herself into! She had actually invited her butler to dine with her! She was definitely a candidate for Bedlam.

Both remained silent until an additional set of dishes was brought and the meal served by the astounded footmen.

"So my cousin, Lord Stapleton, and his friend are coming next week to take you back to London." Oh, dear, that was a bit direct. Isabella stuffed a bite of duck in her mouth. She was really no good at subtlety.

"Yes," he said softly.

"I would assume you are anxious to get back to your life there." She couldn't look at him. He was probably thrilled with the idea of escaping North Bindlefork. She began pushing the food around her plate with her fork. He undoubtedly had numerous women friends at home who were eager to welcome him back. *They* probably wouldn't knock him down if he were to fondle their bottoms. It was too depressing.

"I have thoroughly enjoyed my stay here, my lady. I shall miss North Bindlefork tremendously." He took a sip of the wine. "Perhaps you may wish to visit London one day, and, if you would allow me, I could take you to Gunther's and buy you an ice."

"Who is 'Gunther' and what flavor ice?" The very idea of going anywhere with him was enough to perk up her appetite. Her, go to London? It was absurd. She would be completely out of her element in the bustling city. Perhaps she could learn more about him by coaxing him to speak of things familiar to him.

He laughed. "Any flavor you desire, my lady. Gunther's is a fine old establishment where many people go to enjoy treats. I often take my mother there on Saturday afternoons, when she chooses to reside in the city."

"Oh? Do many butlers go there?" The potatoes were delicious, with just a hint of leeks and rosemary. She didn't bothering commenting on the impropriety of an outing with a butler. Not while she was having dinner with one, certainly.

He chuckled. "I don't really know, my lady. I shall ask Tilbot, when I get home." He helped himself to another serving of the duck.

"Who is Tilbot? You mentioned him, er, before."

"Oh, did I?" He frowned. "He's just a fellow butler, my lady. No one of any consequence."

Isabella nodded, but she had the feeling he was hiding something. "Perhaps he could come with us to Gunther's?"

Easton nearly choked on a forkful of peas. "Well, I can certainly ask him, but I don't think it's his sort of place."

She had had enough of attempting to be subtle. Obviously, it didn't suit her. She was getting absolutely no where with the man. "Just how *are* you acquainted with my cousin, Easton?"

"Well, we met while out on the town. It's a very tedious story, really. It isn't even interesting dinner conversation. I believe the more interesting the table chatter, the better digestion one has." He speared a thick piece of meat. "Don't you agree, my lady?" He popped the bite into his mouth, smiling while slowly chewing.

"I'm quite sure I don't know anything about such a silly idea." She picked up her glass, pleased that her hand didn't tremble. "Would you be so kind as to pour me more wine,

Easton?" He had very neatly sidestepped her direct question. Yes, he was definitely hiding something, and it involved Alex. She had five more days, at the most, to try to find out just what it was he didn't want her to know. But, how to go about it? She had always received direct answers from her father on any subject she broached. She needed to ask Lisbeth what to do.

She studied the man as she sipped her wine and fiddled with her utensils while Easton finished his meal. He was a complicated fellow, to say the least. This need or desire to prevaricate was foreign to her. What would cause a man to be so duplicitous? What was he possibly hiding?

"Are you ready for some dessert, Easton?"

"I should like something sweet to taste, my lady." Easton gave her a wicked grin and watched as she blushed, her hand shaking the barest bit as she set down her wineglass.

"Well, *Cook* has something for you, I'm sure."

"Ah, of course. I'm being dismissed."

"No! I mean, not in the least." Oh dear. She really didn't want him to leave just yet. It was nice having a dinner companion, even if he tended to be a bit outrageous and was hiding some secret. He looked dashing, even virile in the soft candlelight. She toyed with the stem of her glass. He was watching her, a vague smile hovering about his firm lips.

"Would you happen to play, my dear?"

"I beg your pardon?" His eyes were so very blue and warm. She could simply sit here and stare at him for hours.

"Music, my lady. Do you play any musical instrument?"

"Oh, yes." She unconsciously bit her lip as her eyes went to his hands, which rested on the white linen tablecloth her great-grandmother had embroidered. They were very nice hands with long fingers. They had felt wonderful touching her.

"Would you play something for me?"

Her eyes flew to his face. That meant going to the drawing room, and that was much more intimate than the dining room, wasn't it? It was one thing to impulsively invite your butler to join you for a meal, but wouldn't performing for him be quite another?

"All right." Goodness, this new impulsiveness was going to get her into trouble, she just knew. *Serious* trouble, unless she missed her guess.

Isabella nervously sat at the piano. She was all too conscious of him leaning against the doorframe, his arms crossed over his chest, a sinful grin on his face. He was looking at her with such a devilish glint in his eyes she shivered with yearning.

"As I've never entertained a butler before, I don't know what you might prefer to hear, Easton."

He laughed, low and soft, and slowly sauntered toward her. "Whatever you wish, my lady." His deep voice glided over her and she felt tingles alight her skin.

She began to play a French ballad, which was turning out well until her fingers stumbled as he came and stood behind her. She could feel the heat emanating from him against her back and it drove all thoughts of music from her mind. She desperately tried to concentrate on the piece, but it was useless. She was much too aware of him, of his *maleness*.

She tried a jaunty Scottish tune. That didn't come out any better. Finally she stopped and settled her hands in her lap.

"I fear my playing is quite inept tonight." She had only to lean back to make contact with his hard body. She wanted to do nothing more. His masculinity was a palatable thing and its effects drew her nerves taut.

"Not to worry, my lady. Your beauty more than makes up for any lack you may have in musical talent."

That made her snort in a most unladylike way, jarring her back to reality. "Nonsense Easton, don't be absurd." Such practiced words, so meaningless.

"Too forward, my lady?"

"Too obvious, sir."

"Obvious in flattery?"

"Too obvious a lie."

"Now, *you* are being absurd."

Annoyed, and a bit disappointed, she turned around as far as she could on the narrow bench and looked up at him. "Why is everyone suddenly trying to convince me of a falsehood, Easton? Goodness, I've lived long enough being plain to know what I am."

How cruel of him to think to flatter her so falsely, to try to make her think he might actually find her attractive. She had hoped him above such deviousness.

"I beg to differ, my lady, but I feel that I, of all people, would know a beautiful lady when I see one. And I happen to be looking at an incredibly gorgeous young woman." He reached down and pulled her up by grasping her arms. "Isabella, look at me."

She tried to move away from him, but the bench was in her way. She bit her lip and shook her head, refusing to meet his eyes.

"My lady, if you doubt me, surely all those men of last night made it obvious how becoming you are."

"Easton, please," Isabella was close to tears. Was he trying to humiliate her? Why was he saying such things when they weren't true? She knew she was an ordinary woman, with no hope of being thought a beauty. Why, she knew perfectly well those ridiculous buffoons from the ball had only been enticed by her ample estate and, perhaps, the incentive of her equally ample bosom. They weren't truly attracted to her, not like she had begun to hope Easton was.

Gently, he stepped back and taking her hands' led her out from behind the bench over to the sofa and eased them both down. He enfolded her cold hands in his warm ones and waited until she looked up at him.

"I am wholeheartedly serious, my lady fair. You may have been a plain child, but you *are* a beautiful woman."

Isabella found herself wanting desperately to believe him, but it was folly. "Men are only interested in me for my money, Easton. Oh, goodness! I didn't mean you, I mean, well, I don't mean to say that you *are* interested in me, I ... " Oh, dear, she sounded like an idiot. She tried to pull her hands from his grasp so that she could flee, but he wouldn't let go. This was so utterly embarrassing. Blushing madly, she dared to glance at him and their eyes locked. Her pulse raced and her skin burned as she thought she detected wanting in his gaze. She watched his eyes flicker to her mouth. Her lips felt suddenly dry and she licked them breathlessly.

"But, truth be told, my lady fair, I am interested in you." He began stroking her palms with his thumbs. "I really shouldn't have said that, and I shouldn't kiss you either, but I fear I am helpless to do otherwise." He leaned toward her and captured her lips with his own in a tender kiss.

Isabella sighed and leaned into him. Her hands were suddenly free as he again grasped her upper arms, pulling their bodies closer together. He was kissing her as if he couldn't get close enough. Isabella became lost in his embrace and brought her own hands up to encircle his neck. When he touched her like this, she could almost believe she was beautiful, at least to him.

Isabella didn't know what was happening to her body, but it felt wonderful. She hoped he'd never stop. He was delicately nipping and then licking her neck and she wanted to be doing it to him. His finger, feather soft, traced a path between her breasts and she gasped at the intense jolt she felt in between her thighs. And then he actually touched her breast and she arched against him with a soft cry.

He buried his head in her neck with a moan before straightening and pulling her up with him. He dropped a kiss on the tip of her nose, then pressed her head down onto his shoulder.

"Good lord, you'll do me in for sure. I didn't mean to take it that far, my lady fair, but you quite stir me with your responses."

"Is that good?" Isabella felt her brain slowly begin to clear. Goodness, he touched her and she simply melted. She liked it very much.

"Well, yes, certainly. However, for an unchaperoned young lady, it's quite dangerous, as well."

"I think I know what you mean." Oh, my, she hadn't thought of that. Her reputation would be shredded if anyone learned of this. She should *not* be alone with him again. No, she really shouldn't.

"At least, I hope I've proved my point. You are quite irresistible, my dear."

She pulled back from his embrace to look at him. "I think you've given me much to consider, Easton." She couldn't help but grin. He'd said he actually thought her beautiful. Did she really have the power to overwhelm him, an obviously experienced man?

"I think I had best go to bed now." She needed to think about this latest development between them, to understand what had transpired here tonight, if anything.

Just who was this man?

"I think that best, also, my lady. Thank you for this evening." He kissed her lightly, then quickly stepped back.

Isabella left him there in the parlor and drifted up to her room to hopefully relive this surreal evening in her dreams.

Chapter 7

"Why ever are you grinning like a loon?"

The two young friends were trotting away from the manor house. It was mid-morning and the sun was shining down. Luckily, the heat of the day was still hours away.

"Whatever do you mean?" Isabella smiled wider.

"Oh, no, he's been kissing you again, hasn't he?"

Isabella's response was to laugh and break into a full gallop, leaving Lisbeth to try to catch up. She pulled up when she reached the end of the long drive, and Lisbeth was soon at her side.

"What happened this time?" The blonde frowned. "He wasn't drunk again, was he?"

"Not in the least." She patted Dilly's neck. She had to tell *someone* and knew she could trust Lisbeth to keep this bit of gossip to herself. "He did kiss me. He kissed me quite thoroughly, actually."

"Any more bottom grabbing?"

"No," Isabella gave her friend a shy smile. "Just lots of kissing and holding each other close. We decided it best to stop there." She sighed. She hadn't wanted to stop there. She resolved not to mention to the other girl how he had actually touched her bosom, and certainly not how incredible it had felt. "I asked him to join me for dinner." She nudged her horse into a walk, and Lisbeth did the same.

"You did *what?*"

"Well, I wanted to see if I could find out anything more about him and his connection to Alex." That sounded somewhat reasonable. "I finally flat-out asked him, but he danced around the issue."

"You don't mean to tell me he kissed you there at the dining table, do you?"

"Of course not. We were in the drawing room, after dinner, when he started all that."

"You invited him into the drawing room after dinner? He's your *butler*, Bella! At least that's what he's playing at. What were you thinking, for heaven's sake?" Lisbeth looked at the other girl as if she'd grown two heads.

"I did not invite him there," she felt herself blush. "He invited himself. He asked if I would play for him." Her friend still looked disbelieving.

"Well, it was after he thought I was dismissing him, a comment concerning dessert, and I couldn't be rude, could I?" She realized how pathetic she sounded. "Oh, dear."

"Oh, dear, indeed." Lisbeth sniffed. "You're quite in over your head, you know." Giving the other girl a stern look, she continued, "He's toying with you. He's not some young boy, he's a man who is used to women falling all over him." She waggled her finger at Isabella. "You had best stop this right now."

"He'll be leaving soon." The thought dampened Isabella's spirits. Only four more days and she would be all alone again.

"Not soon enough, for your sake." Lisbeth muttered. "Were you at least able to find anything out about him?"

"What? Oh, not really." Isabella thought over her conversation at dinner with Easton. "He said he and Alex met while 'out on the town' and he mentioned a man named Tilbot, whom he said was a fellow butler. He proposed taking me to a place called Gunther's for an ice, if I ever came to London."

"Yes, I've heard of that place. It's frequented by the *Ton*." Lisbeth read the gossip articles of the *London Times* with regularity. "But, what else did you learn?"

"Nothing, really." It was discouraging how little she had been able to glean from him. Isabella remembered her resolve of that evening. "You have to teach me how to wheedle information, Beth."

"What? I wouldn't know how to 'wheedle' anything." The blonde sniffed with mock indignation. "Really, where do you get such ideas?"

"Please," Isabella rolled her eyes, and they both laughed. "You would put a spy to shame with your abilities."

Lisbeth grinned. "All right, but you have to promise to be careful around your Easton. He is a very dangerous man, I think."

ISABELLA went to her day room, as was her habit in the late morning, after Lisbeth left her. It was only a few hours later when there came a knock at her door. Easton entered at her bidding, looking somewhat stern.

"Yes, Easton?" She smiled shyly. He had been elsewhere when she had come down to break her fast that morning. This was the first time she had seen him since last night. Of course, she had done nothing but think of him. Who cared about a flock of sheep when such a man as he was in residence?

"There is a young man to see you, my lady."

"Really?" This was a surprise. "Who is it, Easton?" It obviously wasn't her cousin by her butler's disapproving attitude, which relieved her greatly. She wasn't ready to give up her butler just yet.

"I believe he said his name was Mr. Dalton, my lady. He claims to be of your acquaintance."

"Oh." Why ever would Mr. Dalton be calling on her? With a shrug, Isabella stood and crossed the room. She couldn't help but smile at Easton, looking so proper and handsome. She wished she could kiss him.

"Stop that, my lady."

"Whatever are you talking about, Easton?" She smiled, looking at him from beneath her lashes.

"Lady Isabella." He moved to open the door, being careful to look at the wall opposite him and not her.

Isabella sighed, seeing he was determined to act the proper servant, and walked with him down the curved staircase and toward the front parlor.

Easton opened the door, stepped aside, gave her a warning look, then announced, "Baroness, Mr. Dalton is awaiting you within."

Isabella repressed a giggle at his so very haughty announcement and entered the room. There was Mr. Richard Dalton, just standing to greet her. She eyed Dalton critically for a moment, noting his bright yellow coat, turquoise trousers and white shirt were nowhere near as fine as the material of Easton's own stark attire. Dalton's cravat not nearly so crisp, nor his shoes quite as polished. Goodness, didn't he look like a peacock in those absurdly loud colors! And he tended to slouch. Yes, he was definitely lacking all around.

"Lady Isabella, how very lovely you look this afternoon." Richard Dalton's greedy eyes roamed over her. "I do hope I am not interrupting you?" He took her hand, kissing each finger.

Isabella rolled her eyes as Mr. Dalton slobbered over her hand. Apparently, Easton also thought it was a bit too much as she heard him gruffly clear his throat. Richard released her immediately and moved to take a seat to the side of the settee, obviously offering her the chance to sit next to him. Instead, she chose a chair opposite the sofa. She thought she heard the butler chuckle.

"Is he your chaperone, Lady Isabella?" Richard nodded toward the butler, his tone petulant.

"Easton, please see that tea is served. You will stay for tea, won't you Mr. Dalton?" She had no wish to share a single cup with him, but couldn't be rude. At least, if she offered him tea, she wouldn't be obligated to ask him to join her for lunch. She had never liked the young man, as he appeared much too smooth for her to feel he was ever being sincere in his regard of her.

"Thank you, my lady. I should be pleased to."

Isabella wished she could think of an excuse to send Mr. Dalton away, but nothing came to mind, drat it. He was sitting there, smirking at her in a most annoying manner, his eyes all too frequently darting to her bosom. She thought the yellow of his jacket made his skin appear sallow.

"I enjoyed dancing with you, my dear."

"Why, thank you, Mr. Dalton. It was a lovely party, wasn't it? And how is your dear father?" She was not going to allow him to become too familiar in his speech.

The door opened and Easton entered, pushing the teacart.

"Ah, thank you, Easton."

"Shall I pour, my lady?"

"No, that's quite all right." She could handle Richard better if her handsome butler weren't near to distract her with wicked thoughts. She noticed an errant lock of hair fall across Easton's brow and her fingers itched to reach up and brush it back.

"As you wish, my lady." Easton bowed out of the room, a scowl on his face.

Isabella managed to be polite during Mr. Dalton's visit, but it was a chore, to be sure. He droned on and on about himself, until she thought she'd scream. And the way he kept pulling out that ridiculous bright green handkerchief and fluttering it about was simply too much. Finally, he rose and prepared to take his leave.

"I haven't enjoyed myself more in ages, my dear."

He smiled down at her as she walked him to the door, his pale brown eyes lingering on her breasts. She wished she could slap him.

"I do hope we may visit together again? Perhaps the day after tomorrow I could come and take you riding? I've just purchased a fine stallion."

"Oh," Isabella couldn't think up an excuse to refuse him. Turning away suitors was not a situation she normally had to deal with. "Yes, that would be nice." Heavens, maybe she could get Lisbeth to join them.

Easton was standing just outside the parlor, leaning

casually against the wall, his ankle and arms crossed. He straightened slowly as the two emerged. "Are you on your way, then, Mr. Dalton?" He didn't even try to keep the contempt out of his voice.

Richard gave the butler a glare. "Yes, have my horse brought around." He turned to Isabella and took her hand, bowed over it and placed a kiss on her wrist. "Until Wednesday, Lady Isabella."

Mr Easton walked stiffly out the front door and signaled Harry to bring the man's horse forward.

Isabella breathed a sigh of relief after Easton closed the door on her unwanted visitor. She looked at her handsome butler, standing there with his arms folded across his chest, frowning at her. Goodness, what was wrong with him? He hadn't had to sit there and listen to the fool prattle on and on. It was she who had the right to be cross, if anyone did.

"Wednesday, my lady? You are seeing him again?"

Isabella was taken aback by his angry tone. "Yes, Easton, I am." It was becoming so obvious that he was not a butler it was almost laughable. Never had a servant spoken to her in such a manner! Nor had the audacity to stand before her with such a disapproving look on his attractive face.

"I see."

Whatever did *that* mean? "Well, good. I am relieved things are so clear to you. Would you send a message to Lady Lisbeth, please, requesting she join me for a ride with Mr. Dalton the day after tomorrow?"

He suddenly grinned. "I should be extremely pleased to do so, my lady."

Isabella returned to her day room, once again attempting to review the accounts. It was no use. She kept picturing

Easton smiling at her in the foyer. Who could think about sheep when he was near? She sighed. He was so very handsome. Everything about Easton was handsome. His dress, except for his cravats, which tended to look a trifle rumpled at times, his manners, even his deep warm voice. Goodness.

Just who was this devastatingly virile man her cousin had sent to her? He was, of a certain, not a man used to taking orders. Nor was he in training to see to the running of a household. That was beyond absurd. No, he was a man used to giving the orders, to expecting those around him to heed his direction. His very bearing attested to it with the way he stood so proudly, but with a casual grace, a nonchalance. His deep smooth voice almost always held more than a touch of dry amusement.

And, he was a seducer. How could any doubt that upon setting eyes on him? What man wouldn't be with riveting eyes so shockingly blue, and such a magnificent physique with broad shoulders, lean waist and muscles bulging nearly everywhere, all topped by black hair which, she could certainly attest, was just as thick and soft as it appeared.

Yes, there was much more to Woodrow Easton than she had been told, as yet. What had happened in London to cause his exile to North Bindlefork? And why was Alex aiding him if he was a supposed servant? She would gladly *give* away those fifty silly sheep if doing so would gain her her answers!

Her musings were interrupted by yet another knock on her door. Obviously, she would have no peace today. She was not surprised to see Mrs. Combs enter, looking quite nervous.

"Yes, Mrs. Combs?" Well, it had taken longer than she had thought for her housekeeper to seek her out. She had been expecting this interview at breakfast or very soon after.

"My lady," the older woman curtseyed, clearly uncomfortable and at a loss of how to begin.

"What is it, Mrs. Combs?" Isabella recalled her father's advice about how the servants were people, just as they were, and should be treated with the proper accord. However, they *were* servants and once in a while needed to be reminded who paid them. Father had said there would be times when she would need to reaffirm just who was in charge. She knew this was one of those times.

"I have heard some talk of last evening, my lady."

"Talk, Mrs. Combs? What sort of talk?" She carefully kept her expression bland, her voice cool.

"From the footmen and Cook. They said you actually had the butler to *dinner*, my lady."

She made it sound like some sort of disease. It was quite funny, really. "They did?"

"Oh, yes, my lady! I told them it was preposterous, but they assured me they had seen it with their own eyes."

"And so they did, Mrs. Combs."

The older woman blinked repeatedly. "My lady?"

"Yes, Mrs. Combs? Is there something else?" She let a bit of annoyance creep into her tone and tapped her pen against the edge of her desk.

The housekeeper was clearly confused, trying to fit this bit of oddness into her usually well-ordered world of class and boundaries. "Is this to be a regular occurrence, my lady? Should the table be set for two nightly?" Mrs. Combs quickly recovered her composure and her disdain was comically evident.

Isabella pretended to ponder this idea. "Hmm, I'm not sure, Mrs. Combs. Perhaps you would care to dine with me this evening?" It was hard not to laugh at the appalled expression on the other woman's face.

"Oh, no, my lady! I'm quite sure it's not my place."

"Very well. If I choose to dine with a guest, I shall inform Cook, Mrs. Combs." She gave the housekeeper a stern look and knew she need say no more. The pursed lips of the older woman conveyed she'd been clearly understood.

"Yes, my lady. As you wish."

"I have had a letter from Lord Stapleton. He and a guest shall arrive at the end of this week. Please have two rooms prepared for them. Now, if there are no other household matters, Mrs. Combs ... " She turned back to her desk, obviously dismissing the other woman.

"No, my lady," the housekeeper grumbled.

Isabella heard the rustle of her skirts as she left and cast her eyes heavenward with relief.

"That was well done."

Her back straightened as she recognized his dry voice. "Easton, were you eavesdropping?" Goodness, her pulse was pounding, and she felt quite warm, and from only from hearing his voice.

He snorted and came to stand next to her desk. "Nonsense, my dear, er, my lady. I came with a reply from Lady Lisbeth and saw you were already occupied."

She looked up at him then. He was smiling and his blue eyes sparkled with humor. She couldn't help but smile back, then looked at the paper he held out. As she took it from him, their fingers touched and the jolt she felt at the contact made her eyes fly to his face. She rose and unconsciously leaned toward him.

"Read your note."

"Oh, yes," Isabella said, a bit breathlessly. Goodness, would she ever meet another man who only had to brush her hand and she would want to wrap herself around him? It was terribly unfair that *this* man was the only one, so far. She had felt nothing when dancing with all those others, some of whom had been handsome enough.

Life was a trial. She sighed and unfolded the letter. "Oh, dear, she cannot come tomorrow afternoon."

"Perhaps you could send out two more notes suggesting, instead of riding, dinner on Thursday?"

"Oh, what a wonderful idea! Will you wait while I pen them, please?"

She was done quickly, and, careful not to touch her as he took the notes, he bowed to her then left to find a footman to deliver them immediately.

ISABELLA decided to take a walk in the gardens before dinner, as her room was much too stuffy. It was a lovely clear evening, the twilight only just settling over the land and the stars barely visible. She strolled through the roses, now in full bloom, their heady scent filling the air. Her mother had especially loved the red roses, but Isabella had always favored the white ones. Coming to one of the stone benches situated in front of a huge old rose tree, with a view of the white flowers, she decided to sit for a spell. It was so very peaceful here. She let her thoughts drift, and they again, of course, settled on Easton.

She pondered what Father would have thought of him. He had certainly disapproved of Mr. Dalton saying, "He's a simpering ass, that one is, Bella. Stay away from him or I shall disown you."

No, he hadn't liked Richard at all. But Easton was

anything but an ass, and certainly not simpering. She could imagine her father taking one look at him and scoffing at the butler pretense. He would probably call Easton a womanizer and once again warn her away. Or would he? He had actually encouraged her to flirt once, when a very attractive young lord had come calling on them to inquire about purchasing some land. She remembered looking at him aghast.

"Nonsense, I could not possibly *flirt*, Father!" The very idea was foreign to her. She was not one to act coy or tease with a gentleman, and he knew this. Hadn't he always been so very approving of her directness?

Her father had looked at her a bit sadly and nodded his head. "I know, dearest, more's the pity." She had not understood him.

Would her father think her lovely now, as Easton said? Would he look at her and see some small trace of her mother's beauty shining through? Isabella recalled how often she would come across Father in the hallway, standing in front of Mother's portrait and staring at it intensely. If he spotted his daughter, he would give her a sad smile and say, "Damn fine woman she was," and stroll off to wherever it was he had been going before the portrait had captured his attention. He rarely mentioned Mother's great beauty to his plain daughter.

But, several years had passed now and she had matured. Perhaps he would think she had more to offer a man than the size of her estate and business sense.

Isabella couldn't begin to imagine what he would say if he saw her lusting after the supposed butler. Goodness, it was absurd, she knew, but, what was she to do? The man had only to look at her and she was clay for him to mold as he saw fit. She sighed, knowing there was no way to control these delicious new feelings he stirred and admitted, if only to herself, that she really didn't want to.

She was a practical girl and always had been. She was never one to give over to flights of fancy and had always been rather proud of the trait. But, now ... well, now everything was different. *She* was different. She knew now what it was to feel desire for another, and to wish, beyond all hope, there could be a chance for happiness in the arms of a man quite unsuitable for her. Even if she was right, and he wasn't a servant, he was still not a man she could accept. Even if her body yearned for his touch, and goodness how it did, there was no hope for it. More than likely he was a bastard and would never be acceptable to her Uncle Hugh, Alex's father. And though she held the title of Baroness outright and owned the estate and lands, she would still need the approval of her uncle to be able to marry.

She sighed. What a muddle it all was. She didn't like things to be so uncertain. She wished she knew just how Eaton felt about her, but of course they couldn't speak of it. What a fool she was to even allow her heart to become so attached to the man. She could never have him, and all the wishing wouldn't change that.

Just before dinner, Easton gave her the responses to the notes she had sent. Both Lisbeth and Mr. Dalton would be happy to come to dine on Thursday evening. She told a passing maid to inform Cook that they would have guests, then allowed her handsome butler to seat her for the meal. She was hard pressed not to laugh when every so often a footman would stick his head through the connecting door to the kitchen. She was sure they were dying to see if Easton would be sitting beside her, even though she had not requested even a spare spoon. Although she dared only to surreptitiously glance his way, she had a feeling Easton was amused as well.

After the quiet meal was over, Isabella stood and finally gazed directly at the butler, who had been silently watching her all evening with his smoldering eyes, leaning against the wall with his ankles crossed casually.

"I think I shall go to the library and read. Goodnight, Easton." She saw the surprised lift of one brow and grinned at him impishly. "Yes, I do enjoy reading, Easton."

"Of course you do, my lady. I hear there are quite delightful novels for young ladies and their delicate sensibilities," he said, his voice dry, teasing her back. "Yes, sweet little stories of purity and true love, no doubt. I shall escort you to the library, my lady fair."

Isabella hoped he would keep being silly with her. She did so enjoy his subtle humor. Her father had been an excellent conversationalist, but he was almost painfully direct and grounded to earth. He had not been one to joke about.

Easton ushered her out of the room and toward the large library. "And what is the title of this maidenly little story you plan to read, my lady?"

"Would you be disappointed if it weren't 'Love on the Moors'?"

"I would be appalled."

"Well, then I certainly shan't tell you I'm reading Plato. No, I would hate to crush your genteel opinion of me." Isabella was disappointed to see they had already reached her destination. She had seen him looking at her like he would very much like to kiss her again. However, she doubted he would dare set one foot inside the dim room and be alone with her. "Would you care to come in and select a tome to put you to sleep, Easton?"

Oh, she was wicked.

"Thank you, but no, my lady. I think it best we not offer up any more gossip for the servants." He must have seen her disappointment. "Go on and read, my dear. I shall see you in the morning, I'm sure." He opened the door for her, gently pushed her inside, then firmly shut it.

Chapter 8

It was late when Isabella came to dinner the next evening. Easton had been purposely avoiding her all day and she was angry enough to spit.

To get even, she had spent longer than usual at her bath, knowing he would be standing at the foot of the stairs the whole time. When she did finally come down, she was sorely annoyed to not see him there. Instead, there was a red-faced footman, by the name of Thomas, waiting all this time. Curse him!

"Thomas, where is Easton? Why isn't he performing his duties?"

"My lady," the young man bowed with a jerk. "He claimed he weren't feeling up to snuff and went to town to find a cure, my lady." Another jerky bow. If Isabella weren't so mad, she would have been hard pressed not to laugh at the nervous fellow.

"I would see him when he returns, Thomas. I shall have

to explain the necessity of requesting my permission before abdicating his duties." She turned and stomped to the dining room. Poor Thomas had to run to reach the door before her.

Dinner was miserable. The food even seemed to suffer the loss of Easton's presence. Didn't he realize their time together was drawing to a close? Weren't these last few days as precious to him as they were to her? Even if it was only to spend a few snatched moments here and there together, it meant much to her. She waited in the adjacent parlor for an hour before finally retiring, her fury held close to her.

By morning, her mood had not improved, especially when she remembered her dinner guests would be coming that night. And tomorrow, Alex and his friend would arrive and take her wonderful, if exasperating, butler away. She would be left alone again. Goodness, it was depressing. She decided to go for a ride before breakfast. Perhaps that would lighten her spirits.

She arrived at the stables dressed in a smart brown riding habit. Her long hair was in one thick braid down her back, topped with a small matching hat sporting a white feather that curled down and nearly touched her cheek.

"Harry!" She called out and the fellow was instantly before her, grinning as usual.

"Good mornin', m' lady! You'd like a ride this lovely mornin' 'afore eatin', I'm guessin'."

Isabella couldn't help but return his smile, then laughed as he dashed away, his boyish legs and arms pumping as he ran.

Just over an hour later, she returned from her ride. She had given Dilly her head, allowing the horse to race them across the fields full of wildflowers and her mood was much improved. She headed directly to the table and ate a substantial amount of Cook's delicious fare.

There still was no sign of Easton by the time she had finished.

RAFE watched Isabella return from her ride while sitting on his horse, hidden just off the main path. She looked gorgeous and vibrant astride her magnificent beast. He always admired a woman who could sit a horse well. She moved with natural grace, her bearing confident and bold.

He was just coming back from the quaint town where he had spent the night in the only inns largest bed, which still seemed considerably small to him. A maid there had been tempting, but somehow, it didn't seem right to dally with her. She didn't have glorious auburn hair, for one thing, damn it to hell.

He had managed to stay away from Isabella all of yesterday but knew that it would be extremely difficult to keep the same resolve of the previous night and leave her alone. And so, he thought showing very good sense, he had removed himself from temptation. He knew she would be angry with him, but decided that might also help to keep anything further from happening between them. With luck, which he sorely needed by now, Alex and Whit would come and rescue him tomorrow. With her cousin in the house, she wouldn't dare attempt, in her extremely innocent way, to seduce him further. He had resolve, but he was only a man, after all. How long was he expected to be able to resist her, damn her beautiful eyes?

No, by Sunday, or Monday at the latest, he would safely be ensconced back in his own house, in the heart of bustling London, free once more to go about his daily business. There would be no more threat of being run through by a friend and, no more enticing little country innocents to reduce him to such a randy state. He would immediately find a new mistress and spend several glorious hours making love to her. Rafe frowned as Isabella's image, her face passion dazed, popped into his mind's eye.

Bloody hell.

SHE was furious, again. Easton had come back to the house, a stammering Thomas had informed her, late that morning, and *still* he had not come to see her, despite her orders. Thomas swore he had given the butler the message, but apparently the man had decided to ignore her direct request.

It was too much. And now, she was expecting guests and had no idea if she had a butler who would do his duty. Never mind that she was absolutely certain he wasn't a butler. He was shirking his responsibility, and it was not to be borne. It was the principle of the matter that irked her, nothing more. It certainly had nothing to do with the fact that this would probably be their last evening together before Alex spirited him away again. She would figure out how to make him pay for this insolence. There had to be a way to get under his skin. She smiled, deviously, as an idea came to mind. My, it was wonderfully wicked. Could she possibly pull it off?

RAFE took his place at the entry, heard the sound of hooves clatter on the cobblestone drive and opened the door just as Miss Lisbeth and Mr. Dalton arrived at the same time. He bowed and took their wraps, then directed them to the parlor. He assured them Lady Isabella would be with them in a moment, handed the wraps to a footman after he left them, and waited at the base of the stairs. He didn't have to wait long before he heard the rustle of silk and looked up. His jaw must have hit the floor, it felt it hung so far open at the sight of Isabella descending the staircase. She looked like a goddess tonight, her hair a mass of loose curls, tumbling down from the crown of her head. Her creamy shoulders were exposed, along with a fair amount of cleavage, in a gown of dusky lavender shot through with silver threads. Diamond earrings hung from her dainty lobes, her only enhancement. She was absolutely ravishing and he was going to kill her.

"Ah, Easton," she said smoothly. "So, you *are* still employed here?"

That made his mouth snap shut.

"Have my guests arrived yet?"

Through clenched teeth he muttered, "Yes, my lady."

"Wonderful." She breezed past him, her chin in the air, her haughty mantle firmly in place.

"Isabella!" Rafe hissed at her. "You can *not*—."

She whirled on him, her emerald eyes blazing with anger. "Do not dare to tell *me* what I can and cannot do! This is *my* home and I am the mistress here! Remember your place, sir! You would do well to recall you are still in my employment." She turned and marched toward the parlor.

Rafe's long strides brought him beside her easily. "Do forgive me, *my lady*." Stiffly, he opened the door for her. What he wanted to do was grab her and shake her. She was going to play the haughty little miss, was she?

"Miss Tetherly, Mr. Dalton," he bit out, fuming that he couldn't assert control over the woman and see that she behave properly. She had actually had the nerve to dress him down like any common servant! "The *Baroness* of Kirkwood."

His eyes narrowed as he observed Dalton practically

salivate at the sight of her. He sorely wished the rotter would give him cause to beat him senseless at the moment.

"Goodness, Bella! You do look lovely tonight." Lisbeth looked from him to the haughty mask of her friend. "Although," she muttered, "your color is a bit up, dear."

"I've just been so anticipating this evening, Lisbeth," was Isabella's stiff response.

"Well, lovely, nonetheless. Don't you agree, Mr. Dalton? Mr. Dalton?" Lisbeth stuck her elbow into his ribs.

"My God, yes!"

"Thank you for your enthusiasm, sir." Isabella replied, fairly smirking. The other man moved forward and began kissing each of her knuckles.

"Why don't we go in to dinner? Cook has truly outdone himself this evening, I understand." Mr. Dalton immediately gasped her arm and then, almost as an afterthought, took Lisbeth's also.

"I am truly the luckiest man alive, to have the company of two such charming creatures."

When the three were seated, Isabella at the head of the table, Mr. Dalton on her right and Lisbeth on her left, Rafe gave a nod for the meal to be served. Since there was company, there would be at least three courses and Rafe knew this would be a trying ordeal. He watched Isabella laugh at some remark from Dalton, and felt like slamming his fist in the wall — or the other man's face.

Isabella was flirting outrageously by the time dessert was served, and Rafe was fit to kill. Lisbeth kept rolling her eyes, and stifling an occasional giggle.

Rafe couldn't decide whom to kill first, her or that lecherous bastard receiving all of her charms. He would give her a good piece of his mind, when the bloody sod and Miss Lisbeth left. See if he didn't.

"Let's go into the other room, Mr. Dalton, and allow Lisbeth to play for us." Isabella leaned forward and placed her hand on his sleeve. "She has the most beautiful voice, truly."

Richard, the lecherous sod, could only nod mutely as he peered down her cleavage.

Miss Lisbeth rose and Rafe pulled her chair away for her, all the while watching Dalton do the same for Isabella.

"Easton?" Lisbeth whispered, "the *door*."

Rafe blinked, then gave her an appreciative grin. He stepped away and opened the portal for the trio. His eyes narrowed on Isabella as he caught her giving him a sidelong glance as she walked past. The little vixen was indeed playing with fire. Apparently, she was enjoying this new discovery that her beauty held power over men. She was testing her wiles on the odious Dalton. He would have pitied the other fellow, if he didn't want to strangle him so badly.

"You will sing for us, won't you dear Miss Lisbeth?" Dalton could barely take his greedy eyes off of his charming hostess.

Isabella seated herself on the sofa, and he vividly recalled her passionate responses to his caresses when they occupied that same spot.

Mr. Dalton seated himself beside her.

Rafe was seething by the time Lisbeth had sung three songs. Isabella was sitting much too close to the man, and the bastard keep *touching* her. He was sorely tempted to call a close to the evening himself, his masquerade be damned. Dalton had consumed a copious amount of wine at dinner and was even now finishing his second brandy. Thank goodness the evening finally appeared to be drawing to an end.

"That was wonderful!" Isabella stood and applauded her friend with exaggerated enthusiasm. Her tense stance told him she was feeling the strain of the evening.

"Yes, wonderful indeed, Miss Lisbeth." Richard clapped, following Isabella's lead in rising.

Lisbeth stood and shook the wrinkles out of her skirts, giving Mr. Dalton a pointed look, which he obviously missed, before she left the room, Rafe close behind her.

ISABELLA felt a trill of alarm, which only increased when she looked around and saw that her butler was nowhere to be found. Goodness, she was momentarily quite alone with an obviously enamored and slightly drunk young man. Before she could think of a single thing to distract him, he grabbed her, pressing his body hard against hers.

"Goodness!"

"Oh, my darling Isabella."

To her revulsion, he smashed his thin lips to hers. His arms locked around her and she could scarcely breathe, let alone push him away. Oh, heavens, what was she to do? She'd brought this on herself, really.

The painful kiss continued, now with him trying to jab his tongue into her mouth. She managed to pull her head back, but that didn't stop him. His lips sought the tops of her breasts.

"Mr. Dalton, *stop* that!" She would not shriek. Her servants had already been witnesses to enough gossip fodder from her of late. She didn't care to add to it. "You are too forward, sir!" What was taking Lisbeth so long?

Isabella was in an utter panic. If Richard didn't stop his pawing, she would surely be ill. She attempted to kick his shin, but her delicate silk slippers were useless and she only succeeded in hurting her toes. She doubted he even noticed her assault.

"Stop this, right now. *Stop it*," she hissed through clenched teeth. God, who would have thought a foppish man would be this strong? She feared he was bruising her ribs and it was getting more and more difficult to draw a breath. She squirmed in an attempt to break free.

Richard chuckled. With his teeth, he tried to pull her bodice lower.

"What *do* you think you are doing? I say stop this this instant, sir!" She squeezed her eyes shut as he continued, despite her pleas, terrified of what he might do next. She heard the rending of fabric. Heavens, she was just going to have to scream. There was no hope for it. She tried to draw in a breath and opened her mouth.

Suddenly, she was released from his painful grip and toppled backward, luckily landing on the sofa, what little breath she'd managed to draw whooshing out of her. Goodness! She looked up and saw Richard dangling before Easton, the butler holding him off the floor with one hand by a fistful of lacy white cravat. She couldn't see the other man's face, but Easton looked fit to kill.

"You scum! You bloody bastard!" Her butler who was no butler, shook the other man as if he were only a dirty rag.

Richard made a squeaking noise as Easton shook him yet again.

"You filthy little rotter! How dare you molest Lady Isabella!" He was shouting in the man's face, oblivious that he now had quite an audience attending him. "I should kill you, here and now, you puling son of a bitch!" Another head wobbling shake and a hard fist in the nose was what the scoundrel got.

Isabella wished she could conveniently faint. There, behind Easton, crowded in the doorway, was not only Lisbeth, but her huge cousin and another gentleman, too.

"Oh, good lord." Could this evening get any worse? "Easton, please put him down. Hello, Alex. I assume this is your friend, Lord Langley? How do you do, sir?"

Easton hit Dalton again, then dropped him onto the hard floor, and looked at her. "Alex? Whit? They're both here? *Now?*"

Isabella nodded. "Right behind you." She pointed over his shoulder, then looked down at Richard, who lay unconscious in a crumpled heap. "Does anyone have a sturdy shoe I may borrow? I wish to kick him." She looked up at Easton. "I did try before but my slippers are simply no good."

Her hero didn't even spare his friends a glance, but went straight to her side, sat and pulled off his shoe, presenting it to her with a flourish. "Will this do, my lady fair?"

She started to laugh, then her voice hitched and tears threatened to spill.

Easton embraced her, easing her head down onto his broad shoulder. She knew she should protest, especially with such an audience but she hadn't the strength.

He heard the snort from her cousin and looked over, appearing surprised to see he other two men still hovering in the doorway. He waved them in impatiently, his concern focused on her as she still lay cradled in his strong arms.

Lisbeth pushed her way through the two young lords, anxious to see that Bella was truly all right. "Oh, Bella, dearest."

Isabella felt wonderfully safe in her butler's muscular embrace, but pulled back to look at her friend. Her smile felt watery. "I'm fine, now." She looked up at the man holding her so tenderly. "Thank you, Easton." He had actually hit Richard, and for her sake! How very gallant.

"You're quite welcome, my dear."

Isabella looked down at the body again and grimaced. "Would someone please remove *that?*"

Mr Easton brushed a tear from her cheek, released her and stood, calling out the names of several of the more burly servants. Finally, he looked at his road-weary friends. Cousin Alex appeared dumbfounded as he stared at her.

"Good God, Bella," Alex said, looking her over from the top of her head to toe of her slippers peeking out from the hem of her gown.

"Oh dear, Alex. I know I'm quite a mess." She patted at her tresses, now a bit the worse for the wear. "If you'd come when you were *supposed* to, you'd not have had to witness this absurd spectacle I've caused."

The three men laughed.

"Leave it to a woman to apologize and blame the men in the same breath," the one named Whit chimed in. "I believe Alex was only taken aback by your beauty, my lady, not your mussed hair." He chuckled. "Lord Stapleton has been so worried about his 'plain' cousin, you see. And well, here you are, presiding like Guinevere while men are slain at your feet." He snickered and pointed at her butler. "Your knight!"

Mr Easton gave his friend a warning look, which of course, was ignored as the other man continued to chuckle. The servants arrived and looked to him for direction. "Remove this bloody sod, and none too gently, lads. He has abused our dear lady."

The men looked at their mistress, eyes darting from the torn bodice to her tear-stained face. They scowled down at Mr. Dalton. In a manner not even remotely gentle, they picked him up, nodded to their lady, then hauled him out. The sound of the body hitting the cobbled drive was quite clear.

"Easton, your shoe."

"Thank you, my dear."

"Good God, Rafe, what's been happening here?" Cousin Alex fairly shouted.

Lisbeth, seated beside her friend, squeaked in surprise.

"Don't fret, dear lady," Whit smiled at the pretty blonde, "he's just a very loud bear, not a vicious one."

"'Rafe,' Easton?"

"A nickname, my lady."

"An odd one, Easton."

"Not at all. One of my names is Raefiel."

"Still odd, but better than Woodrow, I suppose."

"Thank you so much, my lady. I am relieved you deign it sufficient," he said. "Back to the practical little general, I see. Now," he scowled seriously, "did the blighter hurt you?"

Isabella blushed and shook her head. "He may have bruised me, just a bit, he was holding me so tightly." She frowned. "I couldn't move, couldn't do anything. It was quite unnerving."

"Are you sure you're not hurt? Should we call for the doctor?"

"Goodness, no!" Isabella jumped. "He's Mr. Dalton's *father!*"

Whit started to laugh again.

"I just want to know one bloody thing!" Cousin Alex

bellowed. "Have you compromised me little cousin!" And with that he grabbed a fistful of Rafe's shirtfront.

Chapter 9

A short while later, they were all calmly seated at the dining table, a feast of cold fare spread before them. Cousin Alex was placid now, finally believing Isabella's assertions that she had not been compromised by anyone. While Whit and Alex ate, the others filled them in on the scene they had come upon.

"It really was my fault for behaving so silly," Isabella confessed. She glanced sideways at Easton, who was now being called 'Rafe' by everyone, including Lisbeth, and being treated quite like a peer. "I was attempting to flirt. It wasn't well done of me, I admit." She could feel the blush burning her cheeks.

"Nonsense, me dear," Alex said around a mouth full of chilled roast beef. "No matter how much a lady flirts, a gentleman doesn't attack her in her own bloody drawing room."

Whit and Rafe both raised a brow at him.

"What? Oh, I do mean *attack*, me lads, not finesse."

Isabella watched how easy the three were together. It said much. Rafe was certainly no commoner. No, he was somehow closely related to the peerage. He was too comfortable, too relaxed, sitting here and supping with them all. His manners and comportment were refined, even surpassing the other two gentlemen. Could he be related to royalty?

"You're not a butler, so why did Alex send you to North Bindlefork, Rafe?" She liked the sound of his new name. It was somehow dark and dangerously attractive, just as he was.

The three men exchanged looks.

"Oh, come now, I'm not a ninny. I've realized for some days you are not a servant."

They still wouldn't answer her.

"You're a bastard, then."

"Really, cousin! No need to get nasty."

"No, I mean he's actually the baseborn offspring of a lord. Goodness, Alex!" Isabella threw a roll at her relative, who deftly caught it. She couldn't help but grin at his surprised expression.

"Ah, well then, yes he is."

While the two young ladies exchanged a look that declared triumph, Rafe punched his friend in the arm. Alex shrugged in response, looking confused.

"Oh, goodness!" Lisbeth's small white hand fluttered to the base of her throat. "My poor father! I quite forgot about him. He expected me home some time ago. He shall be worried sick."

Isabella frowned. "It is too late to travel back home. You shall have to stay here."

Isabella found herself immediately looking to him, seeking his counsel.

Smiling, he turned his gaze to the blonde. "I've already sent him a message, Miss Lisbeth. I said you would be staying the night, to help sooth Lady Bella's nerves."

"My nerves are quite fine, thank you."

"Well, then," Whit wiggled his light brown eyebrows suggestively at Lisbeth, "perhaps she can sooth me? My nerves are terribly frayed."

"Really!" Lisbeth smiled coyly, then giggled.

"Oh! I just thought of something else." Isabella jumped up from the table and ran out of the room, leaving everyone staring after her. She was back in a few moments, smiling and shaking her head. Her eyes locked with Rafe's.

"I just had *the* most fun!"

"What did you do now?" he asked dryly.

"I just got to tell Mrs. Combs you were now our guest *and* would need to be moved to a better room!"

"WHY the hell couldn't you have told her the truth?"

"What? And have me father here by next nightfall demanding you marry her? Don't be daft, man." Alex looked at Rafe as if he'd taken leave of all of his senses. "And, don't doubt he would, once he heard that the Duke of Devonshire had just spent a fortnight alone with his niece. He knows you too well to think any female as lovely as that chit has become is safe from your wicked ways." He snorted. "Why, she don't even have a butler to protect her. Ha!"

Whit laughed along with him. Rafe, however, was not amused. What he was was frustrated.

It was well into morning, they all having slept in because of the late hour they had retired. Rafe had been apprised of the 'Melanie Situation,' as Alex called it, last night over their brandies after the ladies had gone up to bed. After much flattery and trinkets, Melanie confessed she had never meant it to get beyond Madam Rose about their affair, and that it hadn't. She apparently realized how scandalous their liaison could be. Lyle had returned and found all as it was before he had left. Whit and Alex had quite enjoyed their mission, but were anxious to retrieve their comrade from 'hell and beyond North Bindlefork,' as Whit had put it. They had departed London the next day and rode as quickly as they could, deciding to press on last evening rather than spend an additional night on the road.

Now the three were arguing over how long to remain in the countryside as they descended the stairs to the main floor. Alex was of the opinion they should return immediately.

"There are fisticuffs to attend, damn me, and races to wager on. Not to forget all the lovelies needing our attentions."

"You know, there are a few lovelies right here, old man."

"You'd better not be inferring me cousin."

"No, no," Whit was quick to dissuade the glowering man. He glanced at Rafe, who was relieved, himself. "Your cousin is quite safe from me. I was referring to the adorable little blonde. Now, she'd be fun to dally with."

Alex snorted. "I can't seem to get past them two in plaits, puppy."

"I certainly didn't see a braid last night."

"She's a terrible flirt, you know." Rafe smiled at Whit. "She'll break your heart, then go dancing off without a care."

Whit laughed. "I love that in a girl!"

The three entered the dining room, a place Rafe had begun to develop a love-hate association with, actually, to see the buffet loaded, places set. The air was heavy with the scents of freshly baked bread, sweet pork, and eggs. Rafe's mouth watered.

"Me country cousin does me proud."

They each helped themselves, then took their seats.

"She really does, Alex." Rafe dug into the warm eggs, subtly flavored with nutmeg and cinnamon. "She's been running this place rather well for several years now." He couldn't hide the pride in his own voice.

"Well, of course, she's got a good steward, to be sure." The burly man cut into a thick slab of fried pork with zeal.

"No, she hasn't. She handles matters all by herself."

Alex looked at him like he'd grown horns. "That's preposterous, old sport. She's having you on."

"No, really. It's common knowledge that her father taught her to be self-sufficient, what with her drab beginnings. He was determined what she lacked in her physical appearance could be overcome in other ways, so she could still have hopes of making a decent match one day. I would think you, as her closest relative, would know of this."

"Who told you all this?"

"Why, the servants. Oh, by the by, you don't happen to know just what it is they put in the grog in these parts, do you?"

"Amazing. Uncle Ian was serious about teaching her to run things. I thought he was pulling me leg!" Alex grinned. "Ha! The Bindlefork Brew quite did you in, did it? They'd never tell me. Cook keeps that secret to himself, don't he though." He resumed his attack on the pork. "Me uncle knew. I think he and Cook concocted it together one night when they were young lads."

"God, I've never had a head like that before." Rafe

grimaced at the memory. And then he grinned at another recollection, much sweeter and smelling of roses.

Cook paid Rafe a short visit later that day as he was leaving his new room.

"It's me laird, ain't it?" The squatty older man gave him the once-over, his full face quite red. "Och, I had a feelin' aboot ye. And soon ye'll go off wot wi' them other dandies, leavin' pur wee Lady behind tae pine o'er ye."

Rafe was stunned and it took him a moment to realize Alex's warning was coming back to haunt him.

Cook shook his meaty fist at Rafe. "Ye had ye're bit o' fun, is tha' it, then? We ken ye been at her."

Rafe was quite taken aback at the angry assault. He rather liked the man and it rankled that his opinion of Rafe had sunk so low so quickly. What had happened to the camaraderie of the other evening?

"Is that really what you think?"

The servant deflated before his eyes. "I ken no'. Boot wot's tae be, then? Ye'll be marryin' her?"

Rafe was speechless for a moment. *Marry* Isabella? Bloody hell! "She'd not have me, I'm sure. It's best I leave and she find some placid country gentleman to settle with." The repellent image of Dalton came to mind. "Look, I really am very fond of Lady Isabella, but it cannot work between us. After all, I'm a—" No, he couldn't say it. He couldn't actually tell someone he was a bastard. "In the long run, we just would not suit."

"Ye're a coward, then me fine young laird." And with that, Cook left him.

Rafe scowled after the man. How dare he! He was no coward. He just didn't think he'd marry for a good while yet.

And then, it would have to be a sophisticated London lady, who understood his need for mistresses and would be content to leave him be to lead his life as he saw fit. His future duchess and he would go about their business, only occasionally meeting at the dinner or breakfast table and often in the bedchamber. It was what was expected and what he knew to be proper. Isabella would never agree to such an existence.

She was a rarity, a woman who would demand fidelity, if only because it was honorable. Perhaps if she had been raised among the avarice of London she would have become jaded and hedonistic like the women he was used to. No, integrity and honesty seemed to be a significant part of her personality. It was part of her appeal, part of what drew him to her.

But to have only one woman for the rest of his life? He simply couldn't imagine it would be possible for him. She was incredibly beautiful, granted, and smart as the devil, but marry the proud, independent girl and forsake all others? Just because they had an intense attraction between them? It was bloody nonsense. Maybe Alex was right, maybe they shouldn't remain too long at Kirkwood Manor, after all.

"WHAT am I to *do*, Lisbeth?" Isabella fell back across her bed, her arms flung wide.

"Well, at least he's not a butler anymore. That's something." The usually perky blonde seemed steeped in melancholy, along with her.

The situation seemed impossible.

Isabella snorted. "Yes, he's a bastard, that is just *so* much better, thank you."

"Don't get snippy, Bella."

"I'm sorry." She sighed, raising herself up on her elbows.

"I want him so much, Beth. He just has to look at me that way and I tremble." She slammed her hands down, then bounced up off the bed. "I can't stand this. I'd make a horrid fickle lady. I have to do something."

"What?"

"I don't know." She began pacing, kicking her skirt out of her way with each sharp turn. "There's still something that doesn't seem right about all this. I have to find out whose bastard he is. And just why he came here of all places, pretending to be a butler."

"How are you going to do that?"

She stopped in mid-stride, an idea coming to mind. "You, Lisbeth."

The blonde instantly looked wary.

"Me *what*?"

"Lord Langley thinks you're very pretty."

"You want me to wheedle, don't you?"

Isabella only smiled.

"Oh, Bella! He's certainly handsome, but I don't want to get myself in any trouble and that young man is far better at the game than I."

"Bah! You could have him wrapped around your little finger in a thrice." She snapped her fingers for emphasis.

Lisbeth rolled her eyes. "There is no hope for it, I see."

As it turned out, the only information Lisbeth had managed to gain was that Rafe was connected to the Earl of Easton, somehow. The two ladies sat in the drawing room, waiting for the gentlemen, discussing the situation.

"I'm sorry, Bella." She had taken a ride before dinner with the young man and had been kissed thoroughly, she confessed, but beyond that the things she had learned were meager.

"Well, it's a start."

"A start to what? Or, should I say, a start to where?" Alex sauntered into the room, his huge self immaculately attired, as usual. His jacket was a deep rust color, his vest dark blue and his trousers black as night. Whit followed, wearing muted shades of green and tan, while Rafe brought up the rear, the top of his head visible over Whit's.

"Oh, nothing, really." She caught sight of Rafe — goodness, he was too much in evening clothes! The form-hugging cut of his stark black and white attire only accentuated his perfect form. And she had thought him handsome in his butler's uniform? Oh, dear, she was done in, for sure. How would she ever find someone who could top him?

"Good evening, my lady." Rafe grinned and bowed to her.

"You're no longer my Easton, are you?" she asked sadly. They could never go back to the way things had been between them. Everything had changed now. It was no longer just the two of them.

"Do tell us about this lovely party, Miss Lisbeth," Whit offered into the strained silence. "You were mentioning it earlier to me." He grinned as Isabella's friend blushed tellingly.

"Oh, it was lovely. We only have a few every year, way out here. There aren't that many local gentry who reside year round, you see. Only those that have an interest in overseeing their land, like my father and Isabella."

The others listened while Lisbeth told them amusing stories of the attendees, and the humorous things that had happened that night. She told them how old Mr. Fryer, the former vicar who was very nearly blind, had unknowingly told Lady Hillengard how Lord Hillengard had been seen sneaking off with the widow Brooks, and hadn't Lady Hillengard flown into quite a state! And then, there was young Mr. Cook, who had been publicly dressed down by Mr. Dooley, husband of Sheila who had been Isabella's chaperone previously, for attempting to steal a kiss from the newly married lady. Young Mr. Cook, inebriated on his first taste of champagne punch, had promptly collapsed at the offended party's feet.

"Oh, dear," Isabella chimed in. "Mr. Dalton trod on my feet numerous times. I should have taken it as a sign."

Isabella quite enjoyed the evening, despite the gloom that lingered at the thought of never seeing Rafe again. She had never had such handsome and entertaining company. Yes, Lord Langley was an extremely amusing man, telling them tales of outrageous things the *Ton* had done and her cousin was fun to reminisce with. But it was only when her gaze locked with Rafe's that she felt a surge of hopeless longing that shook her to her core.

The two ladies had offered to allow the gentlemen to linger over their port after the meal was finish, but all three opted to join the women and have brandy instead. Whit and Lisbeth were shortly singing a bawdy duet between fits of laughter. It seemed all too soon when the clock struck, and Lisbeth said she must be on her way home. Whit's offer to escort her was readily accepted, to no one's surprise. Isabella bade her cousin and Rafe goodnight soon afterward. She wasn't even aware of the yearning in her gaze as she looked at her former butler, but he was, all too much.

Chapter 10

Isabella was up and riding early the next morning. She hadn't waited to see if 'her gentlemen' would join her. She needed the time alone. She was horribly dispirited.

Why, of all the men for her to be attracted to, did it have to be the one fellow she couldn't have?

She returned home from her outing feeling no better, even though she had again allowed Dilly to fly with her across the blossoming fields.

What was she to do? This would be their last evening as her guests, she just knew. They might even leave that day! Her gentlemen would return to their exciting lives in London, soon forgetting North Bindlefork and her. She hated this melancholy that sapped her of her usual clear thinking and decisiveness. It wasn't in her nature to feel sorry for herself.

Well then, she just needed to figure out a plan — a strategy with which to resolve this dilemma. Of course, just what the dilemma *was* exactly, was still a subject of confusion.

She wanted to find out the truth behind Rafe's parentage, but, given that he was illegitimate, what good would it do her? He would still be a bastard and it would still cause a scandal if they married.

Marry him?

Oh, goodness!

She was in love with him!

Isabella stood perfectly still, her head cocked to one side. Anyone seeing her would have thought she was listening for something. And, in a sense, she was.

She was listening to her heart and her head, searching for truth. In her practical way, she turned it over in her mind, took stock of her feelings, and concluded that she was indeed in love with Rafe Easton.

Yes, it was true. She loved him for his humor and intelligence. She loved the way he made her feel safe, protected. He seemed to take pride in the way she ran the estate and how she handled her people. And when he touched her, kissed her, her heart soared, that so handsome and wonderful a man should want her.

Oh, goodness! She would be Mrs. Easton! She frowned, shook her head and resumed walking toward breakfast. She was getting way ahead of herself. Marriage was nowhere on the horizon. Uncle Hugh and Alex would never allow her to marry beneath her station, even if the fellow was their friend. And, of course, there was the slightly important question of whether Rafe wanted to marry her. He might not feel the same way.

But if he didn't love her, what made him seek her out more than once? Why was there so often a hungry gleam to his cobalt eyes when he stared at her, a look that seemed to go beyond mere lust? And he was awfully protective of her. How was she to know what to think? After all, he was duplicitous and hiding something, she was sure.

"Damnation," she muttered entering the dining room.

"Beg pardon, my lady?"

She looked up, recognizing the voice of the subject of her fancy. Her heart skipped a beat at the sight of him. He stood and bowed to her and she saw he was wearing a very handsome jacket of fine tan wool with a white shirt and chocolate-brown breeches. She was rather glad he no longer was confined to wearing his serving uniform.

"'Morning, Bella. Been out riding?"

"Yes, Cousin Alex," she answered without thought. Her gaze was locked with Rafe's. His eyes were so bright, and she thought she saw that desire in them that often led to him kissing her.

At least, she hoped so.

"Sit down, Bella. You're miles away, me girl. Come back to the table with us."

Isabella sank into a chair and finally managed to look away from the man she had only just realized had stolen her heart.

"Was it a pleasant ride, my lady?"

"Yes, thank you, Lord Langley." She managed to pull herself together. She started to rise with her plate, but Rafe was suddenly there at her elbow, taking the dish from her and grinning.

"Allow me, my lady. I have done it before."

Rafe filled her plate, then set it before her and took his own seat again.

"We want to thank you for your splendid hospitality, me dear," Alex said, leaning over, placing one huge hand over hers.

"It's been an interesting visit, to say the least, but we feel we shouldn't burden you any longer."

"I see," Isabella said quietly. She stared at the back of her cousin's hand. It was a nice hand, well formed and warm, but it didn't stir her as Rafe's touch could. "You'll be off this morning, then?" She told herself she would not cry. She *never* cried, it was too annoying and useless.

"Oh, no," Whit said, cheerily. "You'll have all three of us at your beck and call until tomorrow morning."

She looked up from her plate at Rafe. "Not until tomorrow? How wonderful." She smiled. At least they would have this one last day. Her only wish was that they could spend some little time together, just the two of them.

"Well, troops, what shall we do now?" Alex said, looking around the table at his companions. He had finally swiped his plate clean, and now leaned back and patted his smooth stomach.

"Isabella still needs a proper butler. Aren't there any to be found way out here?," Rafe asked.

"Only the already employed variety, I'm afraid. I did make inquiries, before you sent Easton to me."

"Yes, Bella," her cousin said. "You are a sensible girl, and of course would try to settle your own problem. We shall simply have to send a real one back to you from London, me dear." Alex gave her an assessing look. "Someone *old*, who won't be tempted by your ample charms, me beauty." He chuckled as she tossed her napkin at him.

"Really, Alex, you are absurd!"

"I quite agree with you, this time, old man." Rafe nodded approvingly at Alex, then turned his gaze back to her. "Someone *very* old. Too old to be able to chase her around the parlor." He ducked to avoid being hit in the head with a freshly baked muffin.

"And nearly blind," Whit joined in. He was thrown a lace trivet, which didn't quite make it across his plate.

"Nonsense! What a lot of rubbish." Isabella felt herself blushing to her roots. "Send me someone from London, then, and I promise not to corrupt him. I'll be my most haughty. He'll positively hate me, I swear." She was still not used to being teased about her appearance. How silly they were! Why would anyone chase her around the parlor, for heaven's sake?

Rafe shook his head and smiled at her warmly. She felt her toes curl inside her boots at that smile.

"Impossible, my dear."

"Quite, little cousin. We shall have to find someone staid and somber, like your Tilbot, Rafe."

"Tilbot is *your* butler?" Isabella's eyes narrowed. Was there nothing he had told her that was true?

"Er, yes." Rafe replied, looking uncomfortable.

"My, you must be getting along quite well to have a butler, what with being, shall we say, born on the wrong side of the sheets."

"Quite. Now, gentlemen, why don't we have a morning ride, before the morning is completely gone."

Isabella watched as Rafe stood, bowed to her, then marched out of the room. Gracious, she must have offended him. He was apparently sensitive about his illegitimacy.

WHILE she carefully prepared for dinner that evening, Isabella again replayed in her mind what had happened after luncheon.

Lisbeth had ridden over and joined them for the afternoon meal, and it had been gay indeed. Later, while her friend and Whit had shared a game of cards, Rafe and Alex had caught up on acquaintances, Isabella listening in. It was apparent he was involved quite closely with the *Ton*, for a supposed bastard — too much so, she thought. Of course, having spent her entire life in the remote countryside, she certainly was no expert in the workings of the elite of the city's society, but gossip traveled, and general rules dictated a basic truth — bastards would never get *too* close inside the ranks, not unless extremely well connected.

After Lisbeth departed, with Whit once again escorting her, Alex decided to look over the small town to see if he could find an amusing trinket to bring back to his current mistress.

For the first time in days, Rafe and Isabella found themselves alone. They were in the parlor, having just seen her cousin off, she on the settee and he leaning against the mantle, watching her, his long muscular legs crossed at the ankles.

"Well," Isabella said, feeling uneasy and anxious, but excited none the less. Attempting to distract her rioting nerves, she said, "Would you like to take a ride? It is warm today, but not overly."

Rafe slowly smiled. She realized she was holding her breath and tried to breathe naturally. She hoped he wouldn't mention they had already had their ride that morning. This would most likely be the last chance they had to be alone together.

"A ride with you would be quite enjoyable, my lady." He chuckled.

She smiled shyly at him. "Shall we, then?"

After she had changed into a riding habit, they walked to the stables and were greeted by the obliging Harry, who immediately fetched their mounts.

Soon the two were flying across the field, a blanket of yellow, red, purple, and white flowers, the warmly scented wind rushing to meet them.

They came to the line of trees and slowed the horses to a walk, then dismounted as the lake opened up before them.

"I do love this place. My parents used to bring me here to picnic when I was little."

"I'm sure you were an imp, a bit serious, but still an imp."

She snorted and pushed back her hair. "I was never an imp. Nonsense. But I was rather serious, I suppose." She plucked a blade of grass and twiddled it between her fingers as she strolled closer to the waters' edge. She looked at him from over her shoulder. "*You* were an imp, if anyone was." She could imagine him as a small boy, a natural charmer, and a wheedler.

He chuckled, leaning back against the trunk of a tree, his arms crossed over his broad chest. "Yes, you're probably right. I do remember my mother telling me how I'd make the cook cry with a sad story so she would feel pity for me and give me treats."

"And what stories work for you now that you are grown?" Isabella teased, sitting down by a clump of blue hyacinth in full bloom.

"Ah," he replied, a sensual, confident smile turning up the corners of his firm mouth, "such stories I have would cause even one of the dowagers of Almack's to weep." He pushed away from the trunk and sauntered toward her.

She smiled up at him and cocked her head to one side. He was so very handsome. "You, sir, are incorrigible, indeed." She patted the ground beside her. "Here, come and tell me a story to make me weep."

"I have a feeling you'd be a tough audience, my lady fair." He sat down, then eased back, supporting himself with one elbow. His gaze settled on her lips. It was insane to have come to this secluded spot with him.

"I think I want to kiss you again, my lady."

"Really?" Isabella could only stare at him, lounging there and looking at her hungrily. He was far too charming for a practical girl's frame of mind.

"Really. Come here, Bella." He held out his hand to her.

"Goodness, Rafe, you know we shouldn't." Her pulse was erratic and it was becoming difficult to breathe. Heaven help her, she wanted his mouth on hers. She wanted those long fingers touching her and making her tremble.

"Come here, Bella." He gave her a wicked grin, then reached out, lightening quick, and pulled her down on top of him.

"Rafe!"

"Hush."

He rolled her over with him, so that she lay beside him, her hair spread out like a fan around her. He lay on his side, propped up with his elbow, and just looked at her. Her tongue darted out to lick her lips and that seemed to be it for him. He leaned down and kissed her hungrily. She trembled, responding back eagerly. He ran his tongue softly against her lips, teasing her until she parted her mouth, then slipped his tongue inside. He moaned as their tongues touched and deepened the kiss. Rubbing his chest softly against her breasts, she groaned deep in her throat. He cupped her cheek with his hand, then slid his fingers down the smooth skin of her throat. With his thumb, he caressed the throbbing pulse, while he kissed her cheeks, her temples, her chin and finally again her lips.

"Sweet, Bella," he murmured against her mouth. "My sweet, sweet Bella."

He used his lips and tongue to trail a path down her throat, while he slid one finger down the valley between her breasts to her stomach. She gasped and pressed against him. He splayed his fingers out across her flat abdomen and her muscles tensed with anticipation. He explored the tops of her breasts with his mouth, and she began to wriggle beneath him in the most delightful way.

Isabella arched against him and wrapped her arms around his neck. She had never thought anything could feel this right. To be in his strong arms, to feel him tight against her, was bliss. Her breasts and the apex of her thighs tingled, and she could feel his arousal hard against her leg. It was wonderfully wicked. She never wanted it to stop. If it stopped, he would leave her. The thought made her clutch him to her tighter still.

"Rafe, your mouth is wonderful," she moaned as his lips and teeth were doing exquisite things to her nerves.

Rafe groaned and buried his face in her neck.

"Rafe? Did I do something I shouldn't have?" He was suddenly so still.

"Yes, no, ... damnation. You're very passionate and have quite overwhelmed me, Bella."

"Oh." She was quiet for a moment. "Isn't overwhelming you a good thing?"

Rafe's laugh sounded somewhat painful. He finally raised his head to look down at her. "Isabella, you have a passionate nature and normally I would be praising the heavens." He reached out and smoothed the hair back from her face. "But this really isn't the proper thing to be doing, at least not for you and me, no matter how much we are enjoying ourselves." He kissed the tip of her nose. "I am not your husband, nor even your fiancé and you are a very proper young miss with no experience." He smiled, wryly. "I, however, should know better." He sighed. "Someday, my sweet lady fair, you will understand." He kissed her, softly, then stood and pulled her up next to him.

Isabella was so disappointed she wanted to scream. She felt more alive when with him than she ever had in her life and he was pulling away. She knew he was right, of course. Even if she did love him, they should not have been lying in each other's arms that way. It was true, he was not her fiancé, and she would be ruined if anyone saw them together. But blast and be gone! It had felt so *right*. Was it at all possible that he could love her too? But what did any of it matter as he was leaving soon? Ah, she was such a fool to allow him into her heart.

Rafe made small talk while he brushed grass from her gown. He deftly rearranged her hair in a simple knot and then inspected her with a mock frown. "Well, I can't do much about the swollen lips, but otherwise you look fairly presentable."

She gave him a curtsy, hoping to appear nonplussed. "You however, sir, need a brushing down as well. Why, you have a twig in your hair." She began to briskly clean him up, her hands only occasionally lingering a bit longer than necessary in places.

He finally shooed her flitting hand away. "That will be fine, I'm sure, my lady." His tone was stern, but his eyes sparkled with amusement.

Isabella gave him what she hoped was a saucy look, then ran to her horse. "I shall race you back, sir." She swung up into the sidesaddle with ease. "The winner shall have whatever her heart desires." She would have him, if she could really have her wish. It certainly wasn't his fault about his parentage.

"Ha! *He* shall, my lady."

It was a tie, they decided, both having reached the stables breathless at nearly the same moment. Their gazes locked, and she wondered what his desire was, hoping that it mirrored her own.

Chapter 11

In her room, while her maid arranged her coiffure, Isabella touched her fingers to her lips, just as Rafe had done when they had separated some hours ago.

"Until tonight, my sweet Bella," he had said so very softly, his blue eyes warmly caressing her face.

Isabella sighed in remembrance. How could a man so incredibly handsome desire her? What was she, that he would want her? She started to shake her head, but was reprimanded by her maid.

"My lady, please!"

"I'm sorry, Alice."

"Gracious, you are a fidget tonight, not that I can blame you, given your ladyship's company. Three such handsome young lords."

Alice helped Isabella into her bronze silk dress, her last suitable evening gown that hadn't yet been worn in any of her guests' presence. It clung to her breasts and waist like a second skin. Isabella thought the color made her eyes appear greener, a feature she had always thought her best physical asset.

"Oh, my lady, I envy you!" The maid sighed dramatically. "Dinner with three such fine young men and you lookin' so lovely. They'll fair to be trippin' over each other to get your attention tonight, you mark my words."

Isabella laughed. "Surely my cousin will not be too affected."

"Cousin or no, he's still a virile young man, my lady." Alice gave her a knowing look and a nod.

Isabella shook her head disbelievingly. Her hair, pulled up at the sides and left loose down her back, swept her bare shoulders. "Nonsense."

"Trust me in this, my lady. A man is helpless against a fair woman's charms."

Isabella rolled her eyes and sat on the edge of the bed to pull on her matching slippers. "Really, Alice, if I was so beautiful, I would have at least one suitor, wouldn't I?" She didn't count the vile Mr. Dalton.

Alice sniffed. "Well, not when you keep yourself stuffed away here." She clasped her hands together and sighed, looking up toward the ceiling. "Now, if you was in *London*, my lady, why, there you would have more beaux than you could shake a stick at."

Isabella chuckled that deep rich sound that, unbeknownst to her, set Rafe's blood boiling. "All right, Alice, if you say so." She stood and inspected herself critically in the mirror. She wanted to make a lasting impression on Easton, one that might haunt him in far away London. She sighed. It would have to do.

"WELL, don't we all look dashing?" Whit chuckled, joining his friends at the bottom of the staircase.

"Of course we do, puppy." Alex flicked a bit of lint from his sleeve. "And we've managed quite well without our valets." He started to snort, but it turned into a choke as he looked over Whit's head and saw his cousin descending the steps.

Rafe was momentarily alarmed, until he followed his friend's line of sight. "Damn me." He sucked in his breath, his heart feeling as if it had stopped altogether.

"What?" Whit turned and saw her. "Oh my."

"Good evening." She smiled, her eyes darting to Rafe.

"Good God, Bella!" Alex boomed out. "How the hell do you keep getting prettier each time I see you? I still can't reconcile you with the skinny little dowd of a child I knew."

"Pretty? You're understating it, old man." Whit looked her up and down. "She's bloody gorgeous. Puts poor Miss Lisbeth to shame."

Isabella laughed. "Nonsense! Beth is by far prettier than I, she's just not here to distract you, is all." She glanced again at Rafe. "Enough silliness. Let us go and enjoy your parting feast."

Rafe was in a bad way and the evening had only just started. His body had reacted the instant he had seen her gliding toward them. She was a vision tonight. The rich bronze gown made her skin glow warmly and her eyes appear more emerald, not to mention how it complimented her glorious hair, which hung down her back, except for a few tendrils curling over her delightful breasts. As he followed the others, he watched the fine silk move seductively with the sway of her hips. The smell of her perfume wafted back; he was more randy than a tomcat and he hadn't even touched her! His self-control would be sorely tested tonight, especially knowing this would be the last time he saw her.

The others were already seated, with Isabella at the head of the table. Rafe took the chair next to Alex, relieved to have a little distance between him and their exquisite hostess. He reminded himself that he had only to make it through this last evening and then he would be beyond her temptation. For some reason, it did not cheer him.

Isabella nodded for dinner to be served.

The footman, whom Rafe had been drinking with in the kitchen only days ago, filled a plate for him from the sideboard. Rafe's eyes flew to Isabella's face as he was served. By God, the little vixen! Memories flooded his mind of that evening only a week past, when they had shared their first meal together — and an extremely passionate encounter. Yes, he could tell by her look, she was remembering how she had melted in his arms.

"Ah! Bloody well done, cousin!" Alex looked up, grinning like a loon. "Duck with raspberry sauce! It's one of your favorites, isn't it, Rafe, me boy?"

Rafe couldn't help it. He saw Isabella's luscious lips quiver and he started laughing. She was quick to join him.

"What's so humorous, you two?" Alex gave them a cross look, then turned to Whit. "What'd I miss?"

Whit smiled. "Don't worry, Alex. They've just been in the country too long."

"Apparently so, old boy, apparently so."

All too soon it seemed, dinner was over, the time having flown by as they joked and teased each other as only good friends could. Isabella saw the gentlemen into the drawing room, then excused herself. Alex did the same a moment later.

Whit poured three brandies and handed one to Rafe, who was leaning against the mantle, feeling quite smug.

"So, my friend, 'out of the frying pan and into the fire'?" Whit retrieved a glass for himself.

"What the hell is that supposed to mean?"

"Alex will make you marry her, if he ever sees past the end of his nose."

"You don't know what you're talking about." Rafe gave Whit a look most men would have quelled at. He did not want to discuss the lady, or what might be between them, with his friend. It was none of his damn business.

The other man only snorted. "Don't give me that look, old friend. I'm no danger to you. It's *her* that's trouble." He shook his head. "I'm certainly not calling her virtue into question. She doesn't even know she's a peril to you. But, you're panting after her, Rafe and that's not like you. Not at *all* like you."

Rafe gave a snort of contempt. "Good God, you make it sound as if I'm trying to seduce her."

"Aren't you?"

"No! It's just that," Rafe raked his fingers through his hair in a frustrated gesture, "she is so bloody irresistible! I mean, how could she ever have thought she was plain? Dear Lord! Just look at her!" Rafe took a swig of his drink.

"And, that dress. Bloody hell, it leaves nothing to the imagination." He caught Whit's stunned expression. "What?"

"Oh, God, you've got it bad!" The viscount doubled over laughing, his brandy spilling onto the floor.

"Damnation," Alex said, striding into the room. "Why on earth are you dumping that fine liquor onto me cousin's carpet, puppy? Are you already foxed?"

"He's just extremely odd, Alex." Rafe's dry tone was back. Whit was being absurd, indeed. Well, perhaps he was right. He was rather taken with Isabella. But, who wouldn't be, the way she exuded sexual appeal? Alex had been right earlier, how it seemed to grow on you, this damn charm of hers'.

Isabella walked in just then.

"Ah, there is the lovely lady now." Whit snickered then, seeing both of his companions' glare at him and managed to swallow his amusement, though his brown eyes still sparkled with humor.

"Am I the brunt of some joke?" Isabella looked at the three in turn.

"Not at all, my lady," Rafe assured her, smoothly. "Whit just had something confused in his small brain matter." He gave his friend a challenging smile. "But, that's all cleared up now, isn't it?"

"Of course, don't give it another thought." Whit pressed his lips together and walked to the bar to refill his brandy. "Here, Alex, I poured you one already." He handed the drink to the other man.

"Me thanks. Now, will you play for us, me dear Bella?"

Isabella and Rafe exchanged looks.

"I'm not very adept, cousin."

"Well, at least you could sing for us, couldn't you?"

"The truth is, my voice is only barely passable."

"Damnation, Bella! You can run this bloody estate but you can't entertain in the drawing room? Whit, go and amuse us."

Whit sat down at the harpsichord and played a lovely Irish ballad. Isabella took the place beside her cousin on the sofa and Rafe continued to lounge against the mantle.

"Ah, there," Alex said when the song ended, "that's the way to round out the evening. Another brandy and then I think it's off to bed for us, me gents. We have to be up and off tomorrow."

Isabella looked at Rafe.

"I think I shall take a stroll in the garden before I retire, gentlemen. I bid you all goodnight and I'm sure I will see you at breakfast, before you leave." She smiled at them, a bit pained. She kissed Alex on the cheek, allowed Whit to kiss her hand, but only nodded at Rafe. "Until tomorrow."

"Sleep well, me dear." Alex smiled after her fondly. "What a lovely girl. I shall have to start thinking about a match for her. Lord knows there's no-one out here suitable."

The three finished their drinks and went up to bed. Rafe, alone in his room, began pacing. He paused and glanced toward the window. Resuming his pacing, he flung his coat off, not caring where it landed. Soon his cravat followed. After a few more minutes, and several more glances out the window and into the moonlit night beyond, he cursed fluently, then left his room, being careful to be quiet.

IT was still warm outside as Isabella strolled among the roses. She leaned over a perfect white blossom and brushed the soft petals against her equally perfect lips.

"Sweet Bella." Rafe said softly, so as not to startle her. The moon was bathing her in its pale light and he'd never seen her look more beautiful and more forlorn.

Isabella turned to gaze up at him. "Hello."

He smiled. "Hello, yourself." Without thought, he reached out to her.

She sighed as she stepped forward into his embrace. "I

was afraid I wouldn't have the chance to say goodbye to you alone. But you came."

"Yes." Rafe held her to him. He had agonized, those minutes in his room, whether or not to seek her out. He knew he shouldn't have, but he, too, wanted this one last chance to be with her. "You're trembling. Are you cold, love?" He held her closer and his body responded immediately to her soft curves.

"No." She raised her face and stared at his mouth. "You make me tremble, Rafe."

He groaned at her sweet words. "Bella, you know you are playing with fire."

"Then let me be singed."

She wrapped her arms around his neck, her fingers sifting through his hair as she pulled his head down to meet her eager lips. At the feel of her mouth, Rafe knew he was lost. Her lips parted and their tongues entwined, just as she had learned from him. He grasped her hips and roughly pulled her flush against his body. Slowly, he moved his hands to knead her sweet, round backside, then lifted her up against him, pleased by her moan and the way she squirmed against him. He kissed her harder, knowing she could feel his rigid member pressing against her soft belly. He trailed kisses along her jaw to her delicate ear. Gently, he tugged on the lobe with his teeth, then sought the sensitive spot of flesh behind her ear. He inhaled deeply and the scent of her made him shiver with desire.

Isabella flung her head back and moaned and he rained kisses on her throat, her ears, her soft white shoulders. She was tugging at his shirt as if trying to touch his bare skin, making little purring noises deep in her throat. Her every movement was erotic. He was panting with desire, God help him, and he wanted to taste every inch of her. He kissed the tops of her breast, hearing her gasps of pleasure. Carefully, he eased them both down, until she was lying beneath him on the lawn. She looked up at him with eyes glazed with desire. God, she was beautiful. He kissed her, taking her full lower lip between his teeth, his free hand roaming up her stomach to cup her heaving breast. She arched against him.

"Rafe, Rafe!"

Rafe fondled first one full breast and then the other, while his mouth explored the tops of her peaks and the cleavage between. God, she was so perfect, and he wanted her so desperately. He'd never felt such raging desire before. His hand moved down to her stomach, then to her thigh. He desperately needed to touch her, to stroke her naked flesh. His mouth closed over one nipple, teasing it through the thin barrier of fabric with his teeth. She jerked against him, pressing his head down. Sweet lord, she was passionate. He suckled the other nipple and felt her thrash her head from side to side, moaning. He slid his hand beneath the hem of her gown and slowly caressed up her bare calf, lifting her skirt as he stroked her leg. He raked the tips of his fingers over the tender back of her knee and she shuddered beneath his touch. Higher and higher his fingers caressed, his mouth continuing to ravage her breasts as he quite skillfully managed to divest her of her undergarment. He doubted she was even aware of it. He resumed caressing her knees and up her soft, creamy thighs until his hand slipped between her legs to her apex, and she bucked against his experienced fingers.

"Rafe, please!"

His fingers found her nub, and he quivered feeling her dampness. He fondled and rubbed her until her body convulsed with ecstasy.

"Oh, my love. Yes, yes, it's all right." Rafe continued to suckle her breasts and to stroke her. He could feel her orgasm cresting and slipped one finger inside her. She was incredibly wet and tight. Her body tensed around him. He heard her cries of pleasure and could tell she was confused and surprised by what was happening to her body.

"Darling, yes, just let it happen. I'm here, love." Finally, he felt the spasms lessening and he gentled his finger's movement. Slowly, he withdrew his hand and he eased her up, pulling her onto his lap and kissing her hard. She gasped and moaned into his mouth. He brought both arms around her and held her tight against his chest. He broke the kiss and buried his face in her neck. He was going mad, trying to contain his own release. It had been fine while he had concentrated on her, but now he wanted only to thrust himself into her moist shaft, to feel her body tighten around his member as it had around his finger. Of course, he couldn't dare. It was bloody well killing him.

He held her tightly and they were quiet for a time. Isabella caressed his hair, her breathing gradually slowing.

"What just happened to me? Are you supposed to touch me like that?"

Rafe chuckled and groaned at the same time. "You just experienced a woman's pleasure, love." He raised his head and kissed her, then stroked her hair cascading down her back. God, she was a marvel.

"It was very nice, Rafe." She frowned up at him, her little nose scrunching. "But what about you? Did you also have pleasure?"

Rafe's eyes nearly crossed. "It was enough that I could

give you yours. If I do to you what I want, Alex will kill me."

"It doesn't seem fair." She was still frowning. "I can feel you, and you're very hard." She wiggled her bottom on his lap.

"Stop that!" Rafe hissed sharply.

"Alright." Isabella kissed him, then laid her head on his shoulder. Her fingers played with the buttons of his shirt and she was quiet for several minutes.

"Will you ever come back here? I, I should very much like to do this again with you. Perhaps, next time, you could also have pleasure?"

"Sweet Bella, I don't think it would be wise. We'd only end up going much farther, if there is a next time. Bloody hell, I hadn't meant it to go this far." He shook his head and looked down into her face. "We are dangerous to each other, love. This cannot happen again, I'm afraid. I have to go back to my life and you must get on with yours. Time must cease to suspend itself for us."

"Nonsense, Rafe. Who is to care if you visit me here?"

"Your large cousin and his equally large sire, are who." He replied dryly. "For the sake of your honor, they should probably kill me for what I have already done to you. I have compromised you quite thoroughly, but not enough that your eventual husband will discover it, thank God." He lifted her off his lap and set her next to him, his arms still wrapped around her. "Come now, Bella. You are a very sensible girl. Be sensible now, I ask you. Each time we are alone together, we take steps further down a path we soon will not be able to retrace. We cannot see each other again — ever. What has happened has happened. Now, it is time to get on with our normal lives and forget all about it. Don't you agree?"

Rafe knew he was spouting nonsense. He could never

forget her passionate responses and sweet taste. He could never forget her cries of abandoned pleasure and the feel of her. He could never forget her beauty, her intelligence, her nobility.

But he was the man, the notorious favorite naughty boy of the *Ton*, the one with so much touted experience at handling these sorts of sticky situations. He knew he could make her see the futility of it. He had to help her to steer her back to common sense. Rafe only hoped she wouldn't start talking about that 'love' rubbish.

"Fine." She pushed against him. "Then let us say goodbye now."

Rafe was so surprised by her fury, he released her and she jumped up to stand before him. Her emerald eyes shone bright and her face was flushed. She was angry, no doubt about it. Well, he should have expected this. No tears and pleas from his country lady, no pouts or sighs of longing. No, she would wrap her haughty mantle about her and withdraw. She was looking at him so contemptuously, it was hard to believe that only moments before she had been crying out with passion, his finger deep inside her. He shuddered at the memory.

Isabella stood before him, her small hands fisted at her sides. "Thank you, Easton, for all the education you have bestowed upon me. I shall never forget you." She turned and fled back to the house.

Rafe stood, sorely tempted to call her back. But what would he say? What could he possibly say to her now?

Chapter 12

"Good morning, all!" Alex sauntered into the dining room to see Rafe and Whit already seated with plates heaped before them. He frowned at the duke. "What's wrong, old boy, meal no good this morning?"

Rafe only pushed the food around his plate. He noticed Whit appeared to find it fine as he shoved a huge piece of fried steak in his mouth.

"Morning, Alex." Rafe dropped his fork, giving up all pretense of eating, and took up his cup of coffee. He hadn't slept a wink last night. He'd only thought about Isabella and how hurt she had been at his rejection. God, she must hate him now. He certainly hated himself. He never should have taken things so far with her.

"Well, where's me cousin? I thought the little lovely would be waiting for us." He loaded his plate from the sideboard piled with dishes of steaming sausages, steak, eggs, kippers and the like.

"I haven't seen her," Rafe replied tersely, then wanted to bite off his tongue. He had to show better control.

"All right," Alex said, taking his chair, and giving his friend a puzzled look. He shrugged. "I'm sure she'll pop in — Ah, there you are, me dear." Alex and the others stood as Isabella walked into the room. "We were wondering about you."

"Oh?" Isabella didn't look at Rafe although she must have known he was watching her. She gave a tight smile to the other two men. "Well, here I am. Fit as a fiddle, as they say. Please be seated, gentlemen." She poured herself a cup of coffee. "I hope that you gentlemen do not mind we only offer coffee. My dear father considered tea a woman's drink."

Was that comment meant for him? Rafe watched her, his eyes narrowed. She looked exhausted and so beautiful it hurt to gaze upon her. So, she hadn't slept either, judging by the dark smudges under her too-bright eyes. The thought certainly didn't make him feel any better. He was a bounder, to be sure. He'd used her. It was *not* well done of him.

Alex chattered on, not realizing he was only getting singular responses from his cousin and nothing from Rafe.

Those who had an appetite, finished their meals. The group then left the dining room, and when they all walked into the foyer, it was to see the footmen taking the gentlemen's saddlebags outside.

"Well, little cousin, you've fed us and put up with us well." Alex crushed Isabella to him. "Thank you for taking such good care of our troublesome friend." He released her and chuckled. "Bet you're glad to see his backside!"

"Quite."

Whit enfolded her hand in his and offered her an oddly

sympathetic smile that Rafe feared he understood all too well.

"Be well, my dear lady. If you're ever in London, please do come and see me. And if ever you have need of aid, send for me and I shall come at once, if only to pat your hand." The edges of his mouth turned up coaxingly.

"Thank you, my lord. I hope your trip has had some enjoyment." She managed to smile, obviously implying Lisbeth.

Whit laughed and squeezed her hand before releasing it. "You'll be fine, I'm quite sure." The viscount took Alex by the arm and the two walked outside, leaving Rafe behind.

Isabella finally looked at him.

"Bella, I ... " Rafe took a step toward her, wanting to offer her some comfort, his hand outstretched, but she backed away and he let his hand fall back to his side.

"We already said goodbye."

"Yes," he sighed. "I suppose we did." God, this was awkward. He suddenly realized he really didn't want to go. He wished he could stay here with her, just a bit longer perhaps. There were so many things he didn't know about her yet. More than anything, he wanted a chance to erase the pain he had caused her, to somehow assuage his guilt for what he had done to the sweet lady.

"You'd best go. They're waiting for you. Your life in London is waiting for you."

"Goodbye, sweet Bella. Try not to hate me too much." He turned and left her, hating himself with each step enough for the both of them. He would always remember the look of sadness and longing in her eyes. She would haunt him for a long time to come.

THE three friends arrived at the inn just as dusk settled, the landscape of gently rolling hills bathed in a mauve glow. They had made good time and were already past the halfway point home. As they had ridden hard, there had not been much chance to talk. Rafe was thankful for that. His mood was black, indeed.

All during the ride, he had been plagued with thoughts of Isabella. Her incredibly passionate responses had been utmost, but he also thought of her intelligence, humor, determination ... God, the list went on and on. She was so lovely, so innocent and so very alone. He had used her horribly. He was a royal ass. She should curse his name forever.

After the men entered the inn and made arrangements with the innkeeper, Alex won the coin toss and got his own room, while Whit and Rafe were to share the small hostel's only other available chamber. After such a hard ride, the three decided cleaning up was necessary before they could fill their bellies.

"Whit, you can go first at the basin." Rafe kicked the door shut to the room they would share and dropped his bag on the floor. He stripped his coat off, draped it over the back of the chair, then loosened his cravat. He heard the thud of his roommate's case as he glanced out the narrow window.

"The weather should hold for us." It was surprising the weather had stayed pleasant for so many days. What was Bella doing now? Was she preparing for dinner? Was she taking a stroll in the garden? Would she caress the fragrant blossoms she loved? He tried to imagine which gown she was wearing.

"I've been wanting to do this all day, Rafe."

Rafe turned toward his friend. In the blink of an eye, the duke lay sprawled on the floor, a bit dazed. He rubbed his jaw and gingerly moved it.

"Damnation, Whit." There had been quite a bit of heat behind that punch. Nothing was broken, at least.

"You goddamn bastard!" Whit stood over Rafe, shaking his fist. "You are an utter fool. Did you see the look in her eyes, Rafe? If you made love to her last night, I'll drag you back there myself and see you married, dense Alex be damned."

"Good God, man, I didn't take her virginity." Rafe said, indignantly. He had never seen Whit so angry. In fact, he didn't think he'd ever seen him angry before now. "Damn me, you've been training in the ring, haven't you? Bloody good shot."

Whit was still glaring at him, but did at least offer him a hand up. Rafe accepted the offer and stood.

"Look, I was a bounder, yes, and I did give her a taste of what she will experience on her wedding night, if she finds a fellow with any finesse at all, but I did *not* take her virginity. All right?"

"She's in love with you. Couldn't you have just left her alone?"

"I tried, believe me. But you saw her." He raked his fingers through his hair. "And it's not love, it's simply lust. I couldn't seem to help myself." He sat down on the edge of the bed, the thin mattress sagging under his weight. "She thought she was plain, and she was so alone. Then she had to go to that damn party." He shook his head. "I got drunk and practically attacked her. Instead of sacking me, she invited me to dinner of all things."

"With duck?"

Rafe snorted. "Don't forget the bloody raspberries. It just kept going from there. I really did try to stay away from her, Whit. I even left Kirkwood Manor for several days. Then

Dalton came to dinner and you saw what happened."

"So, what happens now?"

"It's over." Rafe's voice sounded dead, even to his own ears. It was his guilt. "She asked me to come back and see her again. I refused. She was angry." He shrugged dejectedly. "I'm sure she'd happily see me in hell right now."

"You deserve it. But as long as it's over, I guess we'll not say anything to Alex." Whit snorted. "Right under his nose, and he doesn't have a clue." He walked over to the basin and began washing. "What the hell are we going to tell him happened to you?"

"YOU fell over the chair?" Alex looked incredulously at the pair, one having a swollen jaw. "That was stupid of you."

"Yes, wasn't it?" Whit chuckled. "Thanks for ordering, Alex. Looks tasty enough, though I doubt it will hold up to Cook's food."

"Incredible how your knuckles got bruised helping him up, puppy." The earl raised a bushy brow, but made no more comments.

By dinnertime the following evening, the three gentlemen were riding up to Alex's townhouse, which was situated across from Hyde Park. Whit decided to dine there rather than return to his own bachelor's residence, where they were not expecting him until tomorrow, but Rafe declined the invitation, anxious to sleep in his own bed after so long.

The large Devonshire mansion was a welcome sight, to be sure. It occupied an entire block with its elaborate grounds and rambling structure. He left his horse with the stable hand, and was greeted at the front door by both Tilbot and Simpson.

"Your Grace. How very good to see you." Tilbot bowed

and stepped back to allow the master to enter the golden foyer. "I trust your trip was successful, Your Grace?"

"Goodness, Your Grace, we'd feared we'd never see you again!" Simpson was already wringing his hands and hopping from foot to foot. "It's *Her Grace*, Your Grace." He glanced nervously over his shoulder, as if expecting some horrible creature to descend on them at any moment. "She has been in residence for *three days* now, Your Grace."

"Mother? She's here?" Rafe frowned. Why would she be here, when she abhorred London in season? "Where is she, then, Simpson? Speak up."

After Rafe was divested of his travel garb and grime, he was directed to where Mother was waiting for him in the parlor.

"There's my dear boy." His mother rose from the chair. She gave her only son a wide smile as she walked toward him, her pale rose colored gown rustling with each graceful step. "And just where have you been? The dolts would tell me nothing." The look she sent the two servants was sour.

"I was in the country, Mother. Come, have you had dinner yet? I'm famished." Rafe took her arm and walked her to the smaller eating nook that he preferred. It wasn't often the enormous dining hall was used.

"I was rather hoping you'd arrive tonight. The dolts seemed to think you would." Mother, still quite lovely and vibrant, her black hair barely touched by silver and swept up in a chignon, looked him over before sitting in the chair he was holding for her. Her pale blue eyes were sharp. "You've changed, Rafe. There's something new about you."

Rafe gave a start. "Really, Mother, I don't think so." He leaned down and kissed her soft cheek before taking his own seat. The smell of her was comforting, just as a mother should be. Did Isabella remember the soothing scent of her own mother, dead so many years now? "I'm the same charming son you've always had."

Mother laughed. "You are a tease, my boy." She signaled to the footman. As the soup was served, she eyed him again. "Ah, ha!" She triumphantly waved a bejeweled hand at him. "It's a girl! I don't know why I should be surprised. It's always a girl with you." She lowered her arm. "Was it some pretty country maid you were chasing after?"

"Something like that." Rafe took a hefty swallow of wine. God, his mother had a knack for always knowing what he'd been up to. He wished he knew how she did it. "I was tired of the city and needed a bit of a break. Getting too routine, don't you know."

"Hmm, I wondered if it had anything to do with Baroness du Champs, myself." Anne finished her soup. "Do eat, Rafe, it is very good."

"How the bloody hell do you know about that?"

She laughed. "Madam Rose, dear boy. Didn't you know a confidant needs a confidant?"

"Good God, Mother, you're frightening." Rafe sat stunned. Slowly, he began eating. "What all did she say?"

"Only that Melanie, the little tart, tricked you and when you left her, she got rather bitchy. I think it valiant of you, dearest boy." She raised her wineglass to him. "Your father is proud, no doubt."

Again she smoothly lowered her arm so as not to knock the next course from the servant's hand.

Rafe smiled at her. "Well, it's all over with now, Mother. Whit and Alex helped to clear things up, for du Champs' sake." He shook his head and snorted derisively. "He thinks he actually loves Melanie, the poor sod."

"Rafe, I do wish you hadn't taken seriously that absurd talk from your father about love. It worries me to no end. I *want* grandchildren, son."

"Mother, you'll get grandchildren." Isabella's face appeared in his mind's eye. Her daughter would be so lovely, surely a proud little general like her adorable mother. *Damnation.*

"Rafe? Are you all right? You don't mean to tell me I'm a grandmother already, do you? And, if so, I missed the wedding, hopefully?"

"No, Mother." Rafe smiled wryly and pushed the image of the beautiful baroness away. "I promise you, there are no bastards to come knocking on the door. I am overly tired, let us say, from traveling and being away so long." He nodded to her. "North Bindlefork has short beds," he offered, as if it would explain everything.

"So, why are you here, Mother? Not that I don't always enjoy your visits, but you never come to London when the season is on."

"Oh, there was a fire in the kitchen." She signaled to the footman to pour her more wine.

"Good God, is everyone all right?"

"Of course, dear boy, but the smell is awful. It will take several weeks to make the repairs, I'm told. I hope it is not too long to put up with me?"

"Don't be silly, dearest. Your company is just what I need right now." His mother should keep him properly occupied. He only hoped it would be enough to brace against too many self-recriminating thoughts of his unchivalrous treatment of Lady Isabella.

Chapter 13

"What did you just say?" Lisbeth asked, her teacup paused midway to her mouth.

"I said, I'm going to London." Isabella had spent the last week in agony. She couldn't get thoughts of Rafe out of her head. After yet another sleepless night, she had made up her mind. "I've decided it's high time I saw the city. Besides, I need some new gowns and other things. And, I do have to find a butler." She wondered if she were fooling her friend. By the look she was receiving, she was not.

"Oh, Bella. You can't go after him." Lisbeth set down her cup, her pretty bow mouth pursed in disapproval. "Dearest, it's pure folly. He left you!"

"I know he left me," Isabella snapped. "I was here when it happened, thank you."

Lisbeth bit her lip. "I'm sorry."

"I *have* to go, Beth."

"I suppose, if you feel you must. I would go with you, but

Mother would have a fit."

"I know."

"You can't go alone, though." Lisbeth frowned. "Goodness, who will accompany you?"

"Harry has agreed, and Alice, of course, is dying to come."

Lisbeth picked up her cup, sipped her tea daintily, then set it down. "I see you have quite made up your mind. I won't bother pointing out that a stable hand and a maid aren't appropriate company for a young baroness. So, when are you going?"

"Alice said she couldn't possibly be ready for two days, so that means the day after tomorrow. She's been grousing about all the gowns to pack."

Isabella had been busy all morning making arrangements. She had sent two notes off, one to her solicitor and one to Alex. She had asked her cousin to keep her visit a secret, writing that she wanted to surprise Whit and Rafe. She had also asked him to find her a suitable house for her sojourn, as she couldn't stay in his bachelor's residence. She would give this strategy one month, then, whatever the outcome, she would return home. If four weeks weren't enough time to find out the truth and to ascertain Rafe's feelings, why then, she would have to live with the disappointment and accept being a spinster.

Lisbeth told her the current gossip on the goings on in London society. Finally, she deemed Bella prepared enough.

"Just be careful. I still think you are in way over your head, but it is vastly romantic, I suppose" Lisbeth said, leaving. "I do hope he's worth it, in the end."

IT was lightly raining when Isabella's coach pulled up before

Alex's townhouse five days later. They had left on time and it had taken three days to reach London, just as Isabella had planned. Alex bounded out the door to greet her.

"Cousin! Wonderful to see you, me dear! Come in, come in." He ushered her in the house and into his tastefully understated study. "I'd offer you a brandy, if you were a man but since you're obviously not, I suppose I should offer you tea."

Isabella laughed. "No, thank you, Alex, I am just fine. I don't suppose you have found me a house already? What I would really love is to settle somewhere." She gave him a shrug. "I am not accustomed to bouncing around place to place."

"I quite understand. And, yes, I had remarkable luck. I found you a lovely little place, just minutes away. Shall we go straight there? Oh, hope you don't mind, but I've hired you a cook. A fairly competent fellow," Alex gave her wink. "Not at all like the previous butler."

Isabella loved the quaint little house. There was more than enough room for her small party. She thanked her cousin profusely, agreed to have dinner with him, and then began unpacking. She had much to do in only a month's time and did not want to waste even a moment.

"HOW is Edwards working out for you, cousin?"

"Quite well, thank you." Isabella sat in her charming little parlor with Alex, the rose curtains drawn back to allow in the meager London sunlight. The butler had just brought them tea. "And as you will soon taste, so is Rolands, the cook. I cannot thank you enough, Alex, for all you have done for me these past few days."

"Not at all, me dear. Oh, here," he said, handing her

several envelopes. "Some invitations I thought you might like; one is for a ball tomorrow night. If you'd like to attend, I suppose I could accompany you." He grinned at her. "I rather like the attention I get when I take you places."

Only yesterday, he had taken her to luncheon at a popular spot and they had been quite hounded by his friends.

Isabella blushed, still not used to flattery. "Will anyone I know be there?" And just *whom* would she know besides his two closest friends?

"I don't think so ... Well, actually, I do believe Rafe said something about going. I could ask Whit to join us, also, if you want."

"Well, if you don't think he'd mind." Goodness, was she ready to see her love? What would Rafe do when they met? Oh dear. She would wear the lavender and silver gown.

"Of course the puppy won't mind. He's rather fond of you." Alex gave her hand a fatherly pat.

"He's a lot of fun, isn't he? Lisbeth certainly thought so."

"Ladies find Whit quite amusing, I assure you. I, on the other hand, intimidate them a bit." He chuckled. "But only at first. Once they sample me brain power, they are quite mesmerized."

A short while later, they ended their visit, Isabella saying how she had much to do before the ball. She had an appointment at the seamstress, whom Alex said Whit had assured was *the* best, in an hour for a fitting. After that, she planned on stopping in at the milliner. She declined Alex's invitation for dinner that evening. "You have spent too much of your time taking care of me thus far, Alex. You need a night off. Go and do wicked things to your mistress, who I'm not supposed to know about."

As soon as he was gone, she sought out Alice and found the maid chatting with Edwards. Isabella and the others on her staff had taken an instant liking to the middle-aged butler. He was a quiet fellow, but quite brawny indeed. She felt very safe with him protecting her.

"Alice! I've a ball to attend tomorrow night."

"Oh, my lady, what gown to wear?" Alice gave her a wicked grin. "The lavender, my lady?"

"Definitely." He'd be there, and she would remind him just what he had turned away from.

The strategy she'd thought up was simple enough. She would try to show up every place he did. Given how he had reacted to her before, it shouldn't be long before he was kissing her again. After that, she would just have to wait and see. Somehow, she would find a way for them to be together.

"LORD Stapleton and Lord Langley, my lady." Edwards bowed to Isabella, then stepped aside to allow the young men to enter the parlor.

"Bella!" Alex boomed out. He suddenly stopped mid-stride, causing Whit, who was following close behind, to bump into him. "Good God, it's a good thing there are two of us, with *that* gown."

Whit peeked around his massive friend. "I say, Lady Isabella, it mended quite well."

Isabella laughed at Whit, who was giving her a comically leering smile.

"Stop it, puppy. Are you ready then, me dear? Shall we go and knock them on their collective arse with your beauty?"

They rode in Alex's coach, Isabella nervous beyond belief, and not only about all the strangers she would be meeting in a few moments. *He* would be there. Whit had confirmed it as they were leaving her little house. She chewed on her lower lip as the carriage came to a stop.

"Um, is it too late to change my mind? I think I'd rather just go home and read a book." This was pure folly. She would make an idiot of herself, surely. What if he didn't pay her any attention? What if he had another lady on his arm?

"Don't be absurd, Bella. I didn't put on me fancy togs for nothing."

"Alex, she's just nervous." Whit followed his friend out of the carriage, then turned and offered her his hand. "Come, dear lady, you're far above this worthless lot. Besides, you have two very capable escorts." He nodded to her encouragingly.

"I'm sorry to be so silly, but" she said as she tentatively alighted from the carriage, "I've never been to so large a ball. I'm just your rural cousin, Alex. What if I embarrass you!"

"Damnation, Bella, then we'll all have a good laugh." Alex slipped his arm around her shoulders and gave her a gentle squeeze before proffering his arm. "I can't count the times I've embarrassed meself!"

Whit flanked her on the other side and offered his arm as well. "Shall we, Baroness?"

She gave them a grateful smile, took a deep breath, then allowed them to lead her forward.

"The Baroness of Kirkwood, the Earl of Stapleton, and the Viscount Langley!"

Goodness, Isabella had never seen so many people in one room before. And the jewels! She wondered how many thousands of pounds were on display this evening. She marveled, thinking how much land and supplies she could buy. And these people wore such wealth around their necks? It was quite absurd!

"Alex, Whit! Oh, my, who *is* this vision?" A short red-haired man approached them, openly ogling Isabella.

"Put you tongue back in your head, old sport. She's me cousin," Alex growled, leaning slightly toward the fellow.

"Lady Isabella Fitzhugh, Baroness of Kirkwood, may I present Lord Jeffrey Blake," Whit offered.

"My most sincere apologies, my lady." The little man looked uncomfortable indeed. "I fear your beauty caused me to loose my manners."

"Thank you, Lord Blake," Isabella murmured, not sure she should actually thank him for the remark.

"Do pass the word, Jeffrey, Lady Isabella is to be accorded every courtesy."

"Of course, Alex. I shall make it abundantly clear, have no doubt." He offered her an apologetic grin, his cheeks nearly as bright as his hair. "May I have the honor of a dance, my lady? I promise not to trod upon your delicate slippers, nor shall I allow your stunning beauty to again make me an ass."

Isabella couldn't help but return his smile. "Of course, my lord. I should very much enjoy it, knowing my toes to be safe for once and being well advised I will have to endure no braying."

"Ha!" Jeffrey laughed. "She has a wit. Wonderful!"

"WHAT *is* going on over there?"

"I don't know, Mother. Would you like me to investigate?" Rafe offered.

"Don't bother, dearest. Why don't we slip out soon? It's getting much too crowded." His mother fanned herself. "That is, if you don't mind."

Rafe smiled indulgently. "Not at all." He had only come to escort her. As they had already been there for quite a while, he was more than ready to leave. Numerous times he had caught himself comparing the young women present to Isabella and found them all sadly lacking. None had her glorious hair, her intelligent eyes, her allure. It had been nearly two weeks since he had left Bella and still she consumed his thoughts. Surely it was this unaccustomed guilt that made it so. Isabella was no experienced widow or coquette. He should not have taken such liberties with her.

He glanced across the room to see if the throng was still blocking the entry and was pleased to see the way finally clear.

"Come, Mother, let us make our escape now."

ISABELLA laughed as Lord Blake whirled her expertly around. The man was surprisingly graceful. She saw Whit dancing with a pretty blonde in a bright red dress. Alex stood at the edge of the dance floor, watching her and talking to a group of men. He looked quite smug and she feared she was the topic of his discourse. She hadn't yet spotted Rafe, although Lord Blake had assured her he was in attendance. He had apparently escorted his mother tonight. She had not yet summoned the nerve to ask how a lady could have her bastard son recognized by the *Ton*.

The music finally ended, but before Isabella could catch her breath, she and Jeffrey were surrounded by a dozen lordlings, all asking for the next dance with her.

"Gentlemen, allow the baroness some room, if you please." Jeffrey straightened to his tallest, which had no effect on the crowd.

"Goodness, my lords, I do believe I should dance with my

cousin, Lord Stapleton." She was overwhelmed by their eagerness. Looking to where Alex had been standing, she was relieved to see him striding toward her, a dainty cup of punch in his large hand, his bushy brows drawn together menacingly.

"Step aside, puppies!" Alex frowned at them and they quickly dispersed.

"I leave the lovely lady to you now, Alex." Lord Blake bowed over her hand, then dabbed at his forehead with a bright yellow handkerchief pulled from his dark blue coat pocket. "You are divine, my lady. I shall always be at your service."

Alex watched the small man move away, only to be engulfed by several women, probably to interrogate him on his dance partner. "Bless me, Bella, you're quite a hit. I shall have to hire several guards for you the next time. I can barely handle all these rascals by meself." He handed her the punch, then looked around. "Where did that damn Whit get to?"

Isabella sipped the slightly tart drink. "Oh, thank you, cousin, this quite hits the spot. I saw him dancing with a blonde in a red gown just a bit ago."

"That would be Melanie, I'm sure." He cleared his throat, then took Bella's arm, escorting her further from the dance floor.

As she finished her punch, Isabella surveyed the room. She wished she were taller. He must be here, somewhere.

"Looking for anyone in particular, me dear?" Alex chuckled. "Has some dandy already caught your eye?"

"Oh no, Alex. Don't be silly. I just thought that I might see Rafe. I would like to surprise him. You did say he was coming?"

"Yes, I'm sure he's here somewhere. His mother wanted

to come."

"His mother? Would that be the Lady Anne Lord Blake mentioned to me?"

"Ah, there you are, boy-o!" Alex slapped Whit on the back. "You can't leave me here alone to handle all these idiots drooling over our Bella."

"Nonsense, you've been glowering quite well by yourself. You succeeded in frightening numerous young fops away without my help." Whit grinned down at Isabella. "Are you having fun, my lady?"

"Oh, yes, thank you." She smiled sweetly, wanting to stamp her foot in irritation. She had almost managed to get some information out of Alex, just then. Now, another dance was starting and there were several gentlemen standing about them, trying to catch her eye. Suddenly, she was inspired.

"Whit, would you dance with me?"

"Why, certainly, my dear." He gallantly bowed to her. "I am at your disposal."

Alex took her empty glass and handed it to one young swain who watched with obvious disappointment as Whit led Isabella forward to join the other dancers. "Here, puppy, make yourself useful and get Lady Isabella a fresh cup."

"I don't suppose you've seen Rafe yet this evening?"

"I saw him leaving just a bit ago."

"Oh, too bad." It was hard to hide her crushing disappointment.

"Come, my dear, do try to enjoy yourself. You'll see Rafe soon enough, I'm sure."

"Do you think so?" She looked up at him hopefully.

"He's sure to be at the party Blake is hosting two nights hence."

"Excellent. Ah, that is to say I'm anxious to meet his mother."

"Oh really?"

"Yes. Lord Blake was telling me what a genteel lady she is."

"Jeffrey called Anne *genteel?*"

"Oh, well, perhaps he didn't actually say that."

"I should think not. Anne is nothing if not sublimely cutting and I adore her. But 'genteel'? Never."

The music ended.

"My lord," Isabella said as they made their way back to Alex, a calculating look on her face, "would you come to luncheon tomorrow? I have a favor to ask of you."

"Ah, I thought you might, my dear. Of course, I shall be delighted."

Chapter 14

They sat at her small dining table, which was covered with a delicate white lace cloth and several small plates of food.

"These crab cakes are delicious, my lady."

Isabella watched as Whit finished off his third and reached for another, holding back the cuff of his hunter green day coat as he scooped the patty onto his plate.

"Yes, Rolands is very accomplished." Isabella hadn't even touched her food. She fiddled with the placement of her silverware and occasionally turned her plate to a different angle or sipped daintily at her lemonade. She was trying to think of how to begin. As nothing was coming to her, she took a deep breath and decided to just jump right on in. With practiced nonchalance, she plucked at the sleeve of her pale blue dress. Oh, this was awkward.

"Whit, I don't suppose you'll tell me the truth about Rafe, will you?" She toyed with her fork, held it up to the light streaming through the narrow window and rubbed at an imaginary spot with her finger. Her guest sighed and she dared to look up.

"Dear Isabella, I think it time you and I cleared up many matters."

She exhaled with relief. "Goodness, yes!" Finally, she was to have her answers! "I want to know everything about him, my lord. Please be honest, hold nothing back."

"But first, you must tell me something." His look was so serious, she was afraid. "*Did* he compromise you, my dear?"

Her cheeks flamed scarlet and Whit cursed fluently.

"No! You don't understand, my lord!" Isabella was alarmed, realizing he thought the utmost worst of the situation. "I am still chaste, but ... The things he made me feel, well ... " She couldn't look at him. He must think her awful to have allowed it to happen. Yes, she was a wanton.

"Isabella, I've never involved myself with my friend's romantic dealings before, er, with one recent exception," he cleared his throat," however, it seems to me that I must intervene. For the sake of your honor, if not Rafe's life."

"What do you mean, 'his life'?"

"Your large cousin, my dear, will kill him when he learns of what has transpired."

"How could he possibly hear of it, when he couldn't see it under his very nose at Kirkwood Manor?" Isabella thought he must be teasing her. Alex, for all his 'brain-power', was hopelessly dense about the attraction between her and his friend.

"Because I shall *tell* him, my dear."

"Whit!"

He held up his hand to forestall her protest. "If Rafe has done the things I suspect to your fair person and refuses to do the honorable thing, then I can see no alternative."

Isabella jumped up from the table and began pacing, with each sharp turn kicking her skirts out of the way. "I won't have him if he's forced, my lord. I won't!" Goodness, this was not going how she'd planned. Whit, of all people, should be championing her efforts. He was, after all, the epitome of a rake and therefore should understand lust and love and all it entailed. Why, in heavens name, was he sounding so moralistic?

Whit sighed, eyed the crab cakes longingly, and then also rose. "Perhaps we should continue this in the parlor."

Neither said anything until they sat on the cream-and-rose colored sofa, and Whit enfolded her hands in his.

"Now, my dear, you must tell me something else — do you love him? I do not mean infatuation. I mean really love him. I must know if I am to help you."

Tears of gratitude filled her eyes. "Thank you, my lord. This means everything to me. Oh, Whit, it must be love, this way I feel."

It was onto this scene Alex entered through the open doorway. He blinked repeatedly and was silent for all of five seconds before shaking his fist and shouting at his friend. "Ah, ha! I knew it! You've been bloody well sneaking about behind me back, you dog! You got her to fall in love with you!"

"Alex, please!" Isabella jumped to her feet. Oh dear, what a time for her cousin to visit.

"You're on the wrong track, you dolt. She's not in love with *me*!" Whit, his perverse nature at the fore, started to laugh.

Isabella wanted to cosh him but good.

"What? The devil, you say. I heard her just now." Alex continued to glare at him. "She said she loved you!"

"No, no." Whit doubled over. Isabella hit him in the arm, hard, and he sobered a bit. "Cat's out of the bag, Bella. I'm sorry."

"Whit, we can't tell him. You said Alex would *kill* him!" Isabella frantically tugged on the sleeve of his coat, while glancing between the two, hoping she could get him to stand and do something to ease the situation. She couldn't allow Alex to think she loved Lord Langley, but she was terrified of what he'd do to the man she truly did love.

"Just whom should I kill, if not him." A confused Alex jabbed his finger toward the other man.

"Oh, this is dreadful."

"Now, now," Whit said, as he stood and patted her shoulder with one hand, while the other tried to pry her fingers loose of his best day coat. "He probably won't truly kill him, just bloody him up a bit."

"Alex, you cannot! I forbid you to harm him, do you hear me?"

"How can I help but hear you, me dear?" he asked dryly. "You are shouting at me."

Isabella marched over to him and began poking him in the chest with her finger. "I *love* him, and if you *hurt* him, I'll *never speak to you again!*"

Alex winced at each jab. From over the top of her head, he gave Whit an apologetic look. "Sorry, old sport. It's Rafe, ain't it?"

Whit nodded to him. "Afraid so."

"Well, blast and damn!"

"Now, Alex—"

"Don't you 'now Alex' me, you silly twit!" He picked Isabella up and dumped her on the sofa, then began pacing.

"Good God! Right under me nose! The cad seduced you *right under me nose*! And I *sent* him to you! I should have known I couldn't trust the man. He should be horsewhipped, I say!"

Whit and Isabella rolled eyes at each other as the huge man bellowed.

"That blighter!" Alex continued, now extremely red in the face. "I will kill him! I'll tear him limb from limb! And then he'll marry you, I can tell you that!"

The two conspirators snickered.

"All right, fine. *First* he'll marry you, *then* I'll make you a widow."

"She won't have him if he's forced, old boy."

"What? When did *she* get a bloody choice?"

That got Isabella's dander up. She stood and placed her hands on her hips, her back ramrod straight, her chin thrust forward. "I am my own mistress, Alexander Fitzhugh, and I'll thank you to remember that. The choice is entirely mine. How dare you!"

She ignored the stinging heat infusing her cheeks. She had had quite enough of her cousin's interference.

"You force a fake butler on me after not having seen me in *three* years, leave me in the dark as to why I am harboring the man, and now think to dictate to me whom I am to marry?" She snorted with contempt. "I think *not*, my lord."

"Damn me, she has a grand fire, don't she, boy-o?"

"You have got that right. I rather wished she had fallen in love with me."

"Oh! Both of you are impossible." She threw up her hands in frustration. "I give up on you two idiots. I will handle this myself. Just go about your debauched lives, don't have a thought about me, the one you thrust into this mess." Her glare dared them to do just that. "No, please, go back to your mistresses and drink and gaming. I shall manage splendidly, I'm sure."

Alex sighed heavily. "All right, Bella, what do you want us to do?" He gave Whit a woefully sad frown. "It is our fault. We did send him to her."

"Yes, we are to blame for it." Whit returned his friend's soulful expression.

Isabella took a deep breath. She crossed her arms over her chest and began tapping her foot impatiently. "Well, first I want some answers, then we will start planning."

ISABELLA sat on the sofa, her spine stiff, her hands stapled together in her lap. She was doing her best to appear calm and in control, but her nerves were in a knot of apprehension. Finally, she would have her answers. But what if they were not the truths that would allow her and Rafe to be together? What if it was worse than she thought?

Whit and Alex sat in the matching wing chairs across from her. They looked nervous, uncomfortable, *guilty*.

"All right, you two. I'm waiting."

Alex cleared his throat and glanced at his friend. In return, Whit shrugged.

"Alexander Fitzhugh! I want the truth and I want it now." She raised her brows and tilted her head. Usually, one of these looks had the servants scrambling to appease her. The result on her cousin was to cause him to blush. Isabella thought it telling.

"Look here, Bella," Alex began, refusing her meet her gaze as he tugged at the cuff of his crisp white shirt and then the sleeve of his rust jacket, "it was never a situation meant to involve you."

"Nonsense, Alex. You couldn't have involved me more if you had planned to," Isabella scoffed.

"Now, cousin, we still thought you plain and no temptation to Rafe. How were we supposed to know you'd become a beauty and that the stupid sod wouldn't be able to leave you be?"

"Are you trying to insinuate *I* have some fault in this?" Her eyes narrowed. He grimaced as he looked at her.

"Of course not! It's just that—"

"Alex! The *truth* of who Easton is."

Alex and Whit again exchanged looks but this time it was Alex who shrugged, seeming to be at a loss as to how to continue.

"Isabella, my lady," Whit began, flashing her a charming smile — which slipped at her stony expression. He coughed into his fist before he continued. "Rafe is not a butler."

"That is beyond obvious, Lord Langley."

"He's not of the serving class at all."

"I have already deduced such, my lord."

"Why, he's not even a bastard, actually."

"Then what, pray tell, *is* he, precisely?" Isabella did not try to keep her mounting frustration from her voice. If not a bastard, what could he possibly be that would make him so unsuitable for her? A sudden thought flashed in her mind. Oh heavens! She hadn't even considered it before!

"He is not ... ," she clutched her hands tighter together, afraid to even speak the words aloud but forcing herself to anyway. "He is not ... *married* is he?"

Whit laughed.

"'Course not!" Alex looked shocked at the very idea.

"Thank goodness." Relief flowed through her. "Then why all this nonsense? Why was he pretending to be a butler? Why did he come to Kirkwood Manor?"

"Well," Whit replied, "Rafe got himself in a bit of a situation and needed a place to stay out of sight for awhile."

"But *why*?"

"Listen, Bella," Alex said, leaning forward to rest his arms on his thighs and peering at her intensely, "suffice it to say that Rafe did something he ought not to have, quite by accident, and needed to vacate the city to avoid scandalizing a friend. That is all you need know about that."

"For heaven's sake, cousin, I am not a child. You cannot decide for me what I should and should not know about the man I love. Enough of this nonsense, I say. Tell me the truth."

Alex glanced at Whit, who nodded to him.

"All right, me dear." The earl sighed. "I suppose, given what has passed between you two, you have the right to know the whole of it."

Isabella leaned forward, eager to finally hear the story.

"Rafe's name is not Woodrow Easton." Alex began, then frowned. "Well, actually, it sort of is. His full name is Raefiel Woodrow Atherton."

"Then, he is not related to the Earl of Easton?" Confused, she looked at the viscount, who had supplied her that information through Lisbeth.

"Well, actually, he *is* the Earl of Easton." Whit gave her an apologetic smile. "And the Duke of Devonshire, as well."

"What!" Isabella's mind raced, recalling bits of gossip her friend had told her of the "Debauched Duke," as he was referred to in the gossip columns, and of his many affairs. "Heavens!" Her Rafe was *that* duke? She would be utterly ruined if word got out he had spent two weeks alone with her! She was beginning to understand.

"Cousin, we was only trying to help him out! He was in a spot."

"So you sent this notorious rakehell to me, your drab, simple-minded country cousin? What spot?"

Whit answered. "He unwisely entered into a liaison with a woman. After he ended their 'association,' she threatened to tell all."

"And," added Alex, "if her husband found out, he'd have run Rafe through. We couldn't allow him to be skewered, you understand."

"She is married?" Oh, dear. It was worse than she thought. Her "Easton" was a duke who had affairs with married women!

"Yes, but Rafe didn't know that, my lady." Whit was quick to assure her. "He thought she was an actress."

"An actress." Why did he make it sound as if that explained something? At least Rafe hadn't known this woman was married. That was at least one thing to his credit — one small thing.

"So, what you are telling me is the man I fell in love with is not a bastard, but a duke who is a notorious womanizer?" She remained calm and watched the two men nod to her, their expressions rather sheepish. She gave them a tight smile in return.

"I see." She stood slowly and shook the wrinkles from her skirt with a sharp snap of her wrist. "Is there anything else I should know?" Gracefully, she stepped around to stand behind the couch, resting her hands on the back.

"Well," Whit looked to Alex, then back to her. "He doesn't believe in love."

"Thinks it's bloody rot, me dear." Alex chimed in.

Ah, his comments in the garden that night made more sense now. He may not have been baseborn, but he was still a bastard. What a relief she had not confessed she loved him! He would have had a good laugh over that.

"And that is all?"

Whit shrugged.

"You are taking this rather well, Bella." Alex looked puzzled but relieved by her calm expression.

"How else should I behave, cousin?" She forced a smile on her lips, cold fury welling up inside of her. "After all, I am a *sensible* girl, aren't I?"

"Well, yes, you are."

"I am not the sort of female given to extreme emotions, to fits of temper, am I?"

"Certainly not," Alex replied, beginning to look rather nervous.

"Why, then, would you think I would be upset that you have all lied to me?" She sweetened her smile, her hands digging into the brocade fabric of the couch.

"'Lie' is rather harsh, don't you think, me girl?"

"Oh, do forgive me, cousin. Perhaps I should have said prevaricate? Or do you prefer dissemble? A canard, then?"

"She's angry, Alex." Whit said from the side of his mouth and sat back, crossing his arms over his chest.

"But how can so *sensible* a person like me be angry, Lord Langley?"

"I think you're right, boy-o," Alex muttered, watching her with narrowed eyes. "We're in for it now."

Isabella continued to smile as she relaxed her grip on the sofa and began to smooth the material. She shook her head and stepped around the front of the divan to stand before the two men.

"Cousin," she began cajolingly, then let them both have an earful. "How could you! How could you *lie* to me and treat me as if I was some addle-brained simpleton!" Even the sight of them cringing before her didn't ease her fury. "How dare you send a man to me who is known as the 'Debauched Duke,' even if I was ugly! Had you absolutely no thought for me, for my reputation? The lies!" She threw wide her arms and then began pacing. "The man I love is a cad, a libertine, a seducer of married women. He is so jaded he declares there is no love. He is a conceited, hypocritical fool." She paused to glare at them. "Here I have been torturing myself, thinking his rebuff was made for noble reasons. I excused his behavior as chivalrous, gallant. Since I was above his station and it would have caused me scandal, he was pushing me away despite the love between us — for the sake of my honor. Bosh and rot!"

"Now, Bella—" Alex began.

Isabella held up a hand to forestall him. "Stop! Just stop the lies, Alex. I see the truth well enough now. I was a dalliance, a diversion from the boredom of North Bindlefork. I understand. If he cared at all for me, he could have confessed who he was and offered me marriage. There never was any impediment to our being together." She wanted to crumble into a heap and sob. Instead, she started pacing again. What a fool she had been!

"If it is any consolation, I do think he loves you, my lady," Whit offered softly.

"Enough, I say! I can take no more of this, sir. He obviously does not care for me." Her voice hitched, and she blinked back tears. "If his heart held any tender feelings for me, he would not have left me and rushed back here to his many mistresses." It was hopeless. Rafe didn't want her. Her heart felt as if it was being ripped from her breast. "I want to go home, Alex."

Whit stood and grasped her by the arms, stopping her frantic pacing.

"My dearest Isabella. Come, sit, and let me explain our friend to you."

"What good does it do me now to know of him? I want to return home, sir. I have embarrassed myself enough by coming here." Didn't he understand her humiliation?

"No, you did a very brave thing, my lady. You followed your heart, even when you thought it futile to hope for a future with Rafe."

His look was so earnest, she allowed him to lead her back to the sofa and sat beside him. The least she could do was hear him out. Not that she now had any hopes left.

"What can you possibly tell me that would change anything?"

"I can tell you that Rafe does indeed have feelings for you."

"Nonsense."

Whit gave her an amused frown. "Listen to me, Bella. I have known him since he was a young boy and can see he is in the grips of an emotion he has never come across before. While he may have had numerous liaisons, he has never had an affair of the *heart*."

"Rot. How can a man, loved by so many, never have loved in return? How can he not know what he feels toward me?"

"I tell you, he has never been in love before, Isabella."

"I don't see how that could be possible." She crossed her

arms and glared at the viscount.

Whit smiled gently and patted her knee. "Allow me to tell you about Rafe's father. He was a highly respected peer and brave military man — also, a great libertine in his day. Even after he wed the Dutchess, he continued openly with his many affairs. He was seen often with many beautiful young women and never tried to hide it from Rafe."

"Gracious! His poor mother! To have had to endure such humiliation — why, she must have hated the duke."

"On the contrary. She loves him still. She was never unfaithful, never even brought it up as far as I know."

"Is she such a rug then, that she allowed her husband to trod upon her?"

Whit and Alex laughed.

"Not dear Anne, cousin!" Alex replied, shaking his head.

"No," Whit said. "The Dutchess is a very outspoken woman, actually. I don't know what their agreement was, if they had one, but this was the example Rafe grew up with. His father was the one who gave him the absurd notion that there was no such emotion as love and, by observing the many women his father was with, Rafe himself concluded ladies were a faithless lot. This has been cemented by the numerous married women he has been involved with — women who have had an 'arrangement' with their husbands, that is. He draws the line at seducing the wives of men who think their brides devoted to only them."

"This married lady posing as an actress — her husband is such a man?"

"Exactly."

Isabella sat back, lowering her arms and resting her hands again in her lap. Lord Langley had given her much to think about. "But why did he not ... not take what I offered?" She felt herself blush and glanced at Alex. He was scowling again.

"None of us dallies with debutantes and virgins, my lady. The consequence for such sport is too high," Whit explained.

"Meaning marriage?"

"Quite."

"I see. Does Rafe also view his romances as 'sport'?"

Alex snorted. "He's had the ladies throwing themselves at him since before he was out of short pants. There's not much sport in it when it comes so bloody easy."

"Now, do you understand our Rafe better? Do you still want us to help you win his heart?" Whit was serious again.

Isabella sat staring down at her hands, the thoughts tumbling about in her head. Yes, she still wanted him, still loved him. No matter what they had told her about him, that wouldn't have changed. But could she live with the idea he might not remain faithful to her? If he was so very decadent, what hope did she have that he would come to believe he loved her?

"I suppose I must try. If I don't, I will always regret it." She looked up at Whit, then her cousin. "If you really think he may have feelings for me then, yes, I do still want your help."

She hoped she didn't come to regret this decision even more than she might giving up.

Chapter 15

Rafe sat in his study, sipping at the brandy Tilbot had brought him a short while ago. It had been three weeks now since he'd left Isabella. His gloom had not lessened with the days. In fact, it only seemed to grow.

He missed her. That was it in a nutshell.

He missed the smell of her, the taste of her. He missed how her emerald eyes sparkled and her cheeks softly blushed when he teased her. He missed her sensual chuckle, the endearing way she would cock her head to one side while thinking, and how she trembled in his arms.

It was good his mother was in residence; else wise, he would not go out at all. They were due to attend Jeffrey Blake's soiree this evening, but he still hadn't mustered the courage to face all of those hopeful mamas with their mediocre little misses. It got more absurd the longer that he remained unattached. And this year, given his infatuation with Isabella, was by far the worst.

He had finally acknowledged this annoying passion for his country lady during one of his many recent sleepless nights. Each night as he lay there, the soothing embrace of Morpheus eluding him, he was plagued by visions of Isabella. Most often it was his last sight of her, standing in the foyer, cold, haughty — and so very hurt.

His mother was becoming quite concerned, he knew. Why, she had even brought the doctor home the other day to see if there was any medical treatment for his malaise. Rafe had assured the physician that his only ailment was a case of a guilty conscience. Although the doctor was satisfied, he knew his mother was not.

"Gracious, Rafe," his mother had said the moment the doctor left, "you only pick at your food and you look beyond exhausted!"

"I'm fine, Mother. Just feeling a bit off lately, that's all."

But he wasn't fine.

Sitting in the dark study, he wondered if he would ever feel like himself again. *God, Bella, what have you done to me?* He looked down at the glass in his hand, surprised to see it empty.

Isabella was better off without him. If he had taken her that last night, if he had stripped her naked and made love to her in the moonlight as he had itched to do, she would be cursing him even more than she already undoubtedly was. But at least he might have gotten her out of his system, and the guilt would be a natural and fleeting thing, surely. Yes, the way he felt now was simply enhanced by unfulfilled lust. That was why she claimed his every thought, why he dreamt of her during his brief snatches of sleep. He had never desired a woman as much and had certainly never deprived himself of a willing partner before. She was his forbidden fruit — but, God help him, he still wanted to taste her. He wanted to plunge deep into her and hear her cry out again in wild abandon. He wanted to watch her eyes fill with amazement once more as she reached her release. He raked his fingers through his hair, thinking he was a fool.

He heard the clock in the entry chime the half-hour and sighed. It was time to go up and dress for Blake's party. Well, perhaps tonight he would finally see a woman who struck his fancy and would rescue him from this damned depression he was wallowing in. It was highly doubtful, but still, one never knew when a pretty face would catch one's eye.

"MY dear boy, how very handsome you look!" Anne smiled at Rafe as he sauntered into the drawing room, but there was worry in her soft blue eyes.

"And you look radiant, Mother, as always." He marveled how lovely and young she still looked, despite the tension in her face. She sat on the edge of the small brocade settee, her body stiff. She was studying his face intently, and he could tell she wasn't pleased by what she saw. "You are ready to go, then?"

"Oh, yes. I am quite excited." Anne rose and allowed him to drape her ermine-trimmed indigo cloak over her ruby gown, then she pulled on her red gloves as they left the house. "Lady Stella was telling me at luncheon today about a beautiful young woman that you simply *must* meet."

Rafe rolled his eyes as he assisted his mother into the carriage.

"Apparently, she is newly arrived. A pity we just missed her at the ball the other night. She was a huge success, with absolutely every young dandy vying for a dance with her."

Anne eyed him critically as he settled across from her. "It's just what you need, my boy. A torrid romance will lift your spirits, I have no doubt."

"Please, Mother. Do *not* attempt any matchmaking. I can handle my own affairs, romantic or otherwise."

"Well, you've been handling them rather poorly of late, son. I usually have to make an appointment with you, when I am in town and wish your company, you are so in demand with the ladies. Since I've been here, you've done nothing but mope about. Why, you've turned down more offers these last weeks than most men ever receive!"

"Mother, don't exaggerate so. Besides, is there something wrong with taking time away from amorous pursuits? I do have estates to run, you know."

His mother only snorted derisively. Rafe said nothing in response, glad when they arrived at Lord Blake's home.

"My lords and ladies, the Duke and Dowager Duchess of Devonshire!"

"Ah, good!" Jeffrey Blake was there to greet them. "I was so hoping you'd arrive before too many others, dear Dutchess, Rafe." The redheaded gentleman bowed to Anne, then shook Rafe's hand. "My mother has been anxious to speak with you, Your Grace. She has quite pestered me with each new guest announced to go and see if there was an error and it was really you."

"Your lady mother is a twit, Jeffrey, and well you know it." Humor sparkled in Anne's eyes, despite her caustic words.

"Of course she is, Dutchess, but she is my mother, and so I must put up with her." Jeffrey rolled his eyes, then smiled at the duchess adoringly. "Please do go and sit with her, for just a brief spell, I beg of you."

"All right, but only to get it over with and out of the way." She patted Rafe's cheek. "Do be a love and come fetch me in a half an hour."

"Of course, Mother." Rafe always found it amusing the way Jeffrey and she dealt with each other.

"Your mother's loveliness and sharpness of tongue only seem to increase with each passing year. How lucky a man was your father." Lord Blake chuckled.

Rafe agreed, then, as more newcomers were arriving to claim Jeffrey's attention, moved off to find the champagne. The ballroom was only just now beginning to fill. He saw several acquaintances from his club and decided to pass the time with them until he had to go and "rescue" his mother.

ISABELLA frowned at her reflection. "Are you sure about this gown, Whit?" Her hair was pulled up on top of her head, thick ringlets of auburn tresses spilling down to brush against her shoulders. The style made her face even more attractively angular and gave her a bit more height. She could find no fault with the coiffure, at least.

"For the tenth time, Bella, it is absolute perfection and you simply could not look more beautiful." Whit had selected the evening dress himself, a shimmering, rich gold creation designed just for her.

"Don't you think it a bit *too* daring?"

"Rubbish, it is even a bit more modest in the neckline than your lavender one."

"If you are sure." Isabella was a bundle of nerves. Goodness, Rafe was a Duke! And not just a duke, but the 'debauched duke.' Lisbeth would probably advise her to fly home as fast as she could.

Her cousin entered the parlor, hailing Whit and carrying a black box.

"Stunning, my dear!"

Isabella faced him, smiling at his praise until she saw him frown.

"What's wrong." She began to check herself over, panicking as she looked for a tear or stain.

"You're lacking something." He opened the box and grinned at her gasp. "Just some family baubles to enhance your glory."

"Oh, my! Alex, I cannot wear those." She stepped closer to look at the topaz and diamonds shimmering on a bed of black velvet. "They must be worth a fortune."

"Bloody right they are, and you deserve no less, cousin." He set the box down, removed the dainty necklace and clasped it around her neck. He then handed her the matching earrings. After she had put on the earrings, he fastened a delicate bracelet for her.

"There, I think that's all you need. Don't want to appear gaudy, like so many of them do with tiaras and brooches and rings galore."

"An excellent touch, old man. So very thoughtful of you," Whit said, grinning as usual.

"Well," blustered the huge man, "can't have it said me family lacks enough groats to decorate their females."

"Ha! Like anyone who even knows of your family could think you don't have enough money. Why, Isabella herself could buy plenty of jewels."

Isabella looked at her image in the mirror over the fireplace and was surprised how much the simple jewelry enhanced her appearance. She impulsively turned and launched herself at her cousin, hugging him and planting a kiss on his chin, unable to reach his cheek.

"Oh, thank you so much! And you, too, Whit." His cheek she could reach. "You've both made me feel like a fairy princess." She grinned at their blushes. "Can we go now?"

Alex recovered himself first. "Now, what did we tell you about making a grand entrance? No," he shook his head at her, "don't give me that look. We shall wait just a bit longer."

THE three sat in the coach, just down the block from Lord Blake's residence. They had been there for only some fifteen minutes, and already Isabella thought she would go mad with the suspense.

"Bella, do stop fidgeting, you'll muss yourself."

"Alex, how much longer do we have to just *sit* here? Don't you think it's been long enough?"

"No. There are still too many carriages arriving."

She tried to keep still but that only lasted another ten minutes. She smoothed the fabric of her pure white cape, then tugged at the gold braid, which banded the collar and tied the covering closed.

Whit leaned over and peered out of the window. "You know, Alex, I think it is time." He looked at Isabella, a devilish twinkle in his soft brown eyes. "Remember what we told you, my dear?"

"Of course, of course." Isabella fluttered her hand at him dismissively. "I know perfectly well how you said to behave."

Alex and Whit nodded to each other, satisfied. The larger man thumped his fist against the roof, and the carriage jerked forward.

RAFE escorted his mother back to the party and handed her a glass of champagne from a passing waiter's tray.

"Ah, there is Lady Stella. I shall go and ask her if that new beauty has arrived." She gave her son an impish grin, then moved off to speak with her fellow companion in gossip.

Rafe sighed. He was at a loss of what to do with himself. He had yet to find a lady to even remotely tempt him, and Whit and Alex hadn't yet shown up. The attention of his other acquaintances was now on gaming, something he found a bit boring. He stopped another waiter, liberated two glasses of the bubbly for himself, and downed the first flute in one gulp. He heard the thump of the staff signaling the announcement of some late arrivers. From the corner of his eye, he caught a flash of red and turning, saw his mother racing to his side.

"It's her, I'm sure! Stella said she was not here, as yet." She looked toward the entry which was raised above the main floor by a low flight of stairs, an anxious expression on her face.

"My lords and ladies!"

Rafe could swear the room grew quieter, as if everyone was anticipating that this was the supposed 'new beauty.' He rolled his eyes and his mother poked him in the ribs.

"Look, that *must* be her!"

"The Earl of Stapleton, the Viscount Langley and the Baroness of Kirkwood!"

Rafe was flabbergasted. *Isabella?*

"You see, Lady Stella was right."

What was the hell was she doing here in London?

"My goodness, what a lovely young woman."

How long had she been here? Why hadn't Alex said anything?

"I understand she is Alex's cousin. Odd that he has not brought her around to me for an introduction."

"Isabella," Rafe whispered her name, his pulse racing.

"What dear?"

"Good God, it's really her." Rafe watched her pause there, at the top of the stairs, her fingertips gently placed on the sleeve of the men on either side of her. "Look at her and tell me again she's merely lovely. She is beyond words."

Isabella stood still, the barest trace of a smile hovering about that lush mouth of hers. And then her eyes locked with his and Rafe felt a surge of desire and possessiveness wash over him, the likes of which he had never felt before. He saw her eyes widen, or thought he did, but her gaze left him and she slowly turned her head to survey the room. She was a vision of warm gold topped by her glorious, aureate hair, luminescent with highlights of fire.

What the hell was she doing here?

ISABELLA'S heart was pounding. She'd spotted him easily enough and it was all she could do to keep from running down the steps and flinging herself into Rafe's strong arms. Even without her cohort's earlier warnings, she could not do it, would not do it while the entire assembly was staring at her as they were. She forced herself to look away from his piercing blue eyes.

"Well done, Bella," Whit whispered close to her ear.

"Ah! The ravishing Lady Isabella." Jeffrey Blake approached them, a broad smile on his round face. Stray tendrils of red hair defied his otherwise tidy queue.

Allowing a trace of a smile to curve her lips, Isabella lifted her hand from Alex's arm and held it out to her host, who obligingly kissed it.

"I don't know how it is possible, but you are even more beautiful tonight than I remember, my lady."

Isabella had to remind herself *not* to look toward Rafe as she allowed Lord Blake to lead her forward down the steps. Her two escorts followed close behind.

"Why, thank you, my lord. It was very kind of you to invite me to your home. What lovely decorations." She could feel Rafe's gaze still on her. Her skin tingled with awareness of his virile, commanding presence.

"They pale in your presence, my lady. Even the moon hides tonight, knowing it cannot possibly outshine you."

"Good God, Jeffrey, you're putting it on a might thick," Alex muttered.

Isabella chuckled, low and deep. Her host suddenly had a startled look on his face.

"Do not worry, my lord, my cousin has promised to behave himself this evening. He is to attempt to stop glowering so."

"Ah, champagne, Lady Isabella?" Jeffrey asked, eyeing her guardians standing so close.

"Yes, thank you, Lord Blake."

"Please, do me the honor of calling me Jeffrey."

"As you wish."

Isabella caught Alex exchanging looks with Whit out of the corner of her eye. They looked extremely pleased with her performance thus far. She was acting every bit the regal lady, as they told her to.

Isabella handed her glass to her cousin. "Lord Jeffrey, I should very much like to dance."

"Of course, Baroness. I should like nothing better

myself."

She could feel Rafe's gaze upon her, watching her every move, along with dozens of others, as their host led her onto the dance floor and whirled her about. It seemed the plan was working. Her 'advisors' had instructed her to ignore her love, as best she could, until he approached her. She was to appear receptive to other men's attentions, but still be her most aloof self. Whit had said to act as if she held some great secret that none of the others were yet privy too and that she found vaguely amusing. They had assured her such behavior would intrigue any man. She thought it all nonsense, really, although surprisingly easy to do. She hoped Rafe wouldn't take *too* much longer.

RAFE watched her dancing, his hands fisted at his sides. She looked positively radiant, damn her, in that gold gown which clung to her curves like a second skin. Where the devil did she get those jewels?

"Darling, you look as if you want to kill Lord Jeffrey. Do stop it. Is this my son who had aloofness down to a fine art?"

"Excuse me, Mother." Rafe's gaze narrowed on the couple as Jeffrey's hand slid down Bella's back a bit too far, for his liking.

"Rafe, good God, get ahold of yourself!" His mother placed a hand on his sleeve. "You cannot cause a scene by storming onto the floor and hitting him."

"Why not?" he growled out.

"You are being an ass. Why don't you just take a deep breath and, when the dance is over, partner her on the next?"

"Of course. Thank you, my dear." Rafe decided he would waltz Bella out onto the veranda and strangle her there in the moonlight.

Just what the hell was she doing here?

The music finally ended, but before Rafe could get to her, Lord Northby claimed Isabella in the next dance. Soon, Rafe was frustrated beyond belief as the scene repeated itself. The very moment one partner stepped away, another was there to take his place. After Northby was Smythe, then Cross, and so on. Truly, it was disgusting how they all fawned over her.

"Dearest, I have a headache. Would you see me home?"

"I'm sorry, Mother, what did you say?" Lord Elton was now holding Isabella much too closely. Rafe's eyes narrowed as he watched her smile at some remark from the old lecher.

"Son, I want to leave. I have a headache."

"What, *now?*" For the first time since Isabella had started dancing, Rafe looked at his mother.

"Yes, now."

"Can't you just take a powder or something? No, no, don't say it. Of course I shall take you home at once." He frowned, looking toward his lady fair. "But don't expect me to sit with you."

"Of course not, dearest."

Chapter 16

Alex and Whit sat comfortably in the former's study, sipping fine old brandy and listened to the pounding on the front door. It had been going on for a good ten minutes.

"All right, let him in." Alex finally told his butler, Brisby, who was hovering about, looking morose indeed.

The two lords heard cursing as the front door crashed against the wall then was slammed shut. The force rattled the windowpanes.

"God damn it, Alex!" Rafe stormed into the room, tossing his black cloak back over his shoulders. "Where is she?" He leaned down, placed his hands on either arm of his large friend's chair, and stuck his face into the other's. "She's here, isn't she?"

"Just whom are you referring to, old man?" Alex responded coolly. "I certainly brought no woman here. What about you, Whit? Are you harboring some chit under me roof?" He shoved Rafe away, hard, a dangerous glint in his sable eyes.

"You know very well who I mean, damn your soul!" Rafe shook his fist at the two who just sat there looking as calm as could be. "I went back to Blake's only to find you had spirited her away the moment I left!"

"I do believe he means your lady cousin," Whit supplied and pretended to stifle a yawn behind his hand.

"Oh, *her*. Well, you can't think she would be here in a bachelor's residence, me boy. That's absurd."

"Then what bloody hotel did you put her in?" Rafe raked his fingers through his already mussed hair.

He had panicked upon finding they had already left the party. For several moments, sorrow had gripped him at the thought of never seeing Isabella again. Of course, his good reason had returned, and he'd known just where she would be. Or so he had thought.

"I don't know why I should tell you where she is." Alex leaned forward, his eyes narrowing. "What does it matter to you?"

"Just why is she here in London? Why isn't she safely tucked away in North Bindlefork?"

"She has never been here before," Whit said with a shrug. "That's reason enough for me. You know women. She's been buying new gowns and hats, seeing the sights." He smiled slyly. "Why, I do believe she may even be thinking about making a suitable match while here."

"The hell she is! How could you two allow her to be groped by all those damned dandies tonight?" Rafe was oblivious to the knowing looks that passed between the other two, as he began to pace. "Lord, Alex, what were you thinking, allowing her to wear that dress? It bloody well *clung* to her!

And just who gave her those jewels, I'd like to know? She doesn't own any, save the diamond earrings her father gave her."

"You certainly seem to know a good deal about it. Would you care for a brandy?" Whit asked, his voice bland.

Rafe sank down onto the chocolate brown leather ottoman, holding his head in his hands. "If you won't tell me where she is, at least tell me she's all right." He stared morosely at the tips of his highly polished shoes. He knew he was mad to be doing this, to be seeking her out. Their lust was a dangerous thing to them both, but he could only think of her. Thoughts of her suffering over his rejection had been awful enough. Now he had to endure visions of her earlier enjoyment as one man after another held her in their arms. Could she actually be entertaining thoughts of *marrying* any of those gentlemen?

"What does it matter to you?" Alex asked again, softly, a wary yet curious look about him.

"God, I don't know. Alex, she's all I've been able to think about since we returned." He sat up, realizing what he'd just confessed. "All right, plain speaking. I'm infatuated with her. She quite got under my skin, it seems, and I cannot get her out." Rafe shook his head at the stares from his friends. "I know, it's absurd that a jaded man like myself should develop such a fondness for the girl. Go ahead and laugh."

"I'm not laughing, you sod. And if it is only an infatuation, you can bloody well leave her alone."

"I cannot."

"Then I'll kill you, old man."

It was said with such quiet menace, Rafe quite believed Alex. He looked at his friend, shocked, as a sudden realization came to him. "Good God, she told you about us!"

"She confessed that you took certain, well, liberties with her very lovely person, Rafe," Whit chimed in. "All right, plain speaking it is, my friend. While she's visiting, we shall see to protecting her, from you or any others a bit too eager. If you don't have honorable intentions, then you'd best stay away from the lady. It's as simple as that."

Rafe looked from one face to the other. They were serious! Lord, how could they expect him to stay away from her, when she was all he thought about? He couldn't sleep, couldn't eat, and could barely keep a thought other than her in his head. And now, to find out she was probably only blocks away and they wanted him to refrain from seeing her?

He knew they were right, damn them. If he had a decent bone in his body, he would stay miles away. But he just knew he couldn't. He *had* to see Isabella, if just once more, and damn the consequence.

"Where is she, Alex?"

"Go to hell, Rafe. You'll not paw her again."

"God damn it, man!" Rafe shot to his feet. "Tell me where she is!"

"Take your best shot, puppy, and I'll pound you into the bloody ground!" Alex jumped up, toe to toe with the young duke.

Whit rose and stepped between the two, who where nearly at each other's throats. "Why, Rafe? Do you love her? Can you admit it," he snorted with contempt, "or are you still going to hide behind that idiotic rhetoric your father drummed into your head?"

"Love? Don't be stupid, Whit."

"Then you're a damned coward, and you don't deserve

her. I knocked you on your arse once, don't think I can't do it again."

"Whit, you're hardly the violent type, let *me* knock the muttonhead down."

"All right, fine. If you won't tell me where she is, then I'll just have to find out for myself. At the very least, I shall see her at McPherson's ball next week." Rafe smirked at their obvious displeasure at that idea. "You can't keep me from her forever." He *would* see her.

"No," Alex said softly, his sable eyes narrowing dangerously, "but we can keep you in bed for a good while." His meaty fist landed directly in Rafe's face.

"WELL, what happened? Did he come to see you?" Isabella could hardly sit still. She, Alex and Whit sat at breakfast in her cozy house. While the two men devoured the meal, Isabella only sipped at her tea.

"Oh, yes." Alex paused between bites of the smoked ham omelet and gave her an assessing look. "He, of course, came looking for you." He shook his head with obvious annoyance at her radiant smile.

"So, when is he to come calling on me?" She was so excited she wanted to dance a jig. Just as they'd planned, he'd come for her! How long would it be now before he held her in his strong, warm arms and kissed her? Before he was again teasing her in that dry mocking way of his? She couldn't wait!

"We didn't tell him where you were."

"What? Why ever not?" Isabella gave her cousin a confused frown.

"Bella, dear," Whit said, wiping his mouth with the linen napkin. "He won't admit to loving you and wouldn't agree to marry you." He shrugged. "That only left one other reason to see you and we cannot allow him to further his corruption."

"The damn rotter."

"Well, that is just fine!" Isabella slammed her cup down so hard, it was amazing it didn't crack apart. "Just what am I supposed to do now? Accept defeat?"

Whit stroked his chin thoughtfully. "He did say he would either find you himself or see you at McPherson's. As many men as have come calling so far, there will now be twice as many after your performance of last night. I think you should begin accepting them."

"Why bother?" Isabella didn't understand his thinking. There was only one man she wanted. She didn't want to waste time on a bunch of dandies when she only had another few weeks.

"When I hinted you may be considering making a match, he was furious. Let's continue to eat at him through jealousy."

"I see." Isabella wasn't sure about the plan, but it couldn't hurt to try. "If you really think he would be jealous of others, then I suppose I could begin by accepting a ride in the park with Lord Elton tomorrow."

"Ah, best wait a few days."

Whit exchanged a look with Alex that did not go unnoticed by Isabella.

"What do you mean? Why should I wait?" She was sure she saw guilt in their eyes. "Just what have you done?"

"He was being an ass, Bella, so we, er, hit him a bit."

"Alex!"

"Don't worry, me pet, nothing's broken — at least, I don't think."

"Goodness! I shall go and see him at once." Isabella

started to rise, only to have each man grab an arm and yank her back down into her chair.

"You most certainly will *not*," Whit said.

"Don't be a twit, dear girl," Alex huffed.

"Just what were you two thinking? I was perfectly serious when I said I would not have him if he were forced." She glared at them. "Really, I don't know what to do with you two. Now I shall have to sit around for several days while he mends."

As it turned out, Isabella had much to do in the two days before she had agreed to accompany Lord Elton. She had several more fittings at the dressmaker, went to the opera with Alex and ordered numerous household items to be sent to Kirkwood Manor.

Finally, Tuesday arrived and she was dressed in a new riding habit of light brown with ecru trim when her escort arrived. He gushed over her appearance, but it only irritated Isabella who was anxious to be out and seen. She had accepted another invitation, for dinner with Lord Northby for that evening, and didn't have time to stand about listening to the older man wax poetic.

"Shall we be off, my lord? I fear my horse grows restless," she said sweetly, mentally rolling her eyes.

They rode through the tree-lined avenues of the park, nodding to various lords and ladies also out to enjoy the sunny day. Unfortunately, she saw so sign of her love. It was a disappointing outing, to be sure.

That evening, when Lord Northby arrived with his carriage to escort her to dinner, Isabella was ready wearing another new gown, this one a soft smoky blue. Lord Northby had chosen a popular restaurant, wanting to show off his beautiful companion to the *Ton*. Isabella was polite but reserved with the man. He was a better conversationalist than Lord Elton, but tended to drink a bit more than she thought appropriate. Once again, there was no sign of Rafe.

"Alex, where is he?" Isabella asked her cousin the next day at tea. "You said he would be mended by now. Have you checked to see if you did more damage than you thought?"

"Bella, he's sulking. I have a spy in his household, and she tells me he's been grousing about, unable to locate the hotel you're supposedly staying in." He chuckled. "The stupid sod."

"Then I've been wasting my time? He doesn't know I'm being courted?"

"Oh, he knows all right. I've seen to it our spy has been keeping him apprised of your conquests." He smiled at her and gobbled down a poppyseed cake. "Delicious. Now, what have you got happening for the next few days?"

Isabella wondered about the reliability of this spy of his, but said nothing. "I am attending a recital at Madam Rose's tonight with Lord Jeffrey. Tomorrow, I have accepted a ride with Lord Northby, and then I'll dine with Lord Cross. And then Friday is the McPherson's ball, of course."

"So," Alex raised an eyebrow at her, "dashing young Cross has thrown his hat in the ring. That should have Rafe gnashing his teeth."

"Do you think?" She nibbled on a lemon tart. "I hope so, cousin. I do hope it's worth all of this silliness."

"Don't worry, me dear. I have a feeling he'll come around soon enough. Our spy is our trump. She'll see he faces his feelings."

Alex looked confident, but Isabella certainly had her doubts. Soon it would be her last week, and they hadn't seemed to have accomplished much. Oh, she had plenty of new gowns and the estate was now well stocked with new linens and such, but she still didn't have Rafe. She didn't even know what feelings he had for her.

Chapter 17

It was finally the night of the ball and Isabella considered her gowns carefully, knowing that she would be seeing Rafe.

How the last two days had dragged by! She had to admit that her evening with Lord Jeffrey had been pleasant enough; she did actually like the small man, but Lord Northby was becoming a bore. And Lord Cross had been *much* too forward on the ride home, although up until that point she had enjoyed herself. The problem was, she compared each of them to Rafe. And what man wouldn't be found lacking, held up to him?

Goodness, she was tired of all the drama. It wasn't in her personality to flirt and use duplicity to get what she wanted. Her father had always praised her directness and logical thinking. Perhaps it was the fate of a comely woman to sink to such depths. It was certainly a depressing thought.

Isabella finally decided on a deep lavender gown with a daring neckline and off-the-shoulder cap sleeves. The underskirt, just peeking through the front slit of the gown, was a dazzling white. Alice swept up her hair at the sides and arranged it in tight curls atop her head, with the rest in loose waves down her back. The style was Alice's favorite on Isabella, saying "it brung out them slanty eyes men adore." Isabella didn't argue, as it did seem to complement her.

Anxious, she could not just wait in her room until her two co-conspirators arrived. She decided to greet them in the parlor and had only just seated herself when they arrived.

"Stunning, my girl, absolutely stunning." Alex kissed her cheek fondly and slipped a pearl choker around her neck. "Ah, perfection has been achieved."

"Once again, you've chosen well, Alex. You do look breathtaking." Whit kissed her other cheek. "Tonight's the night, I'm sure. He'll see you and drop to his knees, begging for your hand."

"I shan't hold my breath."

Both men chuckled at her dry response. They confessed their spy, the Duchess of course, had sent Alex a note stating that Rafe was beyond anxious about this evening. He had even insisted she take a headache powder before they leave.

The three plotters left her small house then and once more sat in the coach down the street from the festivity until surely almost every carriage had dropped off its occupants. Finally, the men deemed it was time to make their entrance.

"The Earl of Stapleton, the Viscount Langley, and the Baroness of Kirkwood, my lords and ladies."

Isabella felt his eyes on her the moment they stepped forward. She dared to glance at him. He looked so very handsome, standing beside a lady she fervently hoped was his lovely mother, his dark hair shining in the candlelight and his blue eyes sparkling. What woman could possibly resist him? She saw his firm lips curl in a predatory smile and her pulse raced.

Alex and Whit led her forward after greeting their hosts. Isabella didn't even have time to accept a glass of champagne before Rafe was standing before her. She felt her escorts stiffen, even as her heart thudded erratically in her breast.

"Why, hello, Lady Isabella."

"Your Grace," Isabella managed a slight, elegant curtsey, despite being unable to look away from him. Oh, he looked tired! At least most of his visible bruises were faded, and the cut above his eye was nearly healed. Dear, Alex really would have to apologize for hurting him.

"I would like to request the honor of the first dance, my lady." He lifted one black brow, looking directly at Alex, challenging him.

"I should be delighted, Your Grace." Isabella was *not* about to allow Alex to muck this up now. She quickly stepped forward, placing her fingers delicately on his proffered arm. "I am sure his grace will return me to you after the dance, Alex, so *behave*."

Rafe chuckled at her scolding as he walked her to the dance floor.

"My lady," he said , then bowed to her, and slipped his arm about her waist. He held her hand and began to whirl them about the floor. "You have been rather elusive during your stay in London."

"Your Grace, have I been?" Isabella could hardly think. Finally, he was holding her! She felt the heat of his body through her gown, he was so close. "Why, I have accepted several invitations already, and I do not recall Alex saying any one of the gentlemen complained that I was the least bit elusive."

"Ah, you are sticking to the very boring rules of etiquette, I see. You have the gentlemen go through Alex, then."

"Of course. How could I do otherwise, Your Grace? I do not relish sullying my family name."

"What if I invite you here and now? Would you refuse me?"

"That would depend on the invitation, Your Grace." Goodness, she had best be careful. She loved him so, it would be easy to agree to anything he proposed. He would only have to flash that wicked grin of his, and she'd be tempted to kiss him right here on the floor, if he asked.

"What if I ask you to go riding with me tomorrow? Would that be appropriate enough?"

She appeared to think it over, her head tilted to one side. Then she gave him a teasing little smile. "I suppose I could accept that invitation, since we both know you are not a bastard. I wonder if Alex will insist on chaperoning us, though?"

Rafe laughed, then groaned. "I couldn't bear it!"

"I'm sure that can be avoided, Your Grace."

"Do stop calling me that, my dear. I think we know each other well enough by now to dispense with such formality."

She blushed at his inference.

"Do you realize this is the first time we've danced together? That seems odd."

"Why does it seem odd?" She wanted to lay her head upon his broad shoulder and feel his lips against her temple. She wanted to breathe in the scent of him and hear his heart beat beneath her ear.

"I suppose because we've done so much else besides this one little social custom."

Oh dear, he was grinning *that* grin at her. Her knees threatened to buckle. Luckily, the music ended then, or she would surely have made a fool of herself.

"Come, my lady, I shall return you to your escorts. What time shall I call for you tomorrow and, more importantly, *where?*"

Once back at Alex's side, Isabella at first refused any other offers to dance until, finally, Alex flat out ordered her to accept.

"You're making it too bloody obvious, you twit."

Since Whit had agreed with him, she had danced with the next five gentlemen. Now she was hot, and her feet hurt. She decided to slip outside for a breath of air and a chance to sit for a few minutes in peace. She closed the balcony door after her and sighed. Spotting a bench mostly in shadow, she quickly crossed to it and sat upon the cool marble. A thrill shot through her as she realized that Rafe was actually courting her! She could refuse all others now. She really didn't know if he would actually propose to her or not, but at least she had a chance to be with him. It would have to be enough.

"Why hello, my lady."

Oh dear, Lord Cross. He emerged from the shadows to her left, a sly smile on his face.

"My lord, I was just going to go back in. Would you escort me?" Drat, her solitude would have to be intruded upon. Couldn't she have even a moment's peace to savor her small victory?

The young man advanced on her, slowly reached out a hand and stroked her bare shoulder. "What I would *like* to do is something altogether different, my dear."

Isabella brushed his hand away and stood. The look on his usually handsome face frightened her. She gave him her coldest glare.

"I thought I made myself clear, my lord, that I do not wish you to take liberties with me." She was all too aware of the secluded setting. Would anyone hear her if she yelled? For this time, appearances be damned, she would yell her head off.

Cross grabbed her hand and kissed her palm before she could snatch her hand back. She itched to slap him.

"You are too bold, sir." Isabella gasped as he gripped her shoulders and swiftly kissed her neck. With all her strength, she shoved him back. He was forced to release her but laughed at her indignant expression.

"Come, my dear. Don't be coy." He attempted to embrace her again, but she slipped back out of his reach.

"You are a delicious little piece."

"You are being absurd, Lord Cross. I'm leaving." Isabella turned and tried to move to the balcony doors, but he stepped on the hem of her skirt, and she couldn't move lest she rip her gown.

Isabella rolled her eyes before she turned to face him. "If you don't stop this idiocy, I shall be forced to scream for help."

"Don't bother, my dear." Rafe stepped through the door, his timing impeccable. "Lord Cross, you will remove your foot." Rafe's look was menacing, eyes narrowed, his hands fisted.

Isabella had never seen him look angrier or more deliciously dangerous.

The other man hesitated but an instant before wisely stepping back.

"Baroness."

Rafe continued to glare at the lord as he held out his hand to her. Willingly, she went to him.

"This lady is off limits to you, sir. If you go against my wishes in this and assault her again, I shall see you ruined."

"Do not think to threaten *me*, sir," the young man huffed.

Rafe pulled Isabella behind him and snarled, "It is no threat, sir. If you had accost her again, I shall break your goddamn nose." He gave the cad a cold parting glare, then turned and ushered Isabella back into the crowded ballroom.

Once inside with her, Rafe frowned. "Are you all right?"

Isabella smiled up at him. "You've saved me yet again." She cocked her head to one side. "It's becoming quite a habit with you, *Your Grace*."

"There you two are," Alex stomped up to them, oblivious to the stir he was causing all around him.

Whit was fast on his heels. "Damn it, Alex!" he hissed. "Don't hit him! At least not here."

Isabella knew that look on her cousin's face. She held up her hand to stop him. "Alex, just listen to me. He didn't do anything, except come to my rescue."

"Ha! Try pulling the other leg, Bella." He looked her over from head to toe, even going so far as to turn her around, and was puzzled to see nothing mussed, except for a dusty boot print on the hem of her gown. "You fended him off, then?"

"Rafe was not the one who needed fending off." Isabella turned, noticing Lord Cross sneaking back in through a door further down the length of the room. "It is *him* you should worry about."

The men looked to where she was pointing. The fellow in question happened to glance their way and paled noticeably, then darted away into the crowd, probably to make a wise escape.

"His Grace once again protected my honor, you dolt." She was getting tired of Alex's condemnation of her true love. He had to get past it in case Rafe did eventually want to marry her.

She glanced at the duke, wondering just what had brought him out on the terrace. Had he come looking for her? Did she dare to hope so?

Whit chuckled and punched his large friend in the arm. "Bloody funny, isn't it, old man?" He shrugged at the other fellow's frown. "Well, both times she's been attacked, he's the one to have saved her, and it's only him you seem convinced *will*. Oh, come on, Alex, it is ironic."

"I want to dance. Your Grace?"

"Of course, my dear, but just a moment. Alex, I did warn Cross off her, said I'd ruin him if he went near her again. I thought you should know he didn't seem too contrite, however."

Alex nodded.

"All right, then, love. Let us dance to this pretty tune." Rafe gave Isabella a bedazzled smile and led her away.

"You look gorgeous in that color, my dear. Did you know lavender is my favorite?"

"Really? I thought bronze," popped out of her mouth, and she blushed madly.

Rafe threw back his head and laughed. "I shall not embarrass you further by making a remark. No, I shall be a gentleman and change the subject entirely." He grinned down at her. "So, where has your esteemed cousin taken you so far? Have you yet been to Gunther's?"

"No, he offered but I told him that I had already promised my first visit there to my butler." Isabella gave him an impish grin. It felt so good to be teasing with him again after so long. Now, if only he would kiss her. If only he had been the one to come upon her first outside, to caress her shoulder.

"Isabella," he said, his tone stern, "stop that. If you keep looking at me like that, I'll haul you behind a potted fern and kiss you soundly."

"Promise?" She sighed at the delightful thought.

The music ended, and they reluctantly drew apart.

"Let me fetch us some champagne, love."

Isabella allowed him to lead her back to her cousin and accepted the glass he gave her. She sipped the bubbly beverage and stared at Rafe over the rim of her glass.

"Isabella."

Was there any man as handsome as he? Did any man possess such incredibly blue eyes and hair black as sin? Was any other fellow as noble or possessed of such subtle and dry wit? He was fine, indeed.

"Isabella, stop it."

"What? What did you say, Your Grace?"

"He said to stop it, you little ninny," Alex groused at her.

"Ah, dear boy, here you are." The Duchess joined them, smiling warmly at Rafe, then at Isabella. "So, this is the beauty that has all of London atwitter this season? How do you do, my dear?"

Rafe rolled his eyes, but smiled at his mother. "Her Grace, the Dowager Duchess of Devonshire, my dear mother. Mother, may I present Lady Isabella Fitzhugh of charming North Bindlefork."

"Your Grace," Isabella responded, then curtsied smoothly and returned the other woman's smile. She could see where Rafe got his humor as the lady had mischief dancing in her blue eyes. "I thank you for your compliment, but I hardly think much, if any, of London is twittering about such a simple country miss."

"My, a modest woman. I never knew such a thing existed," Anne said. "I had hoped to meet you the other night, but I developed a terrible headache. You have definitely been the subject of many conversations of late, my dear. Why my dear friend Madame Rose was telling me how you have managed to wrap Lord Jeffrey around your little finger." She chuckled. "He was quite overflowing with praise of you. And I hear Lord Northby, Lord Elton, *and* Lord Cross are sniffing after you, as well."

"Mother, that's being a bit crass, don't you think? Lady Isabella is, I'm sure, not used to such directness from a duchess."

"I have been around you three *gentlemen* long enough to be used to such remarks, Your Grace." Isabella wasn't sure exactly what the Duchess had meant, but she thought she understood the gist of it.

"Now, if you will excuse me for a moment, I must freshen up a bit." Anne gave her a pointed look. "Would you care to join me, Lady Isabella?"

"Of course, Your Grace."

After the women had left them, the three men stood together in an uncomfortable silence. Whit finally broke the tension.

"Good God, Alex, he has been behaving himself. Excellent job of stopping that bounder Cross, Rafe." He held up his glass in salute.

"Well, it was a good thing I saw her slip out, is all. When she didn't return, I became a little concerned." Rafe shrugged it off, but he had felt more than just a little concerned, he had been bloody well concerned. Scenes of Dalton mauling her kept flashing through his mind.

"You saw her leave and didn't chase right after her?" Alex sounded surprised. Surely he was thinking it was usually just the opportunity any of them would have taken if in pursuit of a woman.

"Not with you two watching my every move." Rafe snorted. "It would have been just the chance you're waiting for to bruise me up again. I'm not that stupid, thank you very much."

Alex actually chuckled along with Whit. "Yes, we did you up pretty badly, didn't we? I suppose I should say I'm sorry for it, but, truth is, I'm not. It was just the spleen venting I needed, don't you know?"

"Glad to be of service, old man." Rafe rejoined dryly. "Next time, do try to avoid damaging my face quite so much. It truly upset Mother."

"Why should there be a next time?" Alex narrowed his eyes. "You're going to stay away from her, aren't you, since you don't believe in marriage?"

"I never said I didn't believe in marriage, it was 'love' I took exception to."

Whit noticed the past tense phrasing, but said nothing.

"So, you're thinking of marrying her?" Alex growled.

"Good God, man, don't put words in my mouth!"

LADY Anne and Isabella finished their toilette, but before

leaving the room, the older woman placed a hand on her arm.

"My dear, you love him, don't you?"

"Goodness, you certainly don't believe in mincing words, do you, Your Grace?" Isabella had been fairly sure the Duchess wanted to talk with her, but she wasn't expecting her to be quite so direct. Well, she could certainly deal with it. "My father insisted on plain speaking, also. Yes, I do love your son, Your Grace. I hope that he will feel the same for me, someday. But, if not," she smiled sadly, "then I shall take what I can and not cry in my milk and complain it is watery."

"My son is very lusty, *that* is what you will get. It is obvious he wants you quite badly, my dear. He will not hesitate to bed you, if you allow it. And what if there is a child as the result? Will you be so brave then?"

"How could I help but love a child since I love the father so? I am not being brave, Your Grace. I am being as practical as one can be in matters relating to the heart."

"You risk ruining your family's good name, you understand."

Isabella smiled. "I am the last of my mother's line in all of England so there is no fear of retribution on that front. Alex and his family are my only relatives on my father's side. When I return to North Bindlefork, I will quite soon be forgotten, as if the very earth swallowed me up." She shook her head at the Duchess. "My home is quite isolated, Ma'am; there will be only a minor scandal there. None would touch your son."

Anne blinked several times. "You think it is his reputation that concerns me? Goodness, my dear, he is a man, and it certainly does men no harm to have a few bastards scattered about the country. No, it is how *you* will manage, when this affair ends, that worries me."

Isabella was surprised. The Duchess didn't seem to object at all and was even aiding them in their plot to entice Rafe into marriage. This was really quite odd, standing here discussing her possible bastard child with the Dowager Duchess.

"Your Grace, I fear we are putting the cart before the horse. Your son may be attracted to me, but that does not mean he will risk destroying his friendship with my cousin over a dalliance. He has been extremely proper tonight. Why, he even asked me to accompany him riding tomorrow."

"Ah," Anne grinned wickedly. "So, he begins courting you, now that you're so very popular. It does make one wonder what he will do next. You shall manage him quite nicely, I think, my dear. Yes, I do believe my son has finely met his match."

"I just hope *he* will eventually think so, and soon."

"Is there some rush? Goodness, you're not yet even twenty, I believe."

"Yes, that's right." Isabella liked this woman immensely. She had humor and intelligence and was perfectly comfortable expressing her opinion. Bella's father would have respected her. "I know it sounds silly, but I set myself a time limit. I gave myself exactly one month to discover the truth about your son and what feelings, if any, he may have for me."

"Goodness, you are a practical young thing." Anne only stared at her.

Isabella blushed, perceiving the remark was a compliment. "It is just that, given the obstacles I thought I was facing then, I didn't want to loose sight of the facts. I couldn't afford to spend too much time away from home, and I thought I was in love with a bastard." She shrugged. "My father taught me to put things in perspective, Your Grace. Perhaps he went a bit too far in some things, but I really didn't have the choice not to face up to reality."

"Whatever do you mean, you didn't have the choice? And of what reality do you speak?"

"Oh, I was extremely plain. It was very clear I could not expect to make a match from some young man fancying my physical appearance. My father didn't want my hopes being dashed someday by pretending I was comely, so he made sure I understood how ordinary I was."

The Duchess looked at her as if she'd just proclaimed she was a pixy and could fly. "The devil, you say!"

Isabella laughed. "I cannot get used to everyone's surprise. I swear I look exactly the same as I always have."

Anne looked the young lady over from head to toe. "Good God, Isabella, you have a figure most women have to create with assistance, and your hair is lovely. Even without quite so beautiful a face, you would *never* be considered 'plain'!"

"LADY Isabella is certainly a stunning young woman. Why, she could have her pick of any young man there tonight. I shouldn't be surprised, at all, if Lord Bickers and Lord Smythe should decide to press their suits." She sighed softly while the carriage rolled toward home. "Yes, Lord Bickers was obviously quite taken with her."

"Really, Mother, he's old enough to be her father. I'm sure the lady has better taste than that." He snorted. Bella would never be interested in a man like Bickers. He was an utter bore. How could that old relic make her chuckle in that way that made Rafe want to rip her gown off and take her then and there? It was nonsense. The thought of those wrinkled hands on Bella's soft white skin made him shudder.

"Oh, she did tell me in confidence that she is rather fond of Jeffrey. They would suit well together, I suppose. Although, she would have to accept short children who would probably be cursed with their father's red hair and not her lovely auburn shade." Anne laughed at the glare he sent her way. "Son, your humor has fled! Why so annoyed with me? You usually laugh at my observations after a party."

"Because the subject matter is absurd and fanciful. Bella and Jeffrey? Too ridiculous to consider, Mother. And Bickers, that old sod, with *her*? Bah!" Rafe slouched down further on the carriage seat, his fingers laced behind his dark head. He suddenly grinned at Anne. "Besides, it is *I* who am riding with her tomorrow."

"You, son? Whyever are you courting her?"

"Who said I was courting her?" The frown was back in place. "It's only a ride through the park." Surely asking her for a simple outing was not so drastic a step as to be considered courtship?

"He can't be thinking of *marrying* her, so why bother to court her?" Mother looked with puzzlement out the window, appearing to be talking to herself.

Rafe sat up. "I am not courting her, blast it!"

"Hmm, it is odd." Anne glanced at him. "You did seem rather taken with her, so I suppose I must consider it. You did dance twice with her." She shook her head. "No, it is too silly. Of course, you're not courting her." She leaned across and patted his knee. "Do forgive me, dearest. My, what flights of imagination I sometimes have!"

Rafe grunted in response. Really, the very idea that he

would be courting anyone! Why, he was only just over thirty! He figured he had at least seven or eight years of sampling women before he must settle down and produce an heir.

Isabella and Jeffrey? Utter nonsense.

IN Isabella's carriage, things were quite a bit louder. She had just told Alex that she was to ride with Rafe tomorrow, so couldn't join her cousin.

"The bloody hell you are!"

"Really, Isabella, do you think it wise?"

"Whit, you too? Alex, stop your roaring. It is much too close in here and my ears will soon be ringing." She sat back, frowning at them both, her arms crossed stubbornly. "I accepted, and so I shall go. You two can shout at me all you want. As I only have just over a week left, I intend on doing what I want now. Your plan was to get him jealous and have him pay me court. And so he is!"

Alex leaned forward. "Damnation, he can't be trusted alone with you! He'll haul you off behind a shrub and have his way with you. *You* certainly won't stop him!" He was shouting again and shaking his finger at her. "I saw the way you melted in his arms dancing! He'll take you in a trice, mark my words!"

Isabella rolled her eyes.

Whit tried a more tactful approach. "Bella, dear, things are going along fine, truly. He is jealous beyond belief. But if you succumb to him now, then all will be lost. Don't you see?"

"What I see is that you want him to be so desperate for me, he will marry me just to have me." She felt herself blush madly. "Well, I'll not have it that way. He will only resent me after. He must truly feel something for me and acknowledge it. That is the only way I will marry him. And if he doesn't propose, and I loose my fool head and allow him to seduce me completely, then I shall just return home with my shame for company."

"Bella, don't be such a bloody twit! Why, if he does take your innocence, I'll see that he—"

"No!" Isabella had never all-out shouted before in her life. She sat bolt upright, her hands fisted with anger. "You will not interfere, cousin! This is *my* *life* to decide. I am of age, the mistress of my own estate, and I can make any stupid decision I want! Now, *leave it be!*"

She sat back, her head throbbing. Goodness, outbursts certainly took their toll on a person. She only hoped she had made herself clear and wouldn't have to do it again.

"Bloody hell," Alex grumbled. "You've become a damned shrew, cousin."

Isabella snorted. She was done with allowing them to orchestrate her life. She would handle Rafe from now on, in her own way. She had to work fast, as time was running out.

Chapter 18

Isabella was ready the next day when Rafe arrived. Her brawny butler bowed him in, then stepped aside, allowing Rafe to see her standing at the base of the stairs, a vision in a soft lavender riding habit with tiny pearl buttons marching up the front. A small white hat with a curved lavender feather was perched charmingly on her head.

"You look scrumptious, my dear lady." He crossed the floor to her and took her small hand in his, turning it to kiss her palm. He felt her shiver at his touch.

"You look scrumptious, too, Your Grace."

Rafe felt his blood stir as she looked him over with hunger in her emerald eyes. He cleared his throat. "Men are not scrumptious, my dear. They are handsome and virile." He led her out the door and down the front steps to where their horses stood ready. "Ah, and there is Dilly. I'm glad you brought her with you. She is an excellent mount for you."

"I couldn't bear to leave her behind. Why, she would

have been fed apples all day and become lazy and fat as a stoat."

Rafe chuckled and helped her mount. "Are you a bit homesick, my lady?"

"Oh, no. After all, I will be heading back in a little over a week."

"What's this? How long *have* you been here, then?"

"Let's see. It's been almost three weeks since I arrived. I have become quite fond of my little house. Do you like it?"

They urged their horses forward, side by side.

Rafe thought she sounded awfully flippant. "The house is fine." She had been in London nearly three weeks and hadn't even sent him a note? Damn Alex for keeping them apart for so long! And now he had only, what, eight or nine days with her?

"When, exactly, are you leaving?" It was madness to torture himself this way, to seek out her delightful company when he knew naught could come from it. So just why was he doing it?

"I have planned to leave on Wednesday next. I have had to hire two wagons to haul all my purchases! Goodness, Mrs. Combs will be pleased with all of the things I am bringing home."

"Well, then, I shall have to be sure to take you to Gunther's quite soon, won't I?" So, he would have nine days to be with her. Scarcely any time at all, really.

"Oh, yes! I have been thinking about going there with you. I cannot decide what flavor to have, though. I have asked most everyone I have met what their favorite is, and all seem to be different."

His companion chuckled, Rafe squirmed in his saddle

and as a bolt of lust shot through him. "You shall have to do a sampling to see which you prefer." Even simple thoughts of shaved ice weren't doing much to dampen his passion. He concentrated on pointing out various spots as they turned onto the avenue.

They both turned to look back at hearing her name called. Fast on their heels were Alex and Whit.

"Damnation!"

"Shall we make a run for it?" Isabella frowned at the approaching men.

Rafe sighed, having considered the idea himself for a few seconds. "No, we would only have them chasing us down. I should have known better." He looked into her eyes. "Bella, before those two clods descend upon us, promise me you'll dine with me this evening, *alone*." He prayed she didn't have another engagement. He needed to be with her.

"All right," she said breathlessly. "And just who invited you two along? I believe my day has quite been ruined. Perhaps I shall ride home." She turned her horse and trotted off, as if knowing the gentlemen would follow.

"She's getting bloody lippy." Alex raised one dark brow at Rafe. "I do believe it's your bad influence."

"Nonsense, you old stuffed shirt. I behave excellently in her company."

"Well, I'm going after her. I bet I can have her laughing in a trice. Just see if I don't." Whit grinned at them, then urged his horse forward after Isabella.

The other two, not wanting to be outdone, followed and soon all three had Isabella laughing near to tears.

Isabella was once again ready when Rafe arrived that evening to take her to dinner. Upon seeing her, however, he wanted nothing more than to suggest they dine in. He didn't want to have to share her looking so incredibly beautiful. She was wearing a low-cut gown of deep, shimmering purple. Her glorious hair pulled up only on one side, the other curling against her cheek and neck, then falling over her full breasts. She quite took his breath away.

He took her to an exclusive French restaurant and led her into a private dining room. He had even arranged for a violinist to play discreetly outside for them. As he seated her and then poured them each a glass of champagne, he told her he had already ordered for them.

"I have discovered I truly love champagne," she said, sipping the bubbly drink. "I have to order some to be sent home with me."

"Do allow me. I know of some excellent vineyards."

"Goodness, I haven't had much truly French cuisine. Lisbeth said the French actually eat frog's legs! You didn't order any of those, did you?"

Rafe couldn't help but laugh at her comical look of horror. "I promise you it's only a simple lobster. There should be no amphibian parts anywhere near."

"Lobster! I've never had it. How wonderful. That is the only problem with North Bindlefork — it lacks an ocean."

"That, I cannot order for you."

They were served a creamy soup, rich with shrimp and mussels. Rafe chuckled while Isabella rolled her eyes and smacked her lips.

"Superb," she proclaimed, beaming at the waiter, who instantly fell under her spell with a pining sigh.

Rafe took great pleasure in each of Isabella's reactions as course after course arrived; from rich, plump smoked oysters to delicately sautéed scallops with mushrooms over wild rice. He had remembered Mrs. Combs' remark about how her lady had delighted in having the rare treat of shellfish, so had sent a note to the chef requesting an assortment be prepared for them. Watching her enjoyment, he was exorbitantly pleased with himself.

"Goodness, Your Grace, I fear I shall have no room for the lobster, at this rate." Isabella lamented, looking for a moment as if she were tempted to lick her fingers clean of the succulent food. Instead, she daintily used her napkin.

"Perhaps a respite is called for." Rafe nodded to the smitten waiter, who then reluctantly withdrew. "Would you like to dance or sit feeling contentedly full?" he asked, amused. It would be heaven to hold her in his arms, but he would be satisfied enough to simply sit and stare at her.

"Let us dance," Isabella said, then finished her wine before standing. "I should very much like to feel your arms around me."

Rafe happily obliged, holding her close and gently swaying with her to the music of the lone violinist. Her lush body fit to his and he breathed in her perfume as his hand caressed her back.

Isabella laid her head upon his shoulder. He allowed his lips to brush against her temple, so very lightly, as his fingers stroked up and down her spine.

"Are you falling asleep, my dear?"

Isabella lifted her head, smiling into his face. "No, I was just thinking that I would like to kiss you." She lifted her hand and traced his mouth with her fingers.

Rafe's body, already aroused by the feel of her pressed against him, reacted even more. He watched her mouth part and the tip of her pink tongue dart out to moisten her lips. He knew he was lost, so didn't even attempt to dissuade himself. He lowered his head and kissed her hungrily. Her response matched his own urgency and soon they were breathing heavily, arms wrapped around each other. Her lips parted and their tongues entwined. Rafe moaned at the intense desire raging through him. Her hands slipped beneath his jacket to stroke his sides, his back, trying to press him closer. He kissed her harder still and squeezed her delightful little bottom. She moaned into his mouth and wriggled against him. He knew he had to stop this now or very soon he would have her sprawled out on the fine carpet, her lovely purple gown bunched about her waist. God, even the thought of it made him tremble. Rafe broke their contact so swiftly Isabella nearly fell.

"Sorry, my love." He reached out and gripped her elbows to steady her. "As usual, I loose control with you." He gave her nose a kiss, then seated her at the table. "More champagne?" The lovely girl, still in a lust-induced daze, could only nod at him. "Ah, and here are our lobsters." He gave the blushing waiter a wry smile. "Such excellent timing."

The waiter placed a lobster before each of them, replaced their empty champagne bottle with a fresh one, and then quickly withdrew.

"Goodness," Isabella looked from the large red crustacean to Rafe. "What do I do with it now?" She tapped the hard shell with her fork, eyeing it suspiciously.

He laughed at her puzzlement. "Here, allow me." He took her plate and expertly revealed the succulent meat within, then returned it to her. "Try it with the lemon butter in that warmer. That's it, just dip it in."

Isabella cut off a small piece, did as he suggested, and

gingerly placed it on her tongue.

At the surprised look on her face, he chuckled. "I knew you'd like it. Shall I have some ordered for you to take home?" he teased.

"I wish that you could!" She closed her eyes after popping another bite into her mouth. She sighed, saying, "I shall now have to come visit London often, if only to gorge myself on seafood."

Rafe made short work of his own lobster, then sat back to watch her as she savored each taste. God, she even ate sensuously, slowly licking her lips after each mouthful and making purring noises of pleasure deep in her throat.

Moments after she had finished, their waiter was back to remove the plates and wheel in a small dessert cart, then once again discreetly removed himself.

Isabella accepted a refill of her glass. "If you think I could eat another thing, you're quite mad."

Rafe smiled at her wickedly and reached out, scooping up a finger full of chocolate frosting. "Perhaps I can tempt you." He held out his hand to her.

Isabella quickly dipped her own digit into a dish of raspberry sauce meant to coat one of the delicate pastries artfully displayed on the cart.

Rafe flashed her a heated, sensuous smile before taking her wrist in his hand and guiding her finger into his own mouth. Once again, their eyes locked, and she gasped as Rafe used his tongue to stroke away the sauce while gradually increasing the suction of his mouth. Isabella squirmed in her seat. Rafe watched her as he moved on to finger after finger. Finally, she tried to snatch her hand away.

"It is too much," she groaned, shaking her head but

unable to look away from him. He licked her palm, once, and then released her.

Rafe was aroused, but still in control — just barely. Isabella's lovely face was flushed, and her tempting breasts were heaving, the nipples hard little pebbles straining against the fabric of her gown. He was sorely tempted to pull her dress down and suckle those magnificent breasts.

"Goodness."

"Is that all you have to say?"

"Apparently." She drained another glass of champagne. "I think we should leave, Your Grace."

Rafe chuckled, thinking he had perhaps overwhelmed her a bit. "Yes, it is probably best."

He escorted her out of the restaurant and helped her into the gleaming black carriage embossed with his coat of arms. He took the seat across from her and thumped his fist against the roof to let the driver know to be off.

"Rafe?"

"Hmm, my love?"

"Why are you sitting over there? Don't you want to sit by me, so that I can kiss you again?"

Rafe was speechless for a moment. Why, the little temptress! "Isabella, I cannot make love to you in a coach. Well, I could, but it just isn't seemly."

"Oh."

He smiled at her obvious disappointment.

"It is early, yet. Perhaps you could come into the parlor when we get home? Just for a brandy?" Her head was cocked to one side endearingly, a hopeful smile playing about her lush mouth. She was adorable.

"Just for a brandy?"

"Of course, Your Grace," she said sweetly.

"Isabella, I told you once you were playing with fire," he warned her.

"And," she retorted, leaning slightly forward, undoubtedly to allow him a better view of her breasts, "I believe I told you I wanted to be scorched."

He shook his head at her. "Alex would kill me. I think we have tempted fate enough for one night. Join me tomorrow and we shall see what happens." She would be the death of him. He wasn't sure he had enough willpower to refrain from accepting what she kept offering.

She sighed. "All right, join you where tomorrow?"

The next day, Rafe took her to the cat races where he only kissed her twice and nibbled on her ear. That evening they went to see a very funny play at Drury Lane, then to dinner at the White Swan Inn. They were approached throughout the meal by scores of people who knew Rafe and wanted an introduction to his companion. Finally, after wisely declining dessert, they escaped the unwanted attention.

"My, are you always bothered so?" Isabella asked, innocently, after they were in the coach and headed to her home.

"Only when I'm with such an exquisite beauty, my dear."

"Will you come in for a brandy, Your Grace?" She gave his flattery no heed. "You have not kissed me in a very long time."

He snorted. "I was kissing you only this afternoon, my lady."

"Yes, but only twice." She gave him a determined look. "You have not yet seen my very nice parlor. I am feeling quite neglected."

Rafe laughed. "Very well, my lady, *one* brandy, and then I shall be on my way."

She smiled at him impishly. "Just one. And, perhaps, just one small kiss?"

Isabella led him into the parlor upon arriving at her rented house. After giving Edwards their wraps, she shooed the butler off and poured Rafe his promised drink.

"Now, come and sit beside me." She arranged herself on the settee and smoothed out her deep green skirt. It was another new gown, the neckline as daringly low as the others he had seen her wear. She had said her seamstress had insisted she properly display her 'charming attributes.' He quite agreed.

Rafe watched her with amusement. She was such a delight. It had been interesting watching her handle his various acquaintances, who had all practically dropped to their knees to worship her. She had been gracious, but slightly reserved; as if implying they needed to prove themselves worthy before she would deign to toss them one of her dazzling smiles. As he was the recipient of countless smiles and laughs, he received numerous looks of envy.

Even women seemed drawn to her, even though some showed the usual visual signs of spitefulness. It was if she had been holding bloody court.

"Rafe, stop looking at me with that silly expression and come sit beside me." Isabella gave him a small frown.

"As you wish, my lady." He moved across the room to her and sat down on the small sofa. They were cozy indeed, her knees brushing his. "Isabella, do behave, you aren't leaving for a week yet."

"But that's only seven days, no, six now." She watched him take a drink, her eyes drawn to his mouth. "Won't you give me lots of memories to hold close in the coming winter months?"

"You make it sound as if you're going into seclusion!"

"I might as well be."

"Bella, you will be hounded down by at least half of the young swains you have enchanted while here."

She snorted at him in disbelief.

"Truly. You watch and see how many of your neighbors receive winter guests this year. And how many of said hosts will be talked into giving parties, just in the hopes that you will attend, and they will be able to gaze on your glorious self once more."

She laughed. "Really! How you do go on. You sound just like Alex. Why, he was lecturing me just the other day about the very same thing. It's all stuff and nonsense. When I leave, there will be some other young girl everyone will rave over, simply because she has a new face and an unknown reputation, and I will be quite forgotten, tucked away in North Bindlefork." She chuckled. "Don't you gentlemen think I know how it works?"

"You really haven't a clue to the effect you have on men, darling. God, you quite do us in."

"Rafe," she placed a hand on his leg and pressed her breast against his arm. "Won't you give me one little kiss?"

"One little kiss with you is *never* just one little kiss, love." He set his glass on the low table in front of them, then turned to her. "You're not going to behave, are you?"

"No," she breathed as she parted her luscious lips.

Rafe lost the battle with himself with a groan and crushed her to him, ravishing her lovely mouth. She tasted incredibly sweet as their tongues battled. He nibbled her full lower lip with his teeth, while he eased her down across his lap, one arm supporting her. He kissed her again and again, his free hand caressing her throat, his fingertips brushing the tops of her breasts. She arched against his hand, and he could stand it no longer. He trailed kisses along the column of her throat, down to where her pulse beat madly. His hand cupped her full breast, his thumb brushing across one hardened nipple. She gasped and bucked against him. Rafe shuddered and began nibbling her earlobe, his hand now on the other breast.

"Bella, dear God, you drive me mad. I want you so much I could explode right now." He reclaimed her mouth in a scorching kiss that left them both only wanting more and trembling with need.

"Rafe, please," she begged against his mouth. "I don't know exactly what it is I want, I just know I want more of you." She rubbed her bottom against his rigid member and ran her hands up his chest.

"Sweet mercy," Rafe moaned and then pulled her upright, holding her tight against him and pressing her head onto his shoulder. "Mercy," he said again. His breathing was ragged, and his heart was pounding. "We can't do this, my love." He kissed the top of her head, then laid his cheek upon it. "Listen to me, dearest little one. One of us has to be sane here."

"Does it have to be *now?*" she mumbled against his coat.

Rafe laughed. "Bella, in another moment I would have taken you, I'm quite sure. You simply ignite when I touch you. God, you're so bloody responsive it makes me lose my grip." He let her pull back so that he could look at her face. He was relieved to see she wasn't furious again.

"Rafe, I wish you *would* lose your grip. This is too frustrating!"

He chuckled. "You only know the half of it, my dear."

"Then show me the other half. I want you, if only for a few nights. Is that so wrong?"

"Lord, Bella, don't." He placed his fingers over her swollen lips. "It would be your ruin."

"What do I care what these people think? *They* don't touch my life. Besides, how would they ever know?"

For once he didn't feel so sure of himself, so utterly confident that his view was the right one.

"They are unimportant, Rafe. All that matters is what is between us."

"These people be damned, your future *husband* would know." The word tasted like ashes on his tongue. He couldn't bear the thought of another man touching her, making her moan with passion, having the *right* to do so. It was like a knife in his gut.

"That shan't be a problem."

"Of course it will be! He will know you're not a virgin, damn it."

"No, no, it doesn't matter. What man would call it off, simply because of that, when I have so much money? He would be a fool. Besides, he wouldn't want it known that there had been another, would he?"

Rafe ran his fingers through his hair, incredulous that they were actually having this conversation. He wanted her more than he'd ever wanted a woman in his bloody life. How ironic that she was offering herself to him and for the sake of her honor, he was trying to convince her *not* to.

"No, Bella, I'll not do that to some poor clod. You are beautiful and passionate, and I'll be damned if I'll steal that precious moment from you. The first time you make love should be with your husband and no other. I have already gone well beyond what I should have."

"All right then, I shall accept the first proposal I am offered, have a quick wedding and come to you the night after! Will that satisfy your stupid honor?" She jumped up, obviously finally angry. "You men are absurd creatures! Goodness, you want nothing more than to seduce me and when I say that it's perfectly acceptable to me, please do, you throw up your hands and say you couldn't possibly! You are nothing but a hypocrite, my lord. This is becoming more than I can bear."

"Isabella, you're already compromised just by my being here alone with you. And don't say such ridiculous things about marrying just any man to have it over with. Besides, you should have a care for your husband, and not just a case of lustful infatuation. Thank goodness you're much too sensible to fall for that claptrap talk of 'love.' What an utterly absurd notion! Stuff of fairy tales. Still, you should feel more for your future mate than mindless desire."

"Is that what you feel for me? 'Mindless desire,' Your Grace?"

"Well, it is rather *intense* desire, my dear, but yes, it is mindless as it consumes me. I am rather surprised at how well I lose my finesse around you."

She stood still and looked at him. She took a slow, deep breath, and he saw her pulling her general's mantle around herself.

"Bella—"

"No," she held up her hand and shook her head at him, "I can't keep doing this to us, can I? You're right." She hugged herself, as if suddenly very cold. "We're just playing a dangerous game. And now it's time to call it to an end." She nodded as if he had agreed with her.

"I must thank you, Your Grace, for all of the wonderful things you have shown me and the attention you have paid me. But now I think it best I return to where I belong."

Rafe stared at her a moment, a feeling of dread coming over him. "Isabella, forgive me. I never meant to cause you any harm."

"Well, these things happen, don't they?" He thought he heard her voice crack, just a bit. "I am just sorry things couldn't have turned out differently. I shall have to make do with the memories you've given me thus far, is all." She attempted a smile, but it was a weak replica, without her usual verve. "Please go now, Rafe. There's nothing more for us to say, except goodbye." She averted her eyes from his.

He stood and stared at her a moment longer before wordlessly turning and leaving her standing in her charming little parlor.

Chapter 19

After Rafe left, Isabella retreated to her room and cried, really cried, for the first time since she was twelve and had been told her mother was dead. By morning's first light, she was cried out and exhausted. She drank only tea for breakfast (a woman's drink, a *woman's pleasure*), earning a frown and tongue clickings from Rolands. Alice had already scolded her for her moroseness while helping her to dress. Even Edwards looked down in the mouth. Apparently, they knew that the duke had left on rather final terms.

"Edwards," she asked the butler, who was standing ready to serve her, in case she changed her mind about breaking her fast, "would you care to come to Kirkwood Manor and work for me there? I have no butler, you see." She succeeded in fighting back the tears. She wanted only one butler; she wanted her Easton back.

"I should be honored, my lady. Lord Stapleton said as much when he asked me to serve you here, so long as I pleased you, my lady."

"Fine, then prepare us to leave as soon as you can. The supplies I've ordered should be ready within a few days. Can you manage to pack us up by then?" She wanted to be far away from London. She needed to be home, where surely everything would return to normal. This deep wrenching pain would eventually lessen — it had to.

"You have an engagement this evening, my lady, to attend a soiree with Lord Smythe," Edwards reminded his mistress mournfully.

"Blast!" Isabella scowled at the plate of cold toast on the table. That was the last thing she wanted to do. It was too late to beg off, unfortunately. She would have to attend and hope that she didn't see Rafe. One look at him, and she just knew she would fall apart.

Later, she sent Alex and Whit notes, requesting they join her for dinner the next evening, as a farewell party. She told Rolands to prepare something special, so long as it wasn't seafood or had anything to do with raspberry sauce.

"YOU look divine, Lady Isabella." Lord Reginald Smythe bowed over her hand, folded back the hem of her turquoise sleeve, and pressed her wrist to his mouth.

"You are too kind, my lord." Isabella tried to muster up a smile for the handsome young man with blonde hair and admiring brown eyes, but couldn't even manage a little one. She wanted only to stay home and hug her pain to her breast. She didn't know if she could hold up under the sorrow threatening to bow her spirit.

Reggie, as Lord Smythe said he was called, continued to flatter her all during the ride to the small party. By the time they alighted from his carriage, she had a headache from trying to keep her attention on him. She felt a touch of pity for the man who was being quite charming in his attempts to woo her. She allowed him to take her arm as they walked up the steps and were ushered inside their hostess' house, one Lady Joanna Clark.

"Lady Joanna, allow me to introduce Lady Isabella Fitzhugh." Reggie smiled and bowed to the willowy blonde dressed in a daringly low-cut gown of pink tulle over white silk.

"Welcome, Lady Isabella. I am pleased to finally make your acquaintance."

"Thank you for your hospitality, my lady." Isabella wondered briefly at the look that the other woman was giving her. Was she jealous she was with Lord Smythe? "Your home is lovely." She looked about the tasteful entry and then around the equally elegant drawing room they followed their hostess into. The house was decorated in shades of royal blue and ecru, with elaborately carved burled walnut wainscoting and furnishings.

"Thank you, Lady Isabella."

Isabella quickly scanned the other attendees, sighing with relief upon not seeing Rafe. Reggie, as he insisted she call him, introduced her around, then all found seats as an Italian soprano, tall and thin with a long nose and a sour expression, took her place beside the polished harpsichord to perform for them.

Soon, Isabella was engrossed in the music, oblivious to any around her. She didn't notice a late arrival slip into the room to stand near the back. She didn't realize how many sidelong glances she was receiving from the other guests as they looked from her to the dark lord skulking in the rear of the room. She certainly didn't see how he frowned when Reggie leaned close to her ear to whisper how excellent the singer was, nor how his hands fisted when her escort kissed her hand after she had given him a genuine smile because of her delight with the music. Of course, every other person in attendance noted it with varying degrees of interest.

Isabella sighed when the performance came to a close and applauded heartily. The woman's voice was absolute perfection, truly.

"You enjoyed yourself, my lady?"

Isabella nodded absently when Reggie offered to fetch her a cup of punch when they stood after the completion of the musical performance. She managed a real smile when he kissed her knuckles before moving to the refreshment table. She may not had have much musical talent, but she certainly admired those who did. Lisbeth would be gnashing her teeth in envy when she heard that Isabella had actually been to an intimate performance by so celebrated a singer.

"I see you have made yet another conquest, my lady. It certainly didn't take you very long."

Isabella stiffened, hearing the voice she both loved and hated at the moment. Goodness, the fates were cruel to have them cross paths so soon. Her heart, which she had thought was dead until now, began to thump painfully in her chest, and her throat felt tight. She stared straight ahead, refusing to turn and look at Rafe as she was afraid what she might do at the sight of his handsome face. Surely she would cause a scene as she would either cosh him one or kiss him.

She had finally managed to push his rejection from her mind for so short a while, brief moments really, and now it was all crashing back down on her. His voice was contemptuous and cold, and she wanted to slap him. After all, *he* had rebuffed her. What gave him the right to sound so awfully wounded?

"Is he more willing to oblige you, my lady? Do you think he will suspend his honor when you so prettily beg him to take you?"

Isabella sucked in her breath, hardly able to believe the harshness of his words. How dare he question her in such a crude fashion! Did he honestly think Reggie could have the same effect on her that he did? Did he really think her so wanton that she was only after the experience and didn't care with whom it was? The bastard!

"You say nothing, my lady. Am I to assume my words have hit their mark? Did I make you so hot for it, you will now share your charms with any who asks?"

"Of course you are right, Your Grace." She was amazed how cool and detached her voice sounded to her own ears as cold fury washed over her. If he wanted to be so cruel, then she would happily play his game. She only hoped she could inflict on him the same gripping anguish he was causing her.

"Your efforts indeed left me wanting. He is quite attentive thus far, quite congenial. I'm sure he will not pretend such noble ideals only to make himself feel so much more superior. No, Reggie is at least more honest than that." She paused, wondering why she was doing this, why she was even bothering to verbally spar with him, but unable to stop. "Yes, until this moment, it has been a very pleasant evening, and I have quite regained my perspective, thank you for inquiring, your most benevolent grace."

Just then, Reggie approached them, a puzzled smile on his face. "Devonshire, how good to see you. You know the

Baroness, of course."

"Oh, indeed, I know Lady Bella quite well, actually."

Isabella clenched her teeth and narrowed her eyes as she whirled around to face him. He had incredible gall! He had repeatedly refused her and yet now inferred, in front of Lord Smythe, that he had taken her up on her offers!

"Yes, you think you know me quite well, don't you, Your Grace? After all, you hid at my estate for weeks!"

Rafe scowled at her. "That is not something I will allow you to bandy about, madam. By mentioning it you show your crass country upbringing."

"Now look here, Your Grace!" Reggie looked from Lady Isabella to the duke. "I think you owe Lady Isabella an apology."

Rafe snorted and turned his blazing eyes on Reggie. "Be warned, Smythe, this is none of your concern. What is between the lady and me is quite private."

"Then why are you discussing it so publicly?"

"It is because he lacks the propriety you obviously have, Reggie. He is crude, and I am finished with this conversation. Would you take me for a stroll in the garden, my lord?" Isabella managed to give her escort a tight smile, doing her best to ignore Rafe and his glowering presence. She needed to remove herself lest she begin screeching at the man!

Reggie looked from her to the duke, then down at the cup of punch in his hand. He smiled victoriously as he handed the drink to Rafe, took the lady's hand and walked her to the back of the room and out the doors to the veranda.

"It is a lovely evening, don't you think?"

Isabella wished she were alone. "Yes." Heavens, how could he have been so cruel to her? What had she done to deserve such contempt? Was it only because she was with Lord Smythe?

"Come, Lady Isabella, let me show you the roses yonder. They are especially fragrant, and it will soothe your senses."

"Hmm? Yes, I do like roses." Isabella allowed Reggie to take her arm and walked with him over to an area marked with an arbor. Beyond were a dozen or so rose bushes, their red blossoms appearing black in the night, and she could smell the heady aroma. They walked through the archway.

"So very lovely." She fingered one silky petal. Did Rafe really believe those things he had said? If so, then it was true — he didn't care for her.

Suddenly, Reggie leaned down and kissed her bare shoulder.

Isabella jumped back, startled at the caress. "My lord—" She caught movement from behind Lord Smythe and her eyes grew wide with alarm. Oh, dear! Rafe was striding toward them, his long legs eating up the distance, a thunderous expression on his face.

"I am sorry if I was too forward, Lady Isabella." Reggie mistook the frightened look on her face. "I meant no disrespect." He frowned, seeing her looking over his shoulder. He turned.

Rafe's fist connected directly with Smythe's chin and he smiled with satisfaction as the other man crumpled to the ground. He tossed Isabella an arrogant look, then turned and walked just as purposefully back to the party, leaving her there, staring after him incredulously.

HER two gentlemen co-conspirators arrived early for the farewell dinner, both obviously curious as to why Isabella was leaving ahead of schedule. She told Alex and Whit only that it was clear their plan hadn't worked and she had best just go home. They gave each other knowing looks but were tactful and asked no more questions of her. Whit, being his utmost charming self, even managed to elicit a few weak smiles from her throughout the evening.

Isabella was exhausted, not having slept much the night before. She had kept replaying the scenes with Rafe over and over in her mind, unable to fathom his thinking. He had been angry and hurtful, and she just didn't understand it. It was painfully clear he now held her in contempt.

Her guests did not linger long, seeing her practically falling asleep during dessert. They promised to come and visit her before Christmas, which at least gave her something to look forward to. But, still, that was months away. She would miss them, her very sweet gentlemen who had tried to help her so much.

Isabella slept that night, but only restlessly. She was up early the next morning, anxious to conclude the last of her errands and shopping before lunch. Pleased to have succeeded, she returned home only to find three boxes had been delivered while she'd been out. Just as she thought, one was from each of her gentlemen. From Alex, she received the topaz jewelry. From Whit, there was a lovely double strand of pearls. The third box, which was larger than the other two and was from Rafe, contained a melting lemon ice. She cried again, standing in the entry, Edwards nervously looking on.

"WE could kill him and she'd never know."

"Bloody stupid young sod, of course she'd know. That damned, charming little Lisbeth you like so well would tell her.

She reads the gossips."

"We could beat him again, this time into a truly bloody pulp."

"Damn me, puppy, you seem a bit more upset than meself." Alex eyed his friend suspiciously. "Are you sure you didn't fall for her, too?"

"Damn his black hide!" Whit slammed his fist on the table at White's, causing some of the contents of their glasses to slosh over. A waiter was instantly on hand to mop it up, then stepped back into the shadows, completely unnoticed by the men. "He's broken her tender little heart! And," Whit shook his finger in Alex's face for emphasis, "you can be bloody sure his is breaking as well."

"I just want to break his goddamn nose."

Whit laughed.

Alex scowled in return. "Shut your mouth or I'll break yours, you drunkard."

"I'm not drunk, yet. It's a prediction I made when I first figured out that the two were enthralled with each other. She'd have a broken heart and Rafe a broken nose." Whit stopped laughing as suddenly as he had started. "Damn, it's not so funny now."

Isabella was due to leave in the morning and both men were desperate to contrive of some way to make themselves feel less guilty over the way things had turned out. They'd meddled and helped to bring about this calamity. They'd encouraged and assisted the girl in her pursuit of Rafe. They couldn't stand the thought of their Isabella now so unhappy, but they couldn't seem to find anything to do about it.

"It's us that deserves a beating. We never should have encouraged her."

"That's what *I* said in the beginning, boy-o! But would either of you listen to me?"

Whit glared at his large friend. "So you were right, so what? How exactly does that help us now?"

"Damned if I know," Alex grumbled and tossed back half of his whiskey.

RAFE was drunk, again. He was quite sure it had been four days since he'd refused her and she had again turned him away, and three since he clipped poor Smythe. He, of course couldn't be entirely sure, but was fairly certain.

The pain was worse this time, what with knowing she was still so close by. At least, he tried to convince himself that was why he could find no respite. He sat in his study, almost done with another bottle of brandy. The whiskey had run out at teatime, blast it.

The door opened and in strode his mother.

"Hello, Mother. Do you know what day it is, by any chance?" He was surprised that his words didn't slur. Apparently, he wasn't as drunk as he'd thought, damn it to hell.

"You're a bloody sad thing, my only son." Her voice was as cold as day-old ashes on the grate. "Here you have managed to ruin your life and hers, and you sit a pathetic mess, unshaven, drunk, and self-pitying." She placed her hands on her hips and looked at him with enough disgust that he winced. "I wash my hands of you if you are so stupid as to not realize that you are in love with the girl."

Rafe slammed his hands down on the desktop and stood slowly. "There is no such thing as love," he shouted at Anne. "If there was, then Father would have said he loved you!"

"He did, you dolt! He just never said it in front of you."

"Of course he would say it to you, but it didn't *mean* anything. It was only to please you. They are empty words."

Mother snorted. "If they were empty words, if there is no such thing as love, then why did he give up his mistresses when I asked? Why did he never take another?"

"What?" Rafe sat down heavily and set down his cup. "You knew about his mistresses?"

"Of course I knew, you stupid boy. A woman isn't married to a man for several decades without knowing what is in his heart. I could tell the very day he took the first one." She stepped forward and turned up the lamp on the desk. "I allowed it for a short time. I knew it was only a physical yearning, that she had only caught his fancy. Finally, after a few others, I told him to set them aside." She shrugged at Rafe's astonished expression. "He did and never looked astray again."

"I hate to tell you, Mother, but he did have other mistresses. I heard him talking about it with his friends."

"It was all for show, my dear." Anne smiled at him tenderly. "Your father was afraid I would leave him if he took up with another woman. He begged my forgiveness, said he loved me more than life and would forever on be true to me. From that point hence, he told me at least once a day he loved me."

"And," she said, grinning, "I kept careful accounting of each faux-mistress, just to be sure."

"Mother, Melanie chased after me because she said it was love, and two weeks later was professing the same for Alex *and* Whit!" Rafe raked his fingers through his already disheveled hair. "I've been with enough women to know it's only lust, a temporary obsession of the flesh. They have to justify it by claiming some exalted emotion, some absurd notion that your heart can be captured by one and one only for a lifetime. A lifetime!"

"Son, I wish I had another decade to be only with your father. Finding true love is rare. Most of the women you have dallied with have been infatuated with you, that is all. If it was true love and it ended, they'd be drinking themselves into a stupor and sulking the days away."

"I am *not* sulking."

She snorted again.

"I want her more than any other woman I have ever seen, but does that make it love? I can't be near her and not want to make love to her. I can't stop thinking about her, her passion, her intelligence, her goodness. I see her with another man and I want to kill the poor sod. I can't stop picturing the hurt in her lovely eyes, and it's ripping my gut apart! But, does that make it *love?*"

"Yes, you bloody dolt."

Rafe's mind snapped clear, even though he knew he was still slightly drunk. The almost too brilliant realization struck him. God, what an idiot he had been! What an utter ass! He was deeply, madly in love with Isabella. He couldn't fight it any longer. He certainly couldn't live without her by his side. Somehow, she had crawled into his very soul, and he just now realized he never wanted her to leave it.

"Damnation!"

"Finally!" Anne threw up her arms. "I thought you'd never figure it out. I love you, son, but you're as dense as a stump sometimes."

"I have to go to her, now." Rafe stumbled as he stood,

tripping over an empty bottle of whiskey. He looked down at himself. "God, I need a bath. Simpson!" he bellowed, striding to the door. "Get your arse to my room! I need to bathe and shave and be ready to leave within the hour! If it takes longer, I take it out of your damned hide!"

Anne laughed at he stormed out of the room, now a man with a mission. He was a stubborn boy, always had been. But now, at least, he was on the right track. She wondered, grinning mischievously, what he would do when he learned the lady had already fled London?

Chapter 20

Life in North Bindlefork was quiet and peaceful, just as she had left it, thank goodness. But being surrounded by familiar things and people didn't ease the anguish of her heart as she had hoped. Of course, Isabella had only been home for two days. Perhaps she just needed more time. She had already found it too painful to visit the lake or the rose garden. Rafe was there, the memories still too fresh of him in those places. He was in other spots as well — the drawing room, the parlor, the dining room. Even her little day room brought memories of his smiling face, his teasing, his touches.

Lisbeth was due to arrive at any time now. Her friend would be anxious for all of the details of her disastrous trip. It was going to be difficult to keep anything from her. Well, it didn't matter what she told Lisbeth. Nothing seemed to matter very much.

"My lady," Edwards said, and bowed to her as she reached the bottom of the steps. "Miss Lisbeth is in the parlor and this has just arrived for you." He held out a bouquet of lilies.

"Oh," Isabella said despondently and took the card that was tucked in the wrapping. "They're from Mr. Dalton. Throw them in the rubbish, Edwards."

Isabella had forgotten about Mr. Dalton still residing in North Bindlefork. She hoped he wouldn't make a pest of himself. That was the last thing she needed to have to deal with.

Sighing, she entered the parlor.

"Bella!" Lisbeth jumped up and embraced her friend. Then she stepped back. "It didn't go well?"

Isabella slouched into a chair. "It was both wonderful and horrible. I made an utter idiot of myself, Beth. And he again refused me."

"Oh, dearest!" Lisbeth sat on the sofa near her friend's chair and clasped the other girl's cold hands. "Did he ... ?"

"No, that's just the problem. I asked him to make love to me, I *begged* him to, but he wouldn't. He just wouldn't." The pain was excruciating. "I told him that I wanted to at least have a few nights with him, that the scandal wasn't important, but he said he couldn't take that from my future husband."

Lisbeth sat, stunned. "Well, he did the right thing, Bella. He was honorable."

"His honor be damned!" Isabella was suddenly furious. "He threw it away, Beth! He could have had my love, but he didn't want it! He didn't want *me*! He said love was nonsense."

"Bella," Lisbeth said, kneeling before her. "Darling, there will be other men for you to care for."

"No! Never will there be another. Don't you understand?" Isabella pulled her hands from her friend's grasp. The thought of any other man was abhorrent. "He's the only man I could ever love. He has my heart, my very soul! Don't ever speak to me of loving another."

Lisbeth stood. "But what did he say when you proposed to him?"

Isabella stilled, her eyes wide.

"You did propose to him, after what he said about it being a husband's privilege? Gracious, Bella, you *did* propose, didn't you?"

Flushing, Isabella could only slowly shake her head. "I couldn't, not after what he said. He only admitted to feeling lust for me. I had to salvage some of my pride."

"Well, goodness! You were so busy throwing your virginity at his feet, I'm sure very *proudly*, that you didn't think to offer him marriage? Did he ever propose?"

"No. Look, we were shouting at each other the only time it was discussed." Isabella wanted to smack herself. Lisbeth was right. She should have at least told him she would accept him, even if she had been determined not to reveal her tender heart to him. "He said he was glad I didn't believe in the 'claptrap' thought of as love, and I was hurt."

"Men rarely admit to such tender feelings as love. You should have proposed."

"We had a plan to get him jealous and see if it was enough to make him offer for me. But then I was running out of time, and I became annoyed with the scheme and sped things up a bit, you see, and, well, it got rather intense between us. He was quite nasty the last time I saw him."

"I cannot believe you, Isabella Fitzhugh!" Lisbeth dropped down onto the sofa, not bothering to smooth out the muslin fabric of her dress, unmindful of the wrinkles she was causing, so obviously upset. "You had the perfect opportunity, and you let it slip through your fingers."

"I've got to go back to London. I never even told him that I love him! No matter what he said, I *must* tell him."

"Oh, no, you don't." Lisbeth shook her head, her blonde curls bouncing wildly. "You'll not go chasing after him again."

"But if I don't, then I will have lost any chance! He must know how I feel." God, she had been such an idiot. Why had it never crossed her mind that night to ask him to marry her? Why? Even if he had scoffed at love and said she should save herself for another, she still should have tried.

Lisbeth sat back and crossed her arms over her chest. "You know he will come for you."

Isabella started. "Why should he do that? It was very clear that things were over between us. No," she said and shook her head, frowning, "he will never come here. I've ruined everything."

Lisbeth gave her a knowing look. "Oh, he'll come all right. You said he was jealous? Well, he'll come as soon as he hears who is visiting North Bindlefork."

"Whatever are you talking about? Who in the world is here that would make him come running?" Isabella thought her friend was being ridiculous. Even if Rafe had knocked out poor Lord Smythe for only daring to kiss her shoulder, it was obvious he was through with her.

Lisbeth gave her a smug smile. "Why, only two of the men you mentioned in your notes who were courting you in London. *That's* who!"

"You must be joking! Two of them are here? Which ones?" This was incredible! How did they get here so quickly?

"Only Lord Elton and Lord Cross, two of London's most eligible bachelors. They are staying with Lord Dobbs, the excuse being his fine horseflesh. Of course, the gossip is that they are here to continue paying you court. I do love gossip!"

"But how? I just don't understand how they knew I had left so quickly." Isabella was shocked. She had not thought she'd made such an impression on Lord Elton. Oh, he had obviously desired her, but to come all this way? And Lord Cross had been a toad. Why would he think she was interested in him after the way he had behaved? This was very strange, indeed.

"What does that matter? Your duke will undoubtedly be here in time for the ball being held in the lords' honor tomorrow night." The blonde clapped her hands together and wrinkled her nose in excitement. "It's going to be a very interesting evening, I'll wager."

THE door to Alex's study flew open, and Rafe rushed in. He spotted his two friends sitting by the sluggish fire.

"Hello there, old man."

"Alex! She's gone back home, hasn't she? Will you come with me? We have to leave right away!" Rafe began pacing, slapping the riding gloves he held in one hand against his thigh. "I have to go and fetch her at once. God, I've been such a fool! I only hope she'll still have me. Well, are you two coming or not?" He stopped and stood before them, legs braced and fists on hips, as if prepared to go to battle.

"You want to go after Bella?" Whit asked the obvious. "Why should you want to do that? You want to hurt her even more?"

Rafe shook his head impatiently. God only knew he deserved that remark. "No, no. I never wanted to hurt her. I love her, man!"

Alex and Whit smiled at each other and shook hands.

"Wait," Alex said, sobering, and turned his dark eyes to his friend. "Does this mean you're going to actually marry her? You'd better be thinking along honorable lines here, sport."

"Of course I want to marry her! God, I cannot think of life without her beside me. I *need* her!"

"Well, damn me. Then we'd best be off to stop the others."

"What others?"

"Oh, er, nothing, Rafe. Alex just meant in case any other gentlemen may have followed her home, you know, to continue courting her."

Rafe looked between the two, who were obviously withholding something. "What did you do? Have you been meddling in her life again?"

"She's me cousin! I have every right to do what I think best for her. Even if she will flay me for it," Alex shouted defensively, standing up and thrusting his chin forward.

"Bloody hell!" Rafe rolled his eyes. "You sent them there, these gentlemen suitors. You told them she was easy pickings now, didn't you?"

"Nothing like that," Whit assured him, also rising. "It was only to make you jealous again, so you would go to her. It was the only thing we could think of."

"Good God! Which wolves did you turn loose on her?" Rafe couldn't believe their stupidity. She had no one to protect her at Kirkwood Manor! Well, at least she finally had a real butler. That was a small conciliation.

"Why don't we tell you on the way, old chum?" Alex nervously placed his arm around Rafe's shoulders.

"Bloody hell, I'll kill you both if you tell me you sent

Cross!"

A short while later, the three young lords were riding away from London, Alex with a black eye and Whit sporting a split lip. Rafe had only a few bruised knuckles.

THEY arrived late the next evening at the tavern in North Bindlefork. The innkeeper himself served them their ale.

"Where is your lovely wench, man? Why is the place so empty?" Alex asked.

"All the help's been hired out to the Lord Dobbs tonight, m' lords. Aren't you going there?"

"Is he having a ball?" Rafe scowled, knowing the answer even before the man nodded.

"Oh, aye! It's in honor of the young lordlings come from London to court our dear Baroness." The man beamed at them. "Why, we was surprised that all of 'em came, but she's quite a catch." He winked. "Two of 'em are staying here, the rest at Lord Dobbs'."

"What? How many lords have arrived?" Whit glanced from Alex to Rafe.

"Oh, about seven now, I think."

"*Seven?*"

Whit grabbed Rafe's arm. "I swear, we only sent for three, Rafe. I swear it."

"Just who the bloody hell are they all?" Alex thumped his fist on the table. "I didn't give any *seven* permission to court her, by God!"

The innkeeper looked alarmed. "I don't know, m' lord."

Rafe stood, his ale barely touched. "When does this ball start?"

"It's already begun by now, m' lord."

"Damnation!" Rafe was out the door and striding to the stable, his dark cloak swirling about him, the hem brushing against his dust-covered Hessians. "Saddle him up, lad!" He tossed the stable boy a coin. "And be right quick."

Whit and Alex were fast on his heels. "Rafe," Whit skidded to a halt beside him. "We look a mess. We can't just barge in there. Let's freshen up here, and then go fetch her. It's still early enough, she's probably only just on her way."

Rafe stood still, his jaw clenched. Finally, he nodded. "All right, we've got fifteen minutes so be right quick!" He marched back into the pub. He didn't want to think about how many dances she could have until he got there, surely only one, at most two.

Who the hell were all these men?

"HE'S not here, so I'm not going." Isabella sat before her mirror, absently fingering the topaz necklace already around her throat, while Alice fixed her hair. Lisbeth stood behind her looking cross. "I shall kill Alex for sending all of them here! He's got some nerve."

"I'm sure he only thought to add to Rafe's jealousy, but he did overdo it a bit. Goodness, seven gentlemen all here for you!"

"They are bloody consolation prizes, is what they are. Since I can't have Rafe, I am to choose one of them." She snorted and her eyes blazed with anger. "I can't believe he would send Lord Cross, though."

"Why?"

"He nearly attacked me at MacPherson's ball. Rafe came to my rescue." She sighed and her expression softened. "He always came to my rescue before, but not now. No, I ruined that."

"Oh, do stop that nonsense!" Lisbeth stamped her slippered foot in irritation. "He'll be there and so you are going, and that's final. You're mad if you think I'll miss *this*!"

Lisbeth had insisted she wear the gold gown with the topaz jewelry. Isabella didn't care if she were wearing sackcloth. Rafe wasn't coming.

An hour after they had arrived at the ball and still there was no sign of him. Already she had danced with Lord Jeffrey, who had arrived only that morning, Lord Elton, Lord Bickers, and Lord Smythe. She had refused both Lord Cross and Mr. Dalton repeatedly.

Isabella saw Lisbeth dance by, dressed in the very pretty pale blue gown she had brought her friend, in the arms of Jeffrey and smiled. It was very sweet of him to come, really. He had confided to her that while he was a bit smitten with her lovely self, more than anything had wanted to see what would happen and be sure she was all right. Apparently, most of London had been following her courtship with Rafe. It was embarrassing. At least they all thought she had rejected his suit, not the other way around. Goodness, if the *Ton* only knew the absurdity of their supposed courtship, they would laugh themselves sick.

Isabella sighed and rubbed her throbbing temples. This was all too much. He wouldn't come for her — why should he? He didn't believe in love, and he'd made it clear that marriage wasn't on his mind. He'd even spoken casually of some future husband for her. No, he couldn't love her if he was willing to let another have her.

But he had wanted her, that much she knew. Yes, he'd wanted her, but where had that gotten either of them?

And then, just when she had decided to leave, Isabella knew he had arrived.

It wasn't the murmurs all around her, and it wasn't Lisbeth whispering in her ear, "He's here! He's here!"

No, she could *feel* him close by, could sense his eyes upon her. She took a deep breath and turned. There he was, flanked by his two friends, standing nearly a head above the others crowding forward to greet him, his blue eyes shooting sparks at her. Oh God! He'd come for her! Or had he? She waved her hand absently at whomever was tugging on her other arm. Oh dear, why was he scowling so ferociously? Had he come to further humiliate her with his caustic words? Would he tell them how wanton she was?

Why was he here?

"Please, Baroness, just one dance since I've come all this way to see only you?"

"Yes, all *right*, later then." She couldn't look away from him as he approached. He looked so handsome, and he wasn't even wearing formal evening garb. How could Alex have thought she would accept any of these paltry fellows when compared to Rafe? He was almost upon her. What should she say?

"Take your goddamn hand off of her, you ass!" Rafe didn't wait for the other man to comply, but punched the fellow in the nose.

The other man howled in pain and, still holding Isabella, collapsed to the floor. She was saved from tumbling atop him by Rafe's strong arms grabbing her shoulders.

"Goodness! Where did Lord Cross come from?" Isabella hadn't even known whom it was she had agreed to dance with, she was so bemused. She looked from the bleeding man to her love. "Your Grace. You are here."

Rafe looked down at her. "Yes, my love, I am here."

Whit, standing beside them, cleared his throat. "Lovely performance you're giving the crowd, you two. Hello, my dear Bella. Causing men to fall at your feet again, are you? You *really* ought to let her go now, Rafe."

"Hello, Whit." She blushed but didn't take her eyes from Rafe's face. His warm hands gripped her shoulders and she was tempted to lean into him. He was staring back at her so intently that she felt he must surely see into her very soul.

Just then Lord Elton pushed his way through the crowd. "Look here, Devonshire! What's the bloody meaning in smashing Cross? I think you ought to release the Baroness this instant." He puffed himself up, as if he would continue, his gaunt face quite flushed.

Alex cut him off. "Shut up, you bloody old windbag! This matter don't concern you." He glowered his best at the fellow, then chuckled as Elton huffed off. "Never did like him. Bella, dear, why don't you and this young puppy take a turn out in the garden?"

"Hello, Alex. Yes, all right."

"Come, my dear lady." Rafe placed her hand upon his arm and steered her out onto the balcony, careful to close the door behind them on the crowd of onlookers. He walked her over to a bench, just touched by light spilling out of the windows of the ballroom, and sat her down. He stood before her, absently rubbing his knuckles. "You've led me a merry chase. I want you to just sit there for the time being. No, don't move a hair on your lovely head."

"Rafe! You're really here." Isabella knew she sounded like a complete twit, but she couldn't seem to help it. She had been so sure he wouldn't come. She suddenly frowned at him. "Why are you here?"

"I shall explain, but first, let me just look at you. God, I have missed you."

"Have you?" She tried to keep her pulse from racing. She had to remain calm somehow. For all she knew, he may have finally decided to have her as a mistress, to accept her offer made what seemed so long ago. Perhaps he'd come on occasion to visit her here. Could she settle for that? Would it be enough for her aching heart?

"Bella, first I have to apologize. I behaved horribly to you on numerous occasions. It wasn't well done of me. I'm not proud of it."

"All right."

"I drank myself into a stupor for days after I last saw you. That wasn't well done of me either. I actually *sulked.*"

He sounded so disgusted with himself Isabella wanted to laugh.

"Finally, it was brought to my attention what a sorry state I was in. There was only one answer for it." He stared directly into her eyes. "Do you know what the answer is?"

She only shook her head.

"Isabella Fitzhugh," he stepped closer, then surprised her by dropping to one knee, "I love you with all of my heart and soul. If you can ever forgive me, could you consent to be my duchess?"

"Oh, my goodness." Isabella was momentarily speechless. *Now* he was saying he loved her? He wanted to marry her?

She frowned and looked him over.

She poked him in the ribs.

"Where did they beat you?"

"What?"

"Are you bleeding anywhere?"

"What in the blazes are you talking about?"

"Alex and Whit forced you, didn't they? I thought I would kill them before when they sent all these insipid men, but now they will truly suffer!" Isabella was furious. Did they actually think she would be convinced that Rafe decided now, after so much time, that he loved her? They must think her a dolt.

She pushed him back, and he fell with a grunt onto his posterior. He stared up at her as if she were mad.

"How dare they continue to meddle in my life!" She glared down at him, sprawled at her feet. "Well, you can just tell them it didn't work! You're off of the hook, so to speak. Don't worry, I won't chase you down again. I'm never leaving here again!" Mortified, she turned and fled down the balcony steps and out into the garden. God! How very cruel of them all. If he had loved her, he would have surely professed it before now! She wished all three to the devil.

"Isabella! Isabella, come back here, damn it! I love you!"

She stopped and whirled about to face him. "Stop it! Just stop it! I've heard enough lies! If you loved me then you would not have refused me that last night. You would have come back to me even that first time you left me. No, you made it very clear what you think of love, sir. It is merely 'claptrap,' isn't it? God, I am not a ninny. You don't have to sacrifice yourself on my behalf, Rafe. Tell Alex your duty has been discharged and that I — I do not want you. Just go back to London."

He grabbed her shoulders and gave her a little shake. "You *are* a damned ninny, by God. Listen to me, Bella. I do love you, curse your beautiful hide. I love your fury and your passion and your intelligence. I love everything about you, you silly girl. I was just too stubborn to see it before." His face softened and his eyes showed his anguish. "I was such a fool, an ass. I had myself quite convinced, and would tell anyone who would listen, that there was no such thing as love. I told myself it was something women made up to assuage their guilt at feeling lust." He looked deeply into her eyes. "It was almost too late, but I finally faced the truth, Bella. I love you. I cannot imagine existence without you at my side. Please, please, for the love of God, can you love me back? Can you forgive the way I treated and abused you?" Again he dropped to his knees. Suddenly, as if afraid of her answer, he pressed his face into her silken skirts, his arms wrapped tightly around her.

Isabella stood still, afraid to even breathe. He loved her, he truly loved her. She had seen it in his eyes, could feel it in his touch. She threw back her head and sobbed with the joy of it.

He loved her!

Rafe was instantly on his feet crushing her to him. "Darling, don't, please. If I have destroyed your love, you must not blame yourself. I mucked everything up with my conceit. Me, the great holder of truths!"

"Rafe! Rafe." Isabella pushed at him so that he could see her smile, despite the tears coursing down her face. "I do still love you, I do! Now stop spouting nonsense and kiss me, you idiot."

For once he listened to her and kissed her until they were both breathless. Softly, he licked her salty tears away, holding her face tenderly between his hands. She turned her head and pressed her lips to his palm.

"This *does* mean you'll marry me, doesn't it?"

She gave a throaty chuckle at his dry tone.

"God, did I ever tell you what that does to me?" He kissed her hard. "We'll get a special license tomorrow. Will I possibly last three days?"

"You don't have to."

"Damn it, Bella, I want to do this right. Don't tempt me."

"Well, *I* won't last three days. Come to me tonight, Rafe. Let me finally be yours."

"You are mine, never doubt it. You have been mine since I laid eyes on you, the haughty lady of the manor, and I will kill any man who tries to stand between us."

"Trust me, my love, at this point *I* would kill anyone standing between us. Goodness, three whole days?"

Chapter 21

The morning three days after the ball, Isabella breezed into the dining room, pale but still so lovely both Whit and Alex were envious of Rafe, who was to marry her the day after tomorrow.

"The wedding is off," Isabella said coolly, then took her place at the head of the table. She accepted the cup of coffee Edwards handed her, but waved away the plate of food. "A 'woman's pleasure,' my eye!"

"I beg your pardon, my dear?"

"What bloody nonsense is this, cousin?"

Isabella sipped her coffee, then looked at each of them, her haughty mantle firmly in place and gave them a pained smile.

"The wedding is off — off, off, *off*."

Just then Rafe rushed in, wearing only a shirt, still unbuttoned and wrinkled, and trousers, his feet bare.

"God damn it, Bella! Get up from that table and come

with me."

"I think not, Your Grace."

Rafe raked his fingers through already tousled hair, then gave his friends an apologetic smile and a shrug before turning his ire back on her. "Bella, you can come with me of your own free will and maintain a modicum of dignity, or I shall haul you back upstairs under my damned arm!" His eyes narrowed on her dangerously as she suddenly stood, kicking back her chair.

"You will not order me about, you clod! Alex," she turned desperate eyes on her cousin, "do not let him anywhere near me! He is a brute." She tossed her head at Rafe, challenging him to deny her claim.

"Alex, stay out of this. Bella, get your lovely little arse back up those stairs this instant!"

"I will *not*, sir!" She started to make a run for the kitchen door, but Rafe was too quick. He caught her and tossed her over his shoulder, then, with a salute to each of the astonished fellows, left the room. Isabella could be heard shrieking and pounded on his back for several long moments.

"Good God!" Alex leaned back in his chair after the noises had faded. "What the devil was *that* all about?"

Whit chuckled. "Just a lovers' spat, old man. Not to worry, Rafe will straighten it all out soon enough."

"I bloody well hope so. Me father and his mother are due to arrive today."

RAFE strode into the master's bedchamber, where he had been staying since the night of the ball, when they had announced their engagement. He kicked the heavy door closed behind him and then dumped Isabella onto the rumpled bed.

"Don't you dare come near me!" She scrambled to her knees, her green eyes shooting sparks. She was panting with fury and her hands were fisted.

Rafe watched her through hooded eyes. She looked glorious in her anger, and he wanted to take her that instant. Of course, at this point, she would fight him tooth and nail. God, he'd managed to muck things up again.

"Darling—" he began calmly.

"Don't you 'darling' *me*, you pig! That was horrid, and I'll not let you do it to me again!"

Rafe sighed. He really should have shown more constraint when very early that morning she had crawled into his bed. But he'd been half-asleep, and she had begun touching him so intimately, her little naked body pressing warmly against him, he'd lost control too soon. She hadn't been ready for him and he had caused her pain when breaching her maidenhead. He would never forgive himself.

"Isabella, try to calm down and let me explain." He held up his hand as she opened her mouth, his look so stern she clamped her lips together quickly. "Now, did your mother or father ever tell you about a woman's first time with a man?" He saw her confusion. "No? I was afraid of that." This was going to be difficult, at best. "Look, the first time a woman makes love, it hurts a bit."

"A bit, my eye! I *bled*, Rafe."

"That's perfectly natural, my dear. Trust me, it is." She continued to frown at him. "Virgins have a maidenhead which must be torn through, hence the one time pain and the spotting of blood. I swear to you, it will never hurt again." He slowly stepped forward, watching her face carefully.

"One time pain, you swear to me?" She chewed her lower

lip, digesting what he had said. "It won't ever be that way again?"

He dropped to his knees before her and spread his arms wide. "I swear to you, my love, you may plunge a dagger into my black heart should I ever hurt you again."

She sat back on her heels and crossed her arms over her bosom. Still frowning at him, she tilted her head to one side. "I don't know. Will you sign a paper saying they can't take me to Newgate?"

He chuckled, thankful her reason and humor seemed to have returned. "Anything you wish, my dear."

The frown was slowly replaced by a small smile. "It was rather nice before the pain." She tilted her head to the other side. "Perhaps I could get used to it."

Rafe choked back his laughter. Get used to it, indeed! "Are you horribly sore this morning?"

"Oh, no, not really." She blushed prettily. "I'm fine now."

"Would you hit me if I kissed you?"

She chuckled and patted the place next to her on the bed.

He leaped up and plopped down beside her. Tenderly, he brushed his thumb over her lips. "If I ever do anything you don't like, you must tell me, sweetling."

"To be sure," she breathed against his thumb, then took it in her mouth and sucked.

Rafe shuddered and pulled his hand away. "I said a kiss. If you continue, I shall take you again, Bella. Know that now." He looked directly into her eyes, noting her pupils were dilating already.

"Let's try this lovemaking again, Rafe. Obviously, we bungled it last night. I want to feel again as I did that night in the garden."

"All right, my love, I shall try to go slowly." He claimed her mouth and gently eased her back onto the coverlet. He kissed her thoroughly before letting his hands roam over her stomach and finally up to her breasts. She arched beneath him and wrapped her arms around his head, pulling him closer. He kissed her chin, her ears, her lovely white throat.

Rafe rolled over onto his back, pulling her with him, and began unbuttoning her gown. Her hands slipped his shirt from his shoulders. She moaned into his mouth as his large hands stroked her bare back. She had only thrown a gown on earlier and had not bothered with a chemise.

"Darling, we have too many clothes on." He rolled them back over and smiled down into her flushed face. "Shall we remedy that?"

Soon, he had them both gloriously naked. "You're so beautiful, my Bella."

He kept his distance from her as she looked over his large body. He groaned when she licked her lips as she stared at his swollen member. He could tell she was nervous again, so he began slowly, starting by licking the tender skin of the inside of her elbow, and gradually working his way up her arm and across her shoulder. Finally, he began covering her face and neck with kisses, all the while his hands kneading her luscious breasts. When she was writhing beneath him again, he leaned down and began suckling her hard pink nipples. She was moaning and stroking his back as his hands slid down her stomach to her inner thighs. Gently, he eased her legs apart and with one finger, touched her. She nearly shot off the bed.

"Rafe! Oh, God!"

Rafe trailed kisses over her belly and down to her furry mond, while his fingers touched her pleasure bud. She was incredibly wet and hot, and he had to fight the urge to plunge into her now. He placed his hands under her soft round bottom and lifted her up to his mouth. She bucked and moaned as he suckled her, bringing her to climax almost immediately.

When he felt her tremors lessening, he eased her down and kissed her mouth hungrily. "God, your passion is wonderful to behold. " He kissed her again. "Can you taste yourself, my love?" He fondled her breasts as he continued to nibble on her lips and situated himself over her. "Darling, I'll stop if you say to." Isabella said nothing, only gazed at him with softened eyes. Slowly he eased himself into her tight shaft and gritted his teeth together, it felt so incredible. He had to try to be gentle, but it was difficult. He heard her gasp, and instantly froze.

"Rafe, goodness, don't stop *now*."

"Darling girl, I don't think I could." He tried to steady his breathing. "Do you have any idea how delicious you feel? No, don't wiggle, not just yet."

He kissed her several times and then began slowly thrusting within her. She quickly matched his rhythm, moaning along with him. He was astounded to feel her begin to climax again and slipped one hand between them to increase her pleasure. They cried together as the ecstasy swept over them.

Rafe carefully balanced himself over her, so as not to crush her. Her eyes were closed and her breathing still ragged.

"Bella? Darling?"

"Hmm?" Isabella smiled lazily and opened her eyes to look up lovingly into his face. "My, that was very nice. I think I could get used to doing this. You're still inside me, I can feel you."

"I should bloody well hope so, love. You only have to smile at me, and I become as randy as a goat."

She laughed. "Are goats so very excitable? I didn't know."

He kissed her, then eased himself out of her. "Now, let me clean you up a bit." He rose and stretched, never having felt better in his life. Oblivious to his nakedness, he strolled over to the basin, poured water into the bowl, and picked up a cloth. He returned to her and sat on the edge of the bed.

"Now, hold still."

"Rafe," Isabella said, blushing madly, "I can do this myself."

"Nonsense, it is my duty as your almost-husband to see to your comfort."

He was quick and kept her distracted by talk of the wedding. Soon he was helping her dress, after slipping on his own trousers. He kissed her neck as he buttoned up the back of the gown.

"Your mother and Uncle Hugh should be here soon." Isabella leaned back against his broad naked chest. "Shall I come to you tonight?"

He chuckled and turned her around. "No, you had best get your rest. I don't want you to be sore on our wedding night."

"I'm fine, truly."

He raised one dark brow at her.

"All right, I will behave until we're properly wed." She pulled his head down to kiss him. "But after that, Your Grace, I won't give you a moment's peace."

"I'll hold you to that promise, my dear," he growled, then picked her up and kissed her hard, until they were once again panting. "Damn, it can't happen soon enough."

THE small wedding party toasted the newlywed Duchess and Duke with champagne. The drawing room was filled with the heady scent of the white roses in vases placed throughout the room. Plates of delicate pastries overflowed the sideboard to tempt the guests, and chilled bottles of the wine, carried by the footmen, were constantly at hand to fill an empty glass. The rose brocade drapes were drawn back from the windows, letting in the bright afternoon sunshine.

Isabella looked exquisite in her cream silk and lace gown, her glittering tulle veil flowing over the long auburn hair cascading down her back. Rafe watched her enchant her uncle with one of her dazzling smiles, as he lounged against the fireplace mantle with Alex and Whit on either side of him.

"You're a bloody lucky sod, you know." Alex smiled fondly toward his cousin. "She's already got me father quite wrapped around her little finger."

Rafe chuckled smugly. "She's quite a woman, your plain little county cousin is." He watched Isabella blush at some comment from his mother. He would never grow tired of watching her, of seeing her tantalizing smiles and watching the passion blaze in her eyes. He would never tire of her courage and the kindness of her heart. A lifetime would not be nearly enough time to possibly tire of her or cease desiring her.

"Plain indeed, gentlemen." Whit snorted. "I cannot even imagine her so. It is a shame it was not I who needed to escape London and that I never plan to marry."

"Not in my opinion. Besides," the duke's eyes narrowed on his lovely bride, "she would have unmasked you in a trice and dismissed you as unworthy, my friend."

"Ha! How can you think such a thing? The lady would have fallen madly for me, had I met her first, even if I am only a mere viscount."

"Nonsense, as my dear wife states so often. She needs a stronger hand than you can offer, Whit." Rafe smiled with pure male satisfaction, thinking how well his little duchess responded to his firm hands on her lovely, pale body.

"Oh, ho! So you say, Your Grace. I do not think the lady would agree. Why, I would wager she would say it was you who needs the strong hand!"

"Indeed," Rafe said, his white teeth flashing, "I do enjoy her 'strong hands' quite well."

"Bloody hell," Alex grumbled. "You had best not say such things within me father's hearing, at least until *after* tonight."

Rafe laughed, drawing Isabella's attention from her uncle. He looked beyond handsome in his elegant formal attire. He looked powerful, masculine and a bit dangerous — and he was all hers.

Finally, they were together, blessed by God and this company. His cobalt eyes met hers from across the room and she felt her heart swell with love and pride. He was so wonderful, so honorable and he would someday make such an excellent father, she just knew.

He loved her and she him and they had a future to share together. His sensual mouth curved up in a smile that had her aching to touch him, to feel those lips on her body. Would she never get enough of him? She hoped not.

"You look rather *hungry*, my dear," the Dowager Duchess teased her new daughter-in-law. "Perhaps you would care for a tart?"

Isabella blushed, realizing that her husband's mother had

observed the passionate look between her and Rafe. "I do not think a pastry would suffice, Your Grace."

Anne laughed. "Then you shall have to think of something else to fill this hunger in you."

"Anne, you imply too much to my niece. Surely she cannot understand the things you mean." Hugh Fitzhugh, a large man, whose son closely resembled him, tried unsuccessfully to hide his answering grin.

"Of course, my lord. She could not possibly understand, being only married this day to my own dear and restrained son." Anne snorted. "Go on, my dear Isabella. Go and gaze adoringly at your new husband while he pats your hand."

"As you wish, Your Grace." Isabella smiled at the two and started toward Rafe, who was still watching her with blatant desire shining from his incredibly blue eyes as he leaned so casually against the mantle, his ankle crossed and an empty glass of champagne dangling from his fingers. Oh, how she loved those fingers, the way they could stroke her to such intense heights and tease her flesh until she wanted to scream with passion. Goodness, the room was awfully warm.

"Oh, Bella," Lisbeth said as she stepped forward and placed a hand on the bride's arm. "I am so happy for you. I told you he would come for you." The blonde's voice held humorous glee.

"Yes," Isabellareplaied, tearing her gaze from Rafe's and clutching her friend's hand, "he came for me. Isn't he wonderful?" She looked back to her husband. Tonight, they would again be together. She could explore his magnificent body at leisure, and he could teach her how to please him. She shivered with anticipation, remembering his mouth on her, his tongue touching her in so intimate a place, and how her shock had turned to ecstasy.

"Spoken like a girl in love, all right." Lisbeth smoothed the skirt of her soft green gown, a slightly wistful look on her face. "I hope I can find a man who will inspire such admiration in me."

"Oh, Beth, you will. And he will be wonderful to you and you will want only to be near him, to see his secret smiles meant only for you and feel his embrace." Isabella unknowingly took a step toward Rafe, who was staring at her in such a way she wanted to rush their guests out.

"Goodness!"

"I must go to him." Isabella drifted forward, pausing to turn back and grin triumphantly at the other girl. "I was wrong, you know. Sheila Dooley is *not* a ninny."

The End

Acknowledgments

I must acknowledge my wonderful cast of Beta Readers who helped so much to make this book shine. Thank you to Ruby Popp, Cait Donnelly, Kari Youkey, and Janet Yocum Hollingsworth for your time and invaluable input.

Also, a huge acknowledgement to the wonderful Stella Cameron, not only for the fabulous quote she gave "The Archery Contest" but for all she does to enrich and encourage the writing community.

About the Author

Lori began writing as a young girl, crafting poems, song lyrics, short stories and even the junior high school gossip column. She continued to write, although sporadically, while working, creating a home for her family and raising her son.

After years of studying the craft of writing, Lori is thrilled to now be embarking on her publishing career. Lori gives workshops, has been a founder and presiding member of several chapters of a non-profit national writing organization, has organized book festivals and conferences. She loves to help other writers in any way she can.

Lori, nearly a native, lives in the Pacific Northwest with the Captain and her dog muses.

Website: www.lorilyn.net
Email: writerlorilyn@hotmail.com
Facebook: www.facebook.com/lori.lyn.7
Twitter: @writerlorilyn
Goodreads: www.goodreads.com/lori_lyn
Pinterest: www.pinterest.com/lorilyng/